MW00697903

The Dream

DEBORAH ARLENE

ISBN 978-1-64492-459-4 (paperback)
ISBN 978-1-64492-460-0 (digital)

Copyright © 2019 by Deborah Arlene

All rights reserved. No part of this publication may be reproduced, distributed, or transmitted in any form or by any means, including photocopying, recording, or other electronic or mechanical methods without the prior written permission of the publisher. For permission requests, solicit the publisher via the address below.

Christian Faith Publishing, Inc.
832 Park Avenue
Meadville, PA 16335
www.christianfaithpublishing.com

Scripture quotations marked (NIV) are taken from the *Holy Bible, New International Version*®, NIV®. Copyright ©1973, 1978, 1984, 2011 by Biblica, Inc.™. Used by permission of Zondervan. All rights reserved worldwide, *www.zondervan.com.* The "NIV" and "New International Version" are trademarks registered in the United States Patent and Trademark Office by Biblica, Inc.™.

Scripture quotations marked (AMP) are taken from the *Amplified Bible*, Copyright ©1954, 1958, 1962, 1964, 1965, 1987 by The Lockman Foundation. Used by permission.

Scripture quotations marked (NKJV) are taken from the *New King James Version*®. Copyright ©1982 by Thomas Nelson. Used by permission. All rights reserved.

Scripture quotations marked (NLT) are taken from the *Holy Bible, New Living Translation*, copyright ©1996, 2004, 2015 by Tyndale House Foundation. Used by permission of Tyndale House Publishers, Inc., Carol Stream, Illinois 60188. All rights reserved.

Scripture quotations marked (TLB) are taken from *The Living Bible* copyright ©1971. Used by permission of Tyndale House Publishers, Inc., Carol Stream, Illinois 60188. All rights reserved.

Printed in the United States of America

Contents

ACKNOWLEDGMENTS

Scott, thank you for your love and support. Without the freedom I had to be at home, uninterrupted, to write, this book would have never come to fruition. You know how single-minded I can be. Thanks for having faith that this would happen and thank you for thirty-five years of marriage and counting. God has been good to us.

Andy, thank you for your steady, reliable, calming presence and love. As you know, my firstborn, you are my inspiration for writing about the issue of life. The blessing of "you" has changed me for the better in immeasurable ways. It is amazing to watch you as a daddy; the role fits you beautifully. Jessica and Rylee are blessed. I love you so much, my precious son.

Shaina, thank you for constantly being available to read my writings and offer your editorial assistance, even as you worked and lived on the other side of the planet. Thank you for inspiring me, encouraging me, and praying for me every step of the way. You have soared to heights I could only dream of because you have placed Jesus first your whole life. I love you so much, my precious daughter.

Thank you to my parents and my husband's parents for choosing life and for giving so much of yourselves for the sake of your children. Scott and I love and appreciate you.

Thank you, Loretta, Norman, and Curtis, for reading the manuscript and offering your constructive feedback. The investment of your time has made this book better.

Thank you to so many for praying me through the writing process. There have been a number of you: Shaina, Loretta, Karen, Genesis, Susan, Jane, and more. If you aren't listed, please forgive me, and I sincerely thank you for the prayer covering.

Finally, this book would not exist without my Lord and Savior, Jesus Christ. So many people make this statement, but I can tell you that it is the absolute truth. How do you find the appropriate words to thank Jesus for your life? For your purpose? For *everything?* While I have wanted to be an author for as long as I can remember, it wasn't until I met Jesus that He brought this dream to reality. He has richly blessed me and directed my steps. I am so glad that, daily, He continues to mold and shape me into His image. May every reader of this book be blessed by and come to know the life giver, Jesus Christ!

Create in me a new, clean heart, O God,
filled with clean thoughts and right desires.

—Psalm 51:10 (TLB)

INTRODUCTION

In a dream, in a vision of the night, when deep sleep falls on people as they slumber in their beds, he may speak in their ears and terrify them with warnings, to turn them from wrongdoing and keep them from pride, to preserve them from the pit…

—Job 33:15–18 (NIV)

Seth lunged to a sitting position on the sweat-drenched bed, instantly transitioning from sleep to adrenaline-pumping alert. Blankets twisted and contorted about his limbs like instruments of bondage. Perspiration dripped from his forehead. A damp sheen glistened on his chest in the shimmering moonlight. Pounding heartbeats reverberated loudly in his temples. Stressed lungs heaved air quickly, pumping heavily.

He waited.

Silence.

As he became aware of his surroundings, he forcibly calmed himself, his breathing, his racing heart.

"Another dream," he gritted in frustration, glancing at the stars broadcasting the night's clear presence through open, pale blue blinds. "Why? Why? Why?" he moaned into the still, dim moonlight, pounding fists on the bed in cadence with each strained question while hurling his body back down to a reclining position. He angrily yanked the pillow over his head, fighting tears threatening to spill, choking back sobs determined to wrack his body.

So tired…I'm losing my mind.

A massive yawn filled Seth's lungs, welcomed by his body but despised by his mind. "Why can't I have one…just one week without *this dream?*" he groaned with fatigue.

Tears threatened again. He refused to allow them.

Focus. Brain fog was a constant companion.

The dream was always the same. Exactly the same.

"Be a man. Get a grip. Handle it. What a wimp!" Seth berated himself.

But the dream was relentless. It wore him down. So tired, bone-tired.

He couldn't fight it anymore.

He caved to the tears, hoping relief would follow.

CHAPTER 1

Katy

For a dream cometh through the multitude of business;
and a fool's voice is known by a multitude of words.

—Ecclesiastes 5:3 (KJV)

Katy trounced through the doorway of the stale apartment, flinging her naturally wavy, dark auburn hair over her shoulder. She slammed the door behind her, causing a few loose, curly, peeling white paint chips to swirl slowly to the floor. She stomped directly to the nearest window, wrinkling her nose at the putrid smell as she clicked across the tiles. Her heels looked as though they belonged in trendy downtown New York rather than Seth's apartment.

"Seth, you need to open your windows and let some fresh air in here—it *reeks!*" She shrieked, noticing uneaten pizza crust and an empty, unrinsed, and now very sour milk carton on the overly cluttered countertop.

She grumbled her disapproval as she gingerly picked up the uneaten pizza crust by the very edge, careful not to spoil her perfectly manicured nail art, and dropped it, germs and all, into the garbage can. She dug her mini bottle of apple-scented hand sanitizer out of her purse and squirted a blob in her hand, rubbing it carefully to fully cover both hands while taking in the full range of contents on the counter.

He dumps everything on this mold-colored, crummy green counter-top: apartment keys, checkbook, library ID, mail, calculator, snacks, even a roll of toilet paper!

She snorted in disgust. "When I move in, the windows will be open, there will be air fresheners in every room, you will not be a slob, and this apartment will *not* be gross! I don't know how you can stand this smell!" she yelled.

Reluctantly and unpleasantly pulled from precious sleep, Seth resented Katy's comments. He was proud of his first apartment—his very first place all his own. He secretly wasn't keen to have Katy move in, but he knew such a thought could never be entertained.

Katy would have her way. She always does. He liked his old-fashioned, bright-yellow kitchen walls, lime-green countertop, and white-trimmed doorways just as they were. She wanted to paint and change everything.

She always wants things her way, he thought grumpily while rubbing his eyes and chasing the cobwebs of sleep from his brain. He sighed with resignation. *But her income will help pay the bills.*

She planned to move in after her sister, Merin, got married this fall. They were close, thick as pea soup. Katy and Merin talked daily about wedding details—easier to do when living in the same house.

Katy often said planning Merin's wedding gave her practice for planning her own someday, throwing another marriage hint his way. Seth acted dumb every time he heard it. He wasn't ready to get married. Period. No way.

Maybe never.

Katy flung open the screeching kitchen window with too much vigor, causing it to bang as it reached its widest point. She pushed the dusty white-laced curtains wider apart to allow sunshine to brighten the dark apartment and cool air to flow freely. She breathed the fresh breeze deeply. "Now that's nice."

Seth, annoyed by her sudden appearance and his lack of sleep, barked angrily from the bedroom: "I was trying to sleep, you know. Can't you ever be considerate of me?"

"You are lazier than I thought, Seth. It's eleven in the morning! What is your problem? Why are you still in bed? You know I want to go curtain shopping. I said I'd be here at eleven. I'm here, ready to go. You're still in bed. Just *who* is wrong here? Didn't we agree on this?" announced Katy in her usual barrage of forceful, take-charge complaints.

"*We* didn't agree. You arranged," croaked Seth sleepily.

"What *is* your problem? You are miserable today," said Katy sternly. "I am sick of this. I don't have to take it, you know. I could be shoe shopping. I need shoes. I don't have time to waste!"

"Listen, Katy, I'm sorry, but I keep having these dreams. Can I *please* talk to you about them?" asked Seth pleadingly, rubbing the back of his tense neck and forcibly softening his tone. Maybe if he was nicer, she'd listen this time.

He climbed out of bed and stood in the kitchen, rubbing dirt into the worn tiles with the tips of his bare toes while admiring Katy's breathtaking beauty. She looked real pretty, as usual, in a pair of trim, fashionable jeans. Every detail attended to, her glimmering earrings, necklace, and impeccably ironed blouse all matched her emerald eyes. Suddenly, those strikingly green eyes flashed angrily.

Noticing the dirt under Seth's toes, she yelped, "Seth, that is *disgusting*. When is the last time you cleaned in here? Ran the vacuum? Scrubbed the floor?"

Looking bewildered by the change of subject, Seth nervously pulled his fingers through his curly brown mess of morning hair and floundered. "I don't know? Never?"

"You lazy slob. Go get dressed while I vacuum the dirt off this filthy floor. You can't even tell what color it's supposed to be, with all the dingy gray crud," growled Katy.

Seth turned obligingly and went back to his bedroom to dress and groom a bit, whistling quietly to calm his distress at Katy's onslaught. *Need to get rid of this morning breath—too gross.* He brushed his teeth, combed his hair, and after sniffing his armpits and blanching, he applied some deodorant too. He forgot how much he sweated when he had those dreams.

Gross. Maybe Katy's right. Maybe I am a lazy slob. I'm just so tired. I don't feel like doing anything, even showering.

Looking somewhat more presentable, he emerged from the bathroom to find Katy already efficiently emptying a scrub bucket. His kitchen floor sparkled.

"Thank you. It looks great, better than ever. I'm sorry for being such a jerk," offered Seth politely and sincerely.

"All right, thanks," replied Katy dismissively with thin lips as she ran a brush through her hair. "Let's go."

"Wait. I really want to talk to you about this dream. Please."

"Seth," said Katy, with a voice that shook with anger and grew louder with each sentence, "you have already told me about your dream. I've heard more than I want to hear. I told you that I've moved on. *It* is in my past. I don't want to talk about *it* anymore. If you can't deal with it, find a shrink. Got it? I don't want to hear one more word about your dream. Not *ever*. Let's go!" she screeched in rage, arms flailing wildly.

Wow, thought Seth. He'd read somewhere that demon possession was real. Maybe he really should break up with her because she sure sounded crazy.

What a couple they made! He's a lazy slob. She's crazy possessed. Maybe they deserved each other.

He dutifully followed Katy out the door as she motioned they needed to leave.

"Onward curtain shopping," sighed Seth, mumbling pitifully to himself.

CHAPTER 2

The Appointment

Let the wise listen and add to their learning,
and let the discerning get guidance.

—Proverbs 1:5 (NIV)

Seth walked into the local community library ten minutes before his shift began. Funny. He never had trouble getting to work on time, even though this was an interim job till he could find work as a journalist.

He *loved* working here.

He admired the floor-to-ceiling glass windows where sunbeams streamed across the floor. He could see dust particles glistening in the warm rays. The books had that dusty, musty, ancient, begging-to-be-read smell. The entire place felt like a bedrock of wisdom—a collection of knowledge accumulated across time. He loved reading. Loved learning. Loved books.

And he loved doing research. Digging for truth. He couldn't wait to work as an investigative reporter—his ultimate goal. He had visions of doing famous exposes and documentaries. Exposing corruption. Revealing truth.

His boss and coworkers arrived, one by one. Seth got to work. His duties varied. Usually, he returned borrowed items to their proper places and placed new items as well. Sometimes he worked the desk, answering questions and checking out materials to customers. Every now and then, he even dusted and cleaned bathrooms—not exactly his favorite, but he did what was needed.

Ten o'clock—break time—arrived quickly. Seth always took his break because he used the opportunity to read a book he may have discovered or find new treasures to read.

This time, though, he had a phone call to make. He pulled out his smartphone and walked out the side door for some privacy.

He'd never called a shrink before. His hands shook. His mouth dried up. His mind told him not to do it, but his heart knew he had to. The dream had to stop. He couldn't have this dream every week for the rest of his life! *Someone* would know how to make it stop. He liked the idea of researching the problem with a psychologist. He could dig and find the answer.

He searched for psychologists in his area, and quite a few names appeared. Which one? He examined the list for a while and then just picked the name closest to his apartment.

Convenience. Not the best way to choose. Whatever. I can't think straight with the amount of sleep I got last night. Any psychologist should do. They'll give me some leads, and I'll do the rest myself. One, maybe two sessions tops.

He rubbed his sweaty palms on his khakis and pulled out the small black leather-covered tablet and pen set he always kept in his shirt pocket—a graduation gift from himself. Pocket-sized pen and paper were neatly stored inside a miniature folding case. He liked it. An investigative reporter never goes anywhere without tablet and paper.

Old-fashioned, but, oh well. There's something special about paper.

Writing things down allowed him to look over a whole barrage of information at once, like a puzzle. Sometimes the *way* he wrote something—the handwriting and the doodling—gave Seth clues into his subconscious mind. His emotions poured into note writing. The way he wrote sometimes revealed solutions to mysteries he already knew in the deep recesses of his mind but couldn't yet comprehend because they remained just outside his awareness. Each sense offered clues, the eye honing in on clustered groupings of words, the smell and touch of the paper sharpening senses while the riddle's solution emerged.

Using all five senses enhanced his *genius*. Seth grinned at the thought and once again settled the paper versus technology debate in his mind. He recalled all the times he defended his old-school, nerdy paper-and-pen ways with his technology-addicted friends.

I like technology, but I'm not married to it. Paper and pencil...still the best, he concluded as he brought his thoughts back to the present.

He dialed the number. A perky secretary answered, asking how she could help. Seth's voice shook as he asked to make an appointment.

"Have you been here before?" she asked energetically.

"No."

With more calm and less forced energy, she asked him to explain, in *general* terms only, she added with emphasis, why he sought treatment.

Why? Seth gulped nervously and blurted, "I keep having the same dream over and over."

She waited for further explanation, and when none came, she pressed for more, asking, "Does the dream interfere with your life in some way?"

"Uh, yea, I can't sleep."

"Okay. Does it interfere with your life in any other way?"

"I'm not sure what you mean."

"Does the dream affect your life in any other way? Depression, anxiety, relationships, health issues, job issues?" prompted the secretary kindly at the other end of the phone line.

Seth paused as he ran all the possible scenarios through his mind. "Uh, sure, I guess depression and anxiety, and I guess maybe relationships too."

This answer seemed to satisfy the secretary because she moved on. She asked if he had insurance.

Insurance? "No," he replied tentatively. *Money! Should've thought about that.* He tiredly rubbed the back of his neck and wondered what it would cost. He asked.

In reply, she simply asked another question, this time about his income.

Seth's defenses rose with such a personal question, especially one that always created conflict with Katy. He tersely gave the secretary his meager minimum-wage, part-time earnings. He then grudgingly explained he had rent to pay too, so he didn't have a lot of money.

She then asked how much his apartment cost per month and whether he paid for anything on his own (heat, electricity, garbage removal, etc.).

Is this the third-degree? Seth's anger brewed. *They ask way too many questions.*

He resigned himself to answer, "No, I don't pay extra for that stuff. It's included in the rent. And"—the pitch of his voice rose—"I've got debt from college. And groceries aren't cheap either, you know."

Seeming to sense Seth's growing unease about the price and her line of questioning, the secretary asked him to hold for a few minutes.

She came back on the phone in what seemed like *much* more than a few minutes to say they'd make an exception and give him a discounted first visit. Normally, first visits cost $150, but his would only cost $75—a major concession on their part, she explained. He would need to negotiate future prices with his therapist.

Seventy-five dollars! Seth's face paled, and his heart raced at the mention of the large fee. His mind, in panic mode, conceded *one session only*, though he wasn't going to tell the secretary that.

Instead, he answered as calmly as he could, "Okay, I'll try to pull together seventy-five dollars, but we need to wait until next week to make the first appointment—after I get paid."

They finalized the appointment time: next Wednesday at 4:00 p.m.

Perfect. He'd get off work at 3:30 p.m. so he'd have just enough time to get there by 4:00 p.m.

Now he just had to make it through another week with the dream.

CHAPTER 3

The Psychologist

The person without the Spirit does not accept the
things that come from the Spirit of God but considers
them foolishness, and cannot understand them because
they are discerned only through the Spirit.

—1 Corinthians 2:14 (NIV)

The week passed excruciatingly slow.

Seth had the dream a couple times, but that wasn't his main problem. Something else occurred. Something slightly unsettling. He kept noticing the Bible.

He had a small bookshelf in his living room, which housed a black leather-covered Bible. He never used it. Though he went to church sometimes, he hadn't used that Bible since vacation Bible School one summer—way back when he was a kid. His mom always scrimped and saved to send him to summer camps while she worked, thinking it would keep him out of trouble.

The dust-covered Bible never got pulled off the shelf. Yet he noticed this week that it was slightly dislodged.

He wracked his brain. *I didn't use any book on that shelf, so I couldn't have accidentally pulled it out.*

Seth asked Katy if she'd used his Bible. She looked at him with a withering stare and shrieked "No" in one of her most disgust-filled voices. "Why in the world would I do that? My parents have one, and yours is filthy. It's not like I need a Bible for anything," she explained in her usual demeaning way. "Get a grip, Seth. First you think God's talking to you in your dreams, then you think he's pulling books off the shelves. Really? Isn't that a bit much?"

Seth changed the subject. He didn't want to get into this with her. But it wasn't the only time the Bible jumped out at him. At work, an unusual number of Bibles arrived in the return bins for re-shelving. Each time he encountered one, it startled him, leaving him unsettled.

He shoved these thoughts to the back of his mind as he sat in the psychologist's waiting room completing a new-patient questionnaire. When finished, he whistled quietly to ease his frayed nerves and settled back into his chair to examine the surroundings. With only a few dimly lit lamps, no windows, and a modest number of wooden chairs arranged in several disconnected groupings, the setting appeared drab and uninviting. *Odd. Someone doesn't want appealing or brightly lit surroundings, nor do they want people to sit too closely to one another. Why? So others can't ID the crazy folks who need a shrink?*

Counterintuitively, he recalled when he got physically sick and went to the physician; the chairs always seemed suffocatingly close, and those brightly illuminated lights made him wince, especially when experiencing the aches and fatigue of a fever. He wondered about the close arrangement of the chairs at physician's offices when the person next to you hacked and sniffled incessantly. Surely, their germs could easily spread to those seated alongside. He recalled having the experience and leaning as far away as he could, trying not to inhale any microorganisms. Thankfully, Seth's good health made visits to a doctor's office rare.

But the waiting room for the psychologist's office certainly didn't lend itself to camaraderie. *Why?* His investigative instincts kicked in. *Does a more open, communal atmosphere deter people from coming? Does it make them uncomfortable? What could the reason be? Could it be shame? But why would a counseling center perpetuate the stigma of mental illness in its layout? Was it simply budget issues or thoughtlessness? Or was it unconscious stigma?*

He wondered how many people felt shame in seeking counseling for mental illness. In his own heart, he believed mental and physical illnesses both could be treated, and neither was shameful. Yet the differences in the waiting rooms had him second-guessing his convictions. These thoughts didn't help calm his jitters in the least.

Maybe this was a mistake. I shouldn't have come here.

Just then, one of the doors swung open, and an attractive, petite woman with short sandy-brown hair said his name questioningly. Though only slightly older than Seth, her severe-looking glasses and the professional manner in which she carried herself made her seem older. Seth jumped to his feet, and she waved him over.

"Hello, Seth? I'm Dr. Emily Westnar. Please follow me. Did you have any trouble finding the office?" she asked kindly.

"Hello, ah, no, no trouble," replied Seth quietly as he continued observing his surroundings. They walked briskly down a dimly lit, cramped hallway with frayed, stained carpet. In the semidarkness, its color could barely be discerned. Beige? The sound of muffled voices drifted through the air, and partially closed doors on either side of the musty hallway revealed people seated inside a few of the rooms. With the number of offices and people glimpsed, a lot of people must need this kind of help.

Where do they get all the money? Seth wondered, considering the fees. Upon investigating, he discovered the fees here were pretty normal; in fact, they seemed cheap compared to other places.

"Here we are," said Dr. Westnar gently as she directed Seth into a small room with two chairs, one clearly hers—a gray office chair with wheels next to a desk—and the other his—a small yet comfortably padded living-room-type chair. Visible specks of white fuzz, perhaps from the sweater of the last person who sat there, contrasted loudly and clung to the soft navy-blue fabric.

Katy would hate that.

He plopped himself onto the lint-speckled, cushy chair with some relief. Lusciously soft, fluffy padding overstuffed the cushions.

Nice…very comfortable.

The room was the most pleasing he'd encountered so far. Sunlight streamed through the window next to him, enough to warm the skin.

Glancing through the open, bleached curtains to the pale blue sky filled with puffy white cumulous clouds, Seth noticed that the bright curtain and cheerful inside decor perfectly matched the outside scenery. Inside, the agreeably decorated office showcased several vibrantly colored, whimsical figurines, a few landscape paintings, and a green garden-like statue with flowing water. The peaceful sound of running water was soothing. Seth relaxed.

Maybe this isn't so bad after all. I could almost sleep in this chair. His eyes closed slightly.

Dr. Westnar quietly closed the door and sat in her chair; her movements caused the chair to squeak. Seth opened his heavy eyes reluctantly as she pulled open a file folder. "Before we can begin, we need to take care of some housekeeping tasks," she said softly through a smile, as though speaking to a traumatized child.

He didn't think she meant to sound condescending, but her words and demeanor made him uncomfortable. He wasn't crazy, and he didn't like feeling like he was. He shifted awkwardly in the chair, trying not to take offense since he knew she wasn't intentionally trying to be patronizing. With effort, Seth removed the chip from his shoulder.

"First, company policy requires payment before the session begins, so could I please ask for our agreed-upon discounted payment of seventy-five dollars for today?" asked Dr. Westnar in a kind but business-like manner.

Startled by the early request for payment, Seth jerked his head toward the psychologist in surprise but obediently reached into his back pocket. He unfolded the slightly tattered wallet and dug around for the check he had brought. Not sure how to make it out, he'd left the "Pay to the Order of" part blank. Dr. Westnar held up a self-inking stamp, saying she'd take care of it.

She took the check, stamped it, noted a few things in the folder, and said, "Okay, Seth, thank you. Next housekeeping item—fees. Since you don't have insurance and only have a part-time job, we need to determine how often to meet. As our secretary explained, we gave you a 50 percent discount for today, the maximum discount we can offer, based on your income. Subsequent appointments generally cost less than the first appointment. Normally, our fees are $130 for succeeding appointments, but in your case, we can offer a temporary reduction of $65 for subsequent appointments—an extremely low price, rock-bottom."

She swiveled in her chair to face Seth. "I do care about you and truly want to help. We'll discuss the frequency of our meetings at the end of today's session, but at such a discounted rate, I cannot meet more than once a week. If it's necessary to meet more often, we'll need to renegotiate the rate or try to find someone who can meet with you more frequently at less cost. What are your thoughts on this, Seth?" she asked amiably.

"Uh, okay, I guess. Sixty-five dollars for the next session. I get it. And we can't meet more than once a week, or it'll cost more," Seth repeated dumbly, not knowing what else to say. He still thought it was too much money but felt like a beggar.

This better be worth it.

"Great!" replied Dr. Westnar enthusiastically. She turned back to the desk and scribbled furiously in the folder. "Finally, last house-keeping task. I'd like to review some of the answers you provided on the questionnaire you completed in the waiting room. I'm going to ask some of the questions again, just to be sure. Is that okay with you?"

"Okay," replied Seth dutifully, once again feeling like a child.

"Have you ever tried to commit suicide?"

"No!"

"Have you ever *thought* about committing suicide?"

"No, never, I am *not* suicidal," emphasized Seth clearly.

"Okay, but you *are* depressed?"

"Well, yea, I guess. I don't really know, but I guess I might be. I think it's because I keep having the same dream."

"On a scale from one to ten, where would you place your depression, with one being you barely recognize depression and ten being you're contemplating suicide," asked Dr. Westnar without expression.

"I don't *know*. A two, I guess?" he replied timidly but with some frustration.

"Okay, thank you, Seth. You also indicate you are feeling anxious. On a scale from one to ten, where would you place your level of anxiety, with one being you barely recognize anxiety and ten being highly anxious with anxiety affecting every area of your life to the point of being unable to function," asked Dr. Westnar seriously.

"I don't *know*," said Seth, sighing with exasperation. "I guess maybe a three because I'm more anxious than depressed…maybe the depression would be a one instead of two," answered Seth with confusion.

"Okay, thank you. That is helpful, Seth. We're finished with housekeeping tasks." She closed the folder and shifted gears as she faced him and said brightly, "So, tell me why you're here."

Seth answered with ambiguous, one-sentence replies, revealing very little, for a short while anyway. Finally, he relented and agreed to tell her the dream after she reminded him she couldn't help if he wasn't willing to tell her why he was there.

Feeling embarrassed and awkward at first, Seth tentatively told Dr. Westnar about the dream. As he talked, her expression remained neutral, and he gained confidence as she vocalized encouragement. He recounted his visitor of the night, reliving the emotions; even his racing heart seemed real as he relayed it. He explained he has the dream weekly and that it affects his life and his relationship with Katy too. He ended in a stilted manner, with a still-developing and uncertain explanation about how God was *maybe* trying to communicate something to him.

Dr. Westnar looked deep in thought. The silence lengthened.

Finally, she asked quietly, "How long have you been having the dream, Seth?"

Seth squirmed in his chair uncomfortably. He didn't want to talk about this part, especially not with a woman. He wished he'd thought more about it in advance and had requested a male psychologist. He didn't answer her question for a long time. Finally, he said, "I'm not sure."

She looked at Seth questioningly, as though she didn't believe him, and pushed for a better answer. "Weeks? Months? Years?"

"Nearly a year."

"Is there something that happened around that time, nearly a year ago, that would have prompted the dream?" asked Dr. Westnar gently.

"I don't know."

Sensing his discomfort, Dr. Westnar changed the subject. "How long have you been dating Katy?"

"About a year and a half," replied Seth thoughtfully as he searched his memory. He should know this answer since Katy made such a big deal when he forgot their one-year-dating anniversary. She didn't speak to him for days and carried a grudge for weeks.

"Does Katy know about the dream?" asked Dr. Westnar softly.

"Yes," replied Seth flatly.

"And what does Katy think of it?" Dr. Westnar prodded, leaning forward in her chair expectantly.

"She hates it. She doesn't want to hear anything about it, so I've stopped trying to talk about it."

Again, sensing discomfort, Dr. Westnar changed directions. "Tell me about Katy. How long have you known her? How did you meet?"

Seth launched into a story about how he met Katy at college, along with anything else he could think of to say that might be helpful, which wasn't much. When he stopped, the silence lingered once again.

Dr. Westnar again looked thoughtful. Once more, she changed the subject. "Tell me about yourself, Seth. What do *you* like to do? What was your college major? What's your passion?"

This time, Seth launched into a long-winded explanation of his journalism major, his job at the library, and his investigative reporter dreams. Dr. Westnar noticed Seth's eyes glimmer with excitement as he talked, and he leaned forward in his chair, gesturing animatedly with his arms as he described the things he clearly loved.

When he paused, Dr. Westnar abruptly said, "Okay. Thanks, Seth. We're off to a good start. I do think I can help you. I would like to see you again next week, if that's okay with you. Can you come back next week so we can explore this more thoroughly?"

"Uh, okay," said Seth, startled that the hour had flown by so quickly and things ended so suddenly. Frustrated, he realized all he did was talk. She didn't help at all.

"Can you come the same time next week? Wednesday at four?"

"Yea, sure," said Seth, not happily. He guessed he could pull together sixty-five dollars.

This is crazy!

"During the next week, I would like you to think *real hard* about what might have happened in your life a year ago that would have prompted this dream, okay? I think that piece of information is critical to resolving your unrest. Can you do that for me? That's your homework assignment."

"Okay," Seth replied gruffly. This he did not want to talk about. He stood and walked to the door.

"See you next week," said Dr. Westnar pleasantly.

"See ya," replied Seth with forced courtesy, trying to conceal his frustration.

What a waste of time.

He gulped in the fresh evening air with relief as he stepped out into the street, thankful to put the experience behind him.

Needing to think, he relished the walk home. Grudgingly, he acknowledged that before Dr. Westnar could help him, she needed to know more about his life and the dream. He just didn't look forward to talking about what happened a year ago.

* * *

The past week was insane, thought Seth as he walked to Dr. Westnar's office exactly one week later. He'd had the dream *three times,* the most ever in one week.

Again, though, this wasn't Seth's biggest issue of the week.

Everywhere he looked, he noticed, well…he noticed God.

Church billboards on the lawn in front of churches and their attempt at humorous axioms caught his attention. Actually, some were quite clever. He never paid a lot of attention to those signs before. He recalled thinking in the past they were corny, desperate, and incoherent much of the time.

Not only that, Seth saw a family praying together at a fast-food restaurant before they ate. And at the local coffee shop, he noticed the cashier wore a cross necklace.

Seth became more and more convinced that God was trying to talk to him. He didn't tell Katy. This stuff really played with his head.

He arrived at the psychologist's office, stopping to sign his name at the reception desk before taking a seat. Too lost in thought, he didn't even notice his surroundings today. In no time at all, Dr. Westnar announced his name.

Though not smiling inside, Seth faked a smile in greeting as he approached the doorway.

She asked, "How are you today?"

He replied in the normal way people do, "fine," when both parties know, of course, the ridiculous nature of both question and answer.

If I was fine, I wouldn't be here.

Today, Seth was ready. Before settling into the comfy blue chair, he pulled the check out of his wallet and immediately handed it to Dr. Westnar before she even requested it.

"Oh, thank you, Seth. You are definitely on the ball," said Dr. Westnar with a surprised smile. "Just give me a few seconds." She opened a folder, recorded some items, and placed the check in the folder.

"All right, let's get started. Tell me about your week," said Dr. Westnar with rapt attention.

Seth told Dr. Westnar about the increase in the frequency of his dream.

He paused, wondering if he should tell her about the other stuff—the Bibles two weeks ago. Then this past week, the church signs, the praying family, the cross necklace…

Dr. Westnar noticed his hesitation. "What else would you like to tell me?" she prompted.

Seth didn't say anything.

Dr. Westnar said, "I sense that perhaps you would like to tell me more. Is there something else?"

"You'll think I'm crazy."

"Not at all. I am very interested in what you have to say, and I do not think you're crazy. I can help you better if you are forthcoming with me," explained Dr. Westnar kindly.

Seth quickly explained the past two weeks and how he thought maybe God was trying to give him a message of some sort and how he thought it was the same with the dream—a message from God.

"I don't think you're crazy one iota, but I also don't think this is about God." Dr. Westnar laughed dismissively. She changed the subject. "Now that you have told me about your week, did you do your homework? Did you think about what may have happened a year ago when your dream started? Something that may have been a trigger?"

Seth prided himself on his analytical abilities and felt disappointed she'd brushed his recent experiences and thoughts about God off so quickly. He reluctantly, but obediently, turned his attention to her question.

How to answer?

He'd thought a lot about it. He might as well just jump right in. Seth blurted out what happened a year ago that may have triggered the dream with as little detail as possible.

When he had clearly finished talking, Dr. Westnar said knowingly, "I thought as much, Seth." Her brows furrowed, and she paused for a few moments, thinking. She continued, "You made a completely legitimate choice. Countless others in the same situation have made the same good, necessary, right decision. Could you perhaps be trying to work through some guilt or shame?" asked Dr. Westnar gently.

Seth hesitated a few beats. "Maybe."

"Well, then, please be encouraged. Guilt and shame are completely unwarranted. If you need assurance, I am happy to provide it. In fact, you should take pride in your mature and responsible actions. The alternative would have been thoughtless and certainly not best for all parties. With the alternative, you could not have continued working at the library, honing your research skills. You would have needed a better income, so you would have had to give up your career dreams. Fledgling investigative reporters do not get paid a lot. You made the right decision," said Dr. Westnar passionately. "I believe if you can release yourself from false condemnation or guilt, then perhaps the dream will stop haunting you. In the meantime, I can direct you to a psychiatrist here in the building who can prescribe some sleeping medication, if you would like," said Dr. Westnar authoritatively.

Seth paused. Something bothered him. Her response seemed flip, too easy. He didn't like the recommendation for sleeping medication. He had never taken meds and didn't plan to start now. He made an immediate decision.

Time to move on.

"Maybe since I talked with you about my dream, and the trigger, the dream will stop now, so I'd like to hold off on the meds. I also want to wait a little before I make another appointment, just to see if the dream stops. Thanks for your time, Dr. Westnar," Seth said with finality as he rose from the chair. He reached over and shook her hand. "Take care." He walked to the door.

Dr. Westnar, surprised by the sudden ending of their meeting, said, "Seth, wait, perhaps we should make one final follow-up appointment. I would feel better if we did."

"I'll call you to schedule it. I have to work a few weeks to pull more money together. I've spent all the extra money I had on these last two appointments, so I'll have to get back to you." He acted more confident than he felt.

Better this way. Cool on the outside. She doesn't need to know that my head feels like it's going to explode.

"Okay...well...take care, Seth...I'll look forward to hearing from you," said Dr. Westnar hesitatingly, with a note of chagrin.

"Thanks." Seth turned and quickly walked down the dim hallway, once again relieved to leave. He quietly whistled a tune to calm his swirling emotions.

At his apartment later that evening, Seth's analytical instincts kicked in. He'd figure things out from here. He may not have that dream again, ever. That'd be awesome. Then this chapter of his life could close for good.

But just in case, in the meantime, he wrote his to-do list in his trusty pocket notebook. Seth stretched out on his bed with a couple of pillows propping up his back as he considered the tasks.

    1)   Go see Professor Whitman.

Time to get some other expert opinions. Seth liked his psychology professor, Prof. Whitman, from college. He had his own private practice, so Seth wanted to hear what he had to say about recurring dreams. Why didn't he think of him in the first place? Hmm, probably because he didn't want to get that personal with someone he knew. Maybe he'd tell him he was asking for a friend and wouldn't give too many details.

    2)   Go see Professor Cantor.

While he liked his psych professor, he *really* liked his math professor. Cantor's approachability had resulted in many illuminating conversations about everything under the sun. He considered him a friend. Cantor always told Seth if he ever needed anything to give him a call. Seth used Cantor as a reference and thought he'd run the dream past him. What could it hurt? The man knew a lot about a lot of things. He might at least have some suggestions.

    3)   Research on dreams.

If the dream continues, it's time to get serious. I work in a library, for Pete's sake, what's taken me so long to dig into this myself?
Seth hesitated, chewing on the end of the pen for a while before he wrote the next item on the list. He wasn't sure about it, but if he wanted answers, and he thought God was part of this thing, then he needed to start looking in that direction too. He wrote:

    4)   Research what the Bible says about dreams.

Suddenly, Seth felt very tired. He turned off the lamp by the bed, placed the notebook and pen on the nightstand, and gratefully adjusted his head on the pillow as he closed his eyes. He immediately fell into a deep sleep.

Seth awoke feeling refreshed. He didn't have the dream last night. This was good, but he knew it didn't mean anything. He never had the dream every night.

But still, he had a plan. He'd gotten a good night's sleep. Life was good.

He whistled on his way to work.

CHAPTER 4

The Old Man

The fear of the Lord is the beginning of wisdom, and
knowledge of the Holy One is understanding.

—Proverbs 9:10 (NIV)

As Seth put books back in the stacks, he noticed the white-haired elderly gentleman moving slowly about, his reading glasses on a gold chain around his neck. He'd seen him here a lot.

Towering above the other patrons, the man's height and his thick, shockingly white hair caused him to stand out in the otherwise bland library. He wore a sweater vest over a button-up shirt, over a white undershirt, every day, even now, in the summer. He always wore canvas pants and bright white athletic shoes, so Seth supposed he walked to the library. He seemed in good shape for his age, though Seth couldn't judge age too well. The man could be eighty, ninety... Seth didn't know. He was just "old" according to Seth's point of view.

The old guy busied himself at the library nearly every day, his routine always the same. He read several daily newspapers while sitting at a table where he spread them out across the tabletop. He then moseyed over to the magazine rack to see what was new, sometimes skimmed the history and war nonfiction sections, and eventually settled into one of the library's comfortable chairs to read whatever his searches produced for about an hour or two. Always polite and friendly to Seth, he never missed an opportunity to say hello and engage in small talk, sometimes offering peppermint lifesavers. He always kept a roll in his vest pocket. Seth helped him find books from time to time. He liked the elderly fellow.

The man lumbered slowly toward where Seth carefully placed books on shelves. He greeted Seth with a warm smile and said kindly, "Young man, all this time I have been coming here, and I have never asked your name. Please forgive me. What is your name?"

"I'm Seth. What's your name?" replied Seth in a friendly tone, struck by the unusual pale blue of the man's eyes.

"Harold," said the man in return, smiling, his piercing eyes flickering with light as he gazed intently at Seth's smiling face.

"Seth," said Harold in a suddenly serious tone, his smile changing to a worried frown, deep lines furrowing across his forehead. "I need to tell you something. It's bothered me for a while, and this old man has learned to act on what's in his heart," explained Harold as he nodded his head solemnly and pointed a wrinkled, crooked finger at his own chest. He lowered his hand, sighed deeply, paused for a few seconds, looking uncertain, then blurted gruffly, in a shaky voice quite unusual for the confidence he normally displayed: "You are supposed to write down the dream." Then he turned abruptly to walk away.

Seth literally jumped, and his mouth gaped wide. "What? Wait!" he said more loudly than he intended. Seth's astounded heart raced. "What did you say? Harold! How do you know about my dream? Did you hear me talk about it on the phone?" asked Seth incredulously.

Harold turned back to face Seth. "The phone? What? No…" He hesitated a beat, then blurted simply, "God told me."

Seth's stress level soared. Feeling a headache coming on, he rubbed his fingers across the front of his forehead. He never got headaches.

What's going on?

"What do you mean 'God told you?'" asked Seth. "What does that mean? Did you *audibly* hear the voice of God? Isn't that crazy? Oh, wait a minute, I get it. You know my psychologist, don't you? I thought there was a confidentiality thing. I could sue her for telling others about me," Seth ranted wildly, pointing his finger at Harold. He felt out of control. The room spun.

"What? Sue? No. Let's sit for a minute, could we?" asked Harold with nervous concern and comfort in his voice at the same time, pointing toward a couple of nearby chairs. He gently placed his hand on Seth's elbow and guided him slowly toward the chairs.

Seth wanted to yank his arm out of Harold's grip and tell him to get out of his life. Instead, he drew in a shuddering breath and let it out slowly, then another, steadier. He reminded himself that this was an elderly gentleman, a kind man, and that he needed to stay rational.

What's this all about?

His world rocked. Seth felt his hands shaking and wondered fleetingly if he was dreaming again.

They both sat.

"I apologize for blurting out such peculiar words." Harold paused, putting a finger to his pursed lips as he considered his words. "I'm a Christian. I pray for people all the time. Sometimes people I don't even know, and I've been praying for you. God has put you in my heart for some reason." Harold patted his chest. "He's been telling me to tell you to write down your dream—the dream about the winged babies and the room with pounding rain. That's all I know. And when God tells me to do something, I need to do it. I made too many mistakes by not listening to God before, so now I don't hesitate…no matter how strange it seems."

Seth barely heard most of what Harold said. He focused on a few of Harold's specific words, *The dream about the winged babies and the room with pounding rain.* He felt faint. *How could this man know this?*

Only two people in the world knew about his dream: Katy and the psychologist. Something clicked in the far recesses of his mind: the Bibles, church billboards, people praying, the cross necklace. He'd thought God was trying to talk to him, and now here's this guy saying God told him about his dream! Sweat beaded on Seth's forehead while doubts, confusion, and anger swirled through his mind. But his curiosity was also aroused.

He leaned intently toward Harold, throwing questions at him as quickly as he thought them, "Who told you about my dream? Dr. Westnar? Katy? How do you know them? Why are you talking to people about me?" Seth grilled Harold with desperation.

Harold looked bewildered for a second, then said patiently, "I have no idea who Dr. Westnar is, and I have no idea who Katy is either. I know you don't believe me, but the only person I talked to is God. I don't know anything about you. I'll say it again. God wants you to write down your dream. I don't know why. I don't know what your dream is about other than that one sentence. To be honest, I'm as surprised as you that what I just told you actually means something to you."

Seth sat silent for a few minutes, trying to catch his breath, calm his nerves, and push through to some kind of understanding, something that made sense. "How did God tell you this? Do you hear his voice out loud, like you and I are talking?" asked Seth with doubt and anger still evident in his voice.

Maybe he has dementia.

Nearly a year of sleep interruptions and stress made Seth a ticking time bomb ready to explode. He gulped a few deep breaths, desperately trying to calm his raging emotions.

"No," answered Harold with a shaky voice, pausing as he searched for the right words, again crinkling his brows and pursing his lips as he thought. "I believe Christians can hear from God, in here," he said gruffly while he pointed to his heart, "and here." He pointed to his head. "A kind of knowing you get when you spend a lot of time—many years—with someone. When your dad calls on the telephone, you never have to say, 'Who is this?' because you know your dad's voice. I guess it's like that." Harold paused and then said, "Look, I must come across as delusional to you if you're not a Christian. I understand if that's what you think. I'm just doing what I think I'm supposed to do. I won't pester you anymore. You have a good day. If you ever want to talk, I'm here. I love to talk. I'm a very good listener too. And I'm good at keeping things confidential," added Harold, smiling gently, upward curving crinkles covering his entire face.

He patted Seth on the knee and stood to leave. Turning to Seth, he said, "I'm sorry I upset you. That wasn't my intention. I hope you'll forgive me." Harold walked away, then turned back once again and waved, saying, "See you tomorrow" as he walked out the door.

Seth sat in the chair for what seemed like an eternity, trying to process what had just happened. Overcome with fatigue, he told his boss he didn't feel well and went home.

As soon as he walked in the door of his apartment, Seth crashed onto the bed and fell promptly asleep.

He awoke from the dream the same way he always did—soaked in sweat, heart drumming in his chest.

Okay. So the dream didn't stop. Maybe the old man—Harold—triggered it again. I would've been fine if he didn't have to butt his nose into my life. I may not have had the dream again, ever, if not for Harold.

Seth's anger rose. Once again, frustrated sobs wracked his body. He let them come until, emotionally spent, they subsided.

A glimmer of peace finally settled over him, and he wondered if Harold could be right.

Tomorrow, I'll write down the dream. What can it hurt?

He rolled over to try to get some sleep.

Embarrassed by how he'd reacted to Harold's words, Seth dreaded going to work for the first time ever.

I don't even recognize myself anymore. I flip out at old people now all over a stupid dream.

Seth promised himself not to be a jerk to Harold the next time he saw him. After all, Harold had been kind. Before long, Seth spied him reading a book about World War II. He ambled over and sat in the chair next to him. "Hey, mister, how ya doin?" Seth patted him gently on the back.

Harold glanced up in surprise and grinned broadly when he saw Seth. He closed the book he held in his lap and began animatedly telling Seth about its contents. As a World War II navy vet, the book had prompted his memories. Harold also shared stories about how he met his wife, their marriage and her death. At the mention of her passing, his expression saddened, and he stopped talking. Harold seemed a million miles away as he reminisced.

Seth's heart melted. He really did like this old man, and he seemed lonely. He broke into Harold's reverie. "Look, I'm sorry about how I reacted yesterday."

Jolted back to the present, Harold stared blankly at Seth for a few seconds, trying to figure out what he was talking about. "Oh! That's all in the past now."

"Good. Okay. Well, I have to get back to work. See you later."

Weird. I like him, but now he acts like he forgot he ever said those things to me.

CHAPTER 5

The Dream

If they hear and serve Him, they will end their days in
prosperity and their years in pleasantness and joy.

—Job 36:11 (AMP)

That afternoon, Seth decided it was time to face this thing head
on. His pocket notebook wouldn't suffice; he needed more
room to write. He dug around in his closet until he found a tablet left
over from college classes. Satisfied that it had enough paper, he sat
down at the kitchen table with a pen. He chewed the end and stared
into the distance as he considered the dream's details and its order.
He wrote furiously as memories flooded back. He tried to capture the
dream as fully and completely as possible in words. He rewrote it a
couple of times until he was satisfied of its accuracy.

The Dream

> I am in an enormous room. Bigger than anything
> I've seen before. Somehow I know that no human
> built this place. No ceiling, floor, or walls are visi-
> ble, but I still sense that I am in a room. A giant
> golden throne with extremely intense, blindingly
> bright light emanating in all directions draws

my attention to the center of the room. Due to its intense brilliance, I cannot look directly at the light, kind of like you can't look directly at the sun, but with much greater force. I cannot stand in the intensity, so I fall to my knees from the sheer energy and overwhelming presence of the magnificent light. Someone or something is encased in the center of that most bright and brilliant light. The light lingers above the enormous otherworldly throne. I am aware that this is God, and perhaps this is God in heaven.

Beautiful, translucent winged creatures fly all around the throne. I look closer and realize these lovely opaque beings are babies, tiny human babies…really miniscule…but somehow I can still see them. They have a genuine presence, which is both seen and felt. The babies hover around the throne of God. Sometimes they fly in close to God, disappearing in the light. Other times, they fly around the edge of the light. But they always stay in the light, which somehow I know is God's love surrounding His throne. They stay in the presence of God's palpable love. The babies speak…so many voices, in a childlike heavenly language, in indiscernible words. So many…I could not possibly count them.

The sheer number of tiny winged babies is astronomical. Suddenly, I know these are abortion victims.

Then I hear another sound. At first, it is a distant pattering, but it gets louder and louder, and now the pounding resounds so deafeningly that I feel as though my eardrums will burst, and my heart will simply explode inside my chest from the vibrations. My whole body shakes with the pounding, and though I am on my knees,

I fall completely prostrate because the shaking makes kneeling impossible. I look around from my position lying on my stomach, and I notice that this reverberating pounding is rain. In fact, I am getting drenched, but as the water runs down my face and enters my mouth, it tastes salty. All around the edges of the throne of light, winged babies, and God's love, fall huge raindrops, pounding, pounding, pounding ever more loudly. I am pelted by the rain. I sit up as I realize the source of the quaking and use my hands and arms to brace my body on either side to protect myself from the trembling. It seems as if the surface where I am sitting will break open from the hammering—so great is the torrential downpour and so heavy the raindrops. I begin to worry I'll be carried away in flood currents as water accumulates quickly around me. A flood and an earthquake occur simultaneously. Even the air vibrates.

I hear someone say loudly, directly to me, "This is the room of tears."

Awareness fills me as though someone explains things to me or gives me understanding. I just suddenly know things. A room of grief. Weeping. Torrential tears of heaven gushing forth for the choices made to send these babies here. Deep, profound regret and sadness permeate the atmosphere for so many lost hopes and missed opportunities for each of these lives, but also for mankind. God had strategic purposes planned for each one; their lives beautiful, each as unique as a snowflake, with a matchless purpose and destiny. Many babies were answered prayers. People pray all the time for peace, jobs, money, cures, and health. Answered prayers exist right here in this room with these babies. The room weeps because countless generous gifts of answered prayer for the human race were rejected, along with these precious lives. I am aware of how much God loves these babies.

So many random words, thoughts, sensations, and visions explode at me at once, jumbling, overlapping. It's confusing. Some things make sense; some don't:

Political leaders, affection, cures for diseases, tenderness, ample social security resources, smiles, green-energy solutions, optimism, mothers, bliss, fathers, cheerfulness, siblings, inventions, beautiful music, poverty solutions, laughter, peace makers, beauty, job creators, hope inspirers, love, purpose, art, doctors, transportation solutions, value, new technologies, joy, uncles, belief, aunts, trust, foster parents, courage, pastors, camaraderie, teachers, anticipation, professors, companionship, educational innovations, delight, nutrition solutions, friends, poetry, vibrant colors, health, beautiful sounds, prosperity, architects, nurses, authors, cousins, farmers, dependability, harmony, police, and so many other things.

My mind cannot take it all in. Overwhelming purposes, sounds, expressions, and rainbows of colors reverberate in my head. It is hard to comprehend, let alone try to document in writing.

Each baby had a purpose, set aside before they were even conceived, and these were some of the purposes. The unbearable weight of the weeping and mourning consumes me. So much greater than a mere human can conceive of or imagine; mankind has no idea of the eternal consequences of abortion. Precise awareness of such deeply unfathomable loss is incomprehensible, even as it is shared with me. I cannot fully grasp the profound deprivation.

Then I feel my body pulled away from the pounding rain and toward the light. Just at the edge of the light, a winged baby turns to face me and flies straight toward me, stopping directly in front of my face. He looks deep into my eyes. Somehow I know this is my son. My aborted son. As I look at him, he grows from a tiny baby to a child several months old, in a split second.

I always wake up here, heart racing, drenched in sweat.

The writing process brought some clarity. Seth realized he knew more about the dream than he thought or maybe that he had wanted to admit. He was glad he had written it down.

After closely reading his words, he understood how deeply he regretted the abortion of his child. Seth set the tablet and pen aside and wept. Sobs wracked his body again.

Eventually, despite the pain of discovery, a strange peace enveloped him. Giving words and some understanding to the night visitor that refused to leave for over a year offered a sense of liberation.

But the task also drained Seth of energy.

He crawled onto the couch and fell promptly asleep.

CHAPTER 6

Katy's Job

The human heart is the most deceitful of all things, and desperately wicked. Who really knows how bad it is?

—Jeremiah 17:9 (NLT)

Katy loved her job as a social worker. She returned to her desk with a spring in her step after meeting with a client and directing them to a nearby family planning clinic for an abortion. She regularly encouraged clients to get abortions and took great pride in doing so. She believed abortion eliminated poverty, child abuse, and neglect. She thought she helped women get a leg up in society and helped children by not bringing them into dysfunctional lives. Katy felt it was for the good of everyone that these women chose abortion so they weren't condemned to a life of servitude and mediocrity. Nor was their child relegated to a dismal, pain-filled existence devoid of opportunity. Often clients were alcoholics, drug addicts, gang members, and already had children in foster care. Many had quit school and received government assistance. She tried to help them turn their lives around and make better choices. In her opinion, they weren't exactly mothering types anyway and shouldn't have children.

But Katy realized these women were not typical of all women having abortions. *Many are just like me—terrified college students with a bright future ahead, so it isn't the right time for a child. Abortion must be an option no matter the background or reason.*

Katy rehashed these thoughts in her mind for the millionth time. If she believed all this so forcefully, as she often vehemently verbalized to others, why did she constantly struggle inside?

Anger toward Seth brewed to the surface again. Lately, she despised him. She wanted to put the abortion behind them, but he wouldn't let her, constantly throwing *his* guilt in *her* face.

A hard realization hit. It was time to end the relationship, as much as she hated to do it. Seth represented stability—a future and marriage—and breaking up meant she'd have to start all over again with someone else. *Do I have the energy to start over?* But she knew she had to break up for her own sanity. They weren't compatible. They'd grown apart. He never wanted to go out with their friends anymore. He sat by himself in his apartment, stewing. Or he just slept and worked at that dead-end job, not even looking for a better one. He was content with mediocrity. She wanted more.

Katy didn't need to think about it anymore. Her constant anger made it clear that she'd made her decision a while ago. Why hadn't she done it sooner? Katy resolved she'd stop at Seth's on her way home from work tonight to finally end her misery.

I'm so tired of being angry and stressed. I can finally get rid of the cause—Seth. Five o'clock can't come soon enough.

At five o'clock on the dot, Katy darted out the office door. She felt a bit happy and carefree for the first time in a long time. Probably for the first time since the abortion. She noticed birds singing and the sun shining brilliantly, shimmering against the custom-painted daisies on the side of her gorgeous metallic plum PT cruiser. She jumped into her sparkling, spotless pride and joy, cranked up the radio, and sang loudly along to the pop song blaring from the speakers—even dancing a little—as best she could while driving.

Anxious to get this over with and finally get on with her life, Katy drove too fast, squealing tires as she pulled onto Seth's street. She parked, hopped out of the car, and ran up the outdoor rickety wooden stairs to Seth's second-floor apartment.

She flung the door wide-open, realizing suddenly this may be the last time she might ever do so. A twinge of sadness surprised her, but she shoved it aside. *No changing your mind now.*

"Seth!"

Oh my gosh, he's sleeping. It's only five thirty in the afternoon! Do I really have to wonder if I'm making the right decision? This puts the nail in the coffin.

"Seth, wake up," growled Katy, shaking him by the shoulder.

"I'm awake already," said Seth grumpily as he sat up on the living room couch.

Katy plopped down on the old stained armchair Seth had bought at the Salvation Army. He kept a blanket on it so she wouldn't have to sit on the cruddy thing. She hated the thought of what might have caused all those stains.

"We have to talk," said Katy insistently.

"What's up?" Seth rubbed the sleep from his eyes.

Katy hesitated, chewing on her lip. Her bravado left. She swallowed the lump that had formed in her throat and clasped her hands nervously in her lap.

"What is it?" Seth looked bewildered.

"I need to break up with you," said Katy softly, surprised by a sudden flood of emotions.

"What? Why?" asked Seth, not really sure if she was serious, or if this was a joke. Surprisingly though, he felt nothing at her words.

"I've thought about it for a while. We've grown apart. I'm not happy. Actually, I'm miserable. And so are you. You sleep all the time. We don't do anything together. You don't want to talk about our future. You won't look for a better job. There isn't a future in the cards for us anymore. I know you agree," said Katy patiently, and with more kindness than she'd shown him in a long time.

Now Seth's emotions surged to the surface. "Katy, I think if we could just work through the abortion thing, we'd be okay, but you never want to talk about it. I keep having this dream, and it's wearing me out. I think if we could talk things through, I could get out of this rut, and maybe the dream would go away, and we could be normal again," explained Seth with sadness and fatigue.

As soon as he said the word *abortion*, Katy's anger erupted. "There you go again. I've heard about your dream, and I told you I never want to talk about it again. There's nothing to talk about. We both agreed to that abortion, which was the right thing to do. Stop shoving *your* guilt down *my* throat! I am *done*. Our relationship is over. *Don't* call me. We're *finished*."

She stormed through the apartment, throwing the few belongings she had into a bag: a hairbrush, some makeup and other personal items from the bathroom, a few books, a plastic cup in the kitchen, and a stuffed bear on a shelf in the living room. When she examined the small pile she'd gathered, she realized, once again, that this relationship had really been over a long time ago. They had shared very little of their lives since college graduation.

Suddenly, she felt sad again. She walked to the door, turned, and said, "Goodbye, Seth" as tears welled up. She closed the door behind her, and the tears gushed down her face. Seth never saw them though, which made her feel better.

Seth sat in stunned silence. Then he lay down on the couch and promptly went to sleep.

CHAPTER 7

Professor Whitman

For the wisdom of this world is foolishness in God's sight...

—1 Corinthians 3:19 (NIV)

Seth awoke the next morning, still on the couch. He'd slept through the night. No dream. But then he remembered Katy's visit. He felt a little sad, but mostly—oddly—he wasn't upset. Their relationship had gotten pretty unpleasant and volatile. Still, he was surprised that he felt nothing. He didn't care that she'd broken up with him. Maybe he had secretly wanted this.

Seth's mind went back to their decision for Katy to have an abortion. Though he still wasn't sure what he actually thought about abortion in general, he'd thought it was a good idea at the time for both he and Katy. He never paid much attention to the topic one way or another. Yea, he'd heard passionate debates in college classrooms, but eh, it never really mattered much.

Until he started having the dream.

All he'd wanted to do was talk to Katy about the dream, hash it out or something, but she refused. She freaked out every time he brought it up. The dream put a wall between them. But the dream started right after the abortion, so it wasn't clear if the abortion or the dream created the wedge in the relationship. Maybe both.

Either way, maybe now with Katy gone and having written down the dream, maybe…finally…the dream would stop, and he'd have some peace.

* * *

But it wasn't to be.

The next night, he had the dream again. It was increasing in frequency. Awaking tired and stressed the following morning, he decided the time had come to do step 1 on his list: *Go see Professor Whitman.*

Since Professor Whitman, Seth's Psych 101 professor in college, had his own private practice, he might know something about recurring dreams.

Not wanting to waste any time on his day off, Seth opened his laptop and quickly perused his alma mater's homepage. Finding Professor Whitman, he clicked to view the office hours. Whitman was in the office until 11:00 a.m. today. He could get there by 10:30 a.m. if he hurried.

Seth showered, dressed, and raced out the door in record time. He whistled a fast tune as he walked briskly to the college several blocks away and then began jogging along the walkways of the familiar campus. Though he hadn't stepped foot onto the grounds since graduation, the recognizable landscape flooded his mind with memories. Strategically placed trees, shrubs, vibrant blooming flowers, statues, gazebos and benches offered a beautiful backdrop for learning, and songbirds serenaded the scholars, offering peace and tranquility. A warm breeze caused Seth's temperature to rise as he jogged. Not wanting to get sweaty, he slowed as he neared the building that held Professor Whitman's office. He stopped outside to calm his breathing before walking into the building along with some students. The automatic door slid open quickly.

Seth had made a mental note of the room number, *210.* Even though he'd visited the office before, he'd long forgotten the number. Seth got his bearings inside the familiar hallways, and soon he stood outside a room that housed several offices. He took a couple more deep breaths to calm himself and walked inside.

The small room contained several desks crammed together haphazardly in the center for newer professors while private offices lined the perimeter. Professor Whitman, a tenured professor, enjoyed the privilege of an office, not just a desk clumped together with others. With his office along the inside of the building, he didn't have a window, but in the otherwise cramped environment, a private office with a door that actually closed was quite an honor.

Seth found his office. A quick glance inside the open door revealed no one inside except the professor, who sat motionless at a desk, staring at his computer screen.

Seth knocked lightly on the open door, saying quietly, "Professor Whitman?"

The thin, scraggly, gray-haired professor glanced up blankly and said, "Yes?"

Though briefly disappointed that the professor didn't recognize him, Seth quickly realized this man had hundreds of students each semester. "Hello, Professor Whitman, I'm Seth Siracke. I was in your Psych 101 class a couple years ago. Could I ask you some questions? I won't take up much of your time."

Professor Whitman looked slightly annoyed. "I have 10 minutes tops. Are you in one of my classes now?"

"Uh, no."

"I didn't think so. Though you're vaguely familiar, I can usually recognize one of my current students. If you aren't in my classes, and I know I'm not your advisor, how can I *possibly* help you?" said Professor Whitman hurriedly and with slight annoyance.

Seth lost confidence fast. Whitman seemed real busy. Maybe he was out of line just stopping in like this. *I better talk fast.*

"I always liked your class and respect your views, Professor Whitman, and I know you have a private practice. I have a friend that keeps having a recurring dream, and I wonder if you could tell me something about recurring dreams?" blurted Seth.

Professor Whitman looked surprised and sat back in his chair. "That's not normally the kind of question I get from college students.

Let me think a moment." He shifted in his squeaky, old chair and stared off into space for a few seconds as he tried to get his thoughts in order. "When you say 'recurring dream', how often does your friend have the dream, and for how long?"

"He has the dream a couple nights a week, for about the past year."

Professor Whitman folded his hands on the desk and leaned forward. "Well! That *is* a recurring dream. Such a disorder would fall under the diagnoses of parasomnia." He tapped a pen on the desktop while gazing into space. "I have not had anyone in my practice recently with the issue, but if my memory serves me well, I can tell you that many psychologists believe recurring dreams are one's subconscious trying to tell the individual something important about his or her life, an unresolved or unsettled issue of sorts, something important that the person is trying to suppress or refusing to confront. The dream usually continues until the issue is resolved or understood. Stress can also be a factor. Some recurring dreams are common worldwide, such as falling or being chased or being unprepared for an exam. What is your friend's dream about?" asked Professor Whitman, dropping the pen then rubbing his chin. His eyes alight, demeanor animated, Whitman obviously functioned in his element when facing a counseling opportunity.

After hesitating a few beats, Seth reached into his faded rear jeans pocket and pulled out a folded piece of paper. "My friend wrote down his dream." Seth unfolded the paper and handed it to the professor.

Professor Whitman put on a pair of glasses that lay on the desk, took the paper, and began reading. He read quickly, and as he finished, his face flushed slightly. He took off his glasses, handed the paper to Seth, and said, "This is not one of the routine recurring dreams I referenced earlier. This is different. What does your friend think the dream is about?" asked Professor Whitman, a slight quiver to his voice. Seth noticed one of Whitman's eyes twitching. He seemed agitated.

"He thinks God's trying to tell him something."

Professor Whitman looked at Seth with narrowed eyes for a few seconds, then said, "If you were in any of my classes, then you already heard my opinion about 'god.' Religion is simply an immature form of morality, a crutch invented by man. Does your friend suffer from depression?"

Seth hesitated again, hating to admit this part—seeing his depression as weakness. But he knew he had to be honest if he wanted help. "Yes, I think so. He can't get enough rest because of the dream, so he's tired all the time and sleeps whenever he can. I guess you could say all he wants to do is sleep. He's not interested in doing things with friends, and his girlfriend broke up with him because he stopped trying to get a better job. He has a job, but it isn't a very good one."

In response, Professor Whitman asked another question, "Is your friend a religious person?"

"No," said Seth honestly.

Professor Whitman paused a few seconds, then replied, "Obviously I cannot diagnose anything here. I want to see him in my office. Since your friend isn't religious but he's having a recurring dream where he thinks god is trying to talk to him, I am very concerned about his mental health. I am worried your friend may have been influenced by the dangerous propaganda of antichoice religious zealots. Perhaps he got some of these messages from pro-lifers on campus? I've been opposed to having them here from the start. I knew this kind of thing would happen!" He flailed his arms wildly, bumping his glasses on the table with his hand. He tossed them aside before continuing with vigor, accentuating each phrase with a pointed finger in Seth's direction.

"Loony religious fanatics create false guilt as they thrust their hypocritical morality on others and demonize anyone who doesn't agree with their bigoted, hate-filled beliefs! Abortion is more moral than views held by those haters. Your friend is a prime example of what happens to people who hear close-minded, judgmental, and misguided opinions." Some spittle flew from his mouth just as he finished his angry tirade.

Jumping to his feet, he pulled a business card from a cardholder on his desk. "*Please* give your friend my business card and ask him to call me *as soon as possible*. I know I can help him work through this false condemnation so the dream can stop," said Professor Whitman forcefully, arms flailing again. His voice had gotten a bit too shrill, his face now very red indeed.

Obviously, he feels passionately about this.

Seth took the business card and thanked him for his time.

As he walked down the corridor and out onto the sunny pathways outside, he thought about the visit. The professor's reaction was a little too much like Katy's for Seth's own liking. But he may be right, or maybe not.

Seth knew he had not been exposed to the kind of rhetoric the professor referred to. He had never paid any attention to the issue at all. He did other homework during abortion debates because the discussions bored him. He just wasn't interested. No one filled his head with "nonsense" as the Professor presupposed.

This dream literally had come out of nowhere.

Dissatisfied with the meeting, Seth resolved to visit Professor Cantor on his next day off. If Cantor had the same views as Whitman, maybe then he'd take them both more seriously.

CHAPTER 8

The Accident

Children are a gift from the LORD;
they are a reward from him.

—Psalm 127:3 (NLT)

Katy sat hunched over her desk, breath ragged, eyes closed, the full weight of her face leaning on her two fists, feeling defeated. She expended a great deal of energy just to steady her head, and every last ounce of strength bottled the tears inside. Papers lay haphazardly on her uncharacteristically messy desk. Just looking at the unorganized heaps of documents and folders, now concealing her ever-important appointment book, made her stress level rise further.

A couple of weeks had passed since breaking up with Seth. The initial breakup was tough, but afterward, she'd been so happy—so excited about the future. She tried to remember how she felt in those distant, faraway moments. She strained to recapture the contentment that had enveloped her when the breakup first gave her newfound freedom. But any joy now seemed ancient, elusive.

Katy tried to put a finger on what bothered her so much. She didn't miss Seth, not really.

Why did she keep barking at everyone at work? Her short-tempered reactions to nearly everything clearly annoyed her coworkers. One told her she skated on thin ice. Another, overhearing the comment, remarked snidely, "Yea, she's on my last nerve."

But that wasn't the worst thing. She'd angrily argued with a *client* a few minutes ago. Katy feared a colleague may have overheard the exchange. She could lose her job for that kind of behavior. She knew she'd been wrong but couldn't help herself.

The client was cute and friendly. A thin, young girl of only eighteen who previously had minor behavioral problems at school and with her family. The behavioral problems were trivial, at least compared with some of Katy's other clients. The client and her family had both previously seen therapists at Katy's agency. But the client, now an adult, had an issue of her own. She was pregnant.

Katy, as she normally does, heavily pushed abortion, clearly the most obvious and logical choice, while citing all the usual statistics and reasoning. Yet this girl, with a confidence Katy rarely saw in clients, emphatically told Katy abortion was not an option, and she was trying to decide between having the child or "offering the gift of adoption."

Something about that phrase "offering the gift of adoption" set Katy off. She immediately got angry with the girl. Her voice rose, and she didn't even attempt to look for the list of adoption agencies that she was supposed to utilize in adoption referrals. She rarely referred anyone for adoption.

In fact, Katy realized, she'd never done so. She wasn't even sure where she'd filed her list of adoption agencies. She never used the list since her initial new-employee training.

The client, clearly upset, jumped up and practically ran out the door.

Katy worriedly chewed her bottom lip. *Could I lose my job? I really messed up.*

She rubbed her face in her hands. Trying to comfort herself, she crossed her arms and wrapped them around her waist in an embrace as she bent her torso and leaned forward, her head over her desk, her eyes closed. Trying to will the emotional turmoil to leave.

Emotions overwhelmed every aspect of her life.

She'd even fought with her sister yesterday. A pretty nasty fight too, and Katy never fought with Merin, whom she idolized.

What's going on? Katy banged her head lightly on her desk a few times as she rocked gently, remembering her fight with Merin.

As usual, they talked about Merin's wedding plans. But for the first time in a long while, Merin considered what her life would be like after the ceremony. She talked about having children. She touched her flat stomach and rubbed it, asking Katy what she thought she'd look like with a baby growing inside. "What does it feel like when a baby moves and kicks inside you?" wondered Merin aloud to Katy.

Merin had simply asked a hypothetical question. Katy replayed the exchange in her mind, trying to understand her extreme edginess. Merin hadn't expected Katy to know or answer, but Katy got offended. She lashed out immediately. "How should I know, Merin? Why would I care? You're so selfish! You're always thinking of yourself!"

I shrieked at Merin. Literally shrieked.

Merin had looked stunned, her face white, mouth agape as if she'd been punched in the gut. Merin didn't say anything for a while, then responded gently, "What's wrong, Katy? I don't understand. What did I do to upset you?"

Katy stammered, embarrassed by her own outburst: "I don't know. I guess I'm not feeling well. Sorry."

Merin looked at Katy, uncertain, then asked, "What's wrong? Do you want to lie down?"

Katy said, "No, I just have a headache. I'll be fine."

Katy replayed the incident over and over in her mind.

I lied to my sister. I didn't have a headache.

Merin, thinking the issue resolved, blathered on about having children, what she'd name them, who they'd look like, what kind of parent she'd be, and on and on. At least that's how it seemed. Even now when Katy remembered Merin's words, it hurt. She wanted her to stop saying those things.

Katy finally shrieked again, "Shut up Merin! Just shut up, will you?" and ran out the door.

Katy hadn't seen Merin since. She waited until well past Merin's bedtime to go home yesterday so she could avoid her. Even more unheard of than fighting with Merin was ignoring Merin for the rest of the evening and all of today. Katy ignored every one of Merin's fifteen calls and thirty text messages.

Clearly, Katy upset her sister.

She replayed the argument over and over.

But Merin upset me too. Why?

Katy lifted her head off the desk as tears ran down her face.

Adamantly pro-life, Merin would never understand. Katy could never tell her about the abortion.

Katy also realized at that moment that maybe she wanted a baby after all. She wished she had one *now*. And not *any* baby, but *that* baby.

To top it all off, Katy recognized the pang of jealousy that filled her heart. How she envied her sister's impending marriage and motherhood!

The revelations hurt. Katy blew her nose and dabbed her eyes.

What would it be like to have a baby?

She finally willed herself to rise from the desk and walk out the door, long after quitting time. She had sat alone in the office for a long while, feeling sorry for herself. Lost in thought, she hadn't noticed the sun sink below the horizon or the rain, which now came down in sheets.

Katy ran to her car to avoid getting drenched. She jerked as a bolt of lightning cracked nearby, and thunder roared immediately afterward. Cool rain pelted her bare skin. The darkness prevented her from seeing pools of puddles. She stepped into a deep one and let a few curses fly as the water soaked through her shoes up to her ankles. She plopped herself onto the warm, dry car seat, relishing the sudden comfort and protection it provided. She sat, shivering for a few minutes from the chilly, last day of summer shower and allowed her car's heater to warm up the interior. Hoping the downpour would slow, she sat in the idling car for a few minutes.

Taking advantage of the time, she allowed her fantasy to run full force. She imagined getting married, getting pregnant, and having a baby, or two. Maybe three. She smiled as she considered what her children might look like.

Though she enjoyed the fantasy time immensely, the rain didn't abate, so she reluctantly put the car into gear. *I can't avoid Merin forever.*

She turned up the radio as she pulled onto the ink-black, wet highway, humming a tune and reveling in her daydream about motherhood. But the pleasant daydream was interrupted by regret. What would it have been like to have *that* baby? Tears once again escaped and streamed down her face. A sad sigh escaped her lips as she brushed them aside with the back of her hand.

The rain pounded her windshield, so she fumbled for the controls, turning the wipers on full speed. Katy leaned forward, gripping the steering wheel tightly and peering through the rain-blurred windshield, trying to see into the black night. High beams only made it harder to see in the downpour, so she switched to low beams.

Suddenly, the steering wheel veered, yanked violently from her hands. Tires squealed viciously, and blinding lights thrust at skewed angles confused Katy. Nightmarish honking blared, and her body was tossed like a ragdoll then instantly stilled by a bone-shattering blow.

All occurred simultaneously with an ear-piercing crunch of metal.

Brutish violence ended as quickly as it had begun.

Then silence.

Darkness.

And the rain poured down.

Katy heard voices, foggy, distant, and unclear as if floating in a kind of drug-induced trance or time warp. She strained to open her eyes, but the effort proved too great. She tried moving her hand, but it felt buried beneath a heavy, immovable object. Slow realization dawned. Every body part seemed completely paralyzed. Panic welled. Katy focused her energies on speaking. Silence. Not even her lips moved. Nothing worked except her ears, and they weren't working too well either. Her mind worked though. It raced.

Where am I?
Am I dreaming?
Am I dead?
She lost consciousness again.

The voices were back. This time, a little clearer. Other unrecognizable sounds emerged. Clinking. Swishing. Metal clanging? Footsteps, perhaps. Katy sensed people all around, but they ignored her. She existed in a lonely abyss, in another plane.

Katy once again succumbed to the blackness.

CHAPTER 9

Professor Cantor

For the time will come when people will not put up with
sound doctrine. Instead, to suit their own desires, they
will gather around them a great number of teachers to say
what their itching ears want to hear. They will turn their
ears away from the truth and turn aside to myths.

—2 Timothy 4:3–4 (NIV)

Seth awoke early, thankfully, since he'd had the dream again last night. He rubbed sleep from his eyes, feeling the all-too-familiar sensation of fatigue. *Chronic fatigue.* That's how he felt. *Chronic fatigue syndrome.* He remembered hearing that somewhere. He might have to look that up sometime. Ugh. Too much research. Too tired.

He had to move.

Yesterday, he'd checked Professor Cantor's schedule; he was in the office from eight to nine thirty this morning. Seth wanted to arrive promptly at eight. Hopefully, he could get right in to see the professor and still get to work by ten—his scheduled start time today.

As he'd done when visiting Professor Whitman, Seth darted about his apartment to get ready, ran out the door, bounded down the steps, and jogged up the street. This time, Seth jogged all the way to campus. He hoped jogging would warm his body from the mid-September morning. Seth inhaled deeply. An end-of-summer rain had pelted the ground hard last night, and the earth smelled so fresh. *Enter autumn.* Though the trees weren't turning yet, the crispness of fall filled the chilly morning air. He loved the changing temperatures and uniqueness of each season.

In no time, he arrived at campus, relishing the short nature jog. Most of the flowers still bloomed, but that would end soon since seasons changed quickly in the northeast.

Seth easily found Cantor's office. While in college, he often looked for excuses to visit his favorite professor. He wondered if Cantor would remember him. Whitman didn't, but then again, Seth didn't know Whitman as well.

Seth rounded the corner and discovered Cantor at his desk. Thankfully, no one else had arrived yet; the rest of the desks remained empty. Pleased with his forward thinking, Seth congratulated himself for planning an early arrival. Hopefully, now, they could talk privately.

Cantor didn't have the luxury of his own office. One needed seniority to gain such a privilege. Instead, Cantor's desk, as a junior professor, sat inconspicuously among several rows of aged, grey, dinged metal desks in a crowded room. The desks looked salvaged from a scrapyard. Not exactly prime real estate.

As Seth approached, Professor Cantor glanced up. An initial lack of recognition cleared quickly, and Seth saw clarity register.

"Seth! How are you, my boy?" exclaimed Professor Cantor boisterously as he stood and vigorously shook Seth's hand, with a broad grin on his slightly chubby, boyish face. "What are you doing with yourself since graduation?" he asked with interest, brushing aside an unruly black curl that had flopped in front of his eye from atop his too long, thick head of wavy hair.

Seth took in the sight of Cantor—the familiar wild mustache, jowls moving with every word, and buttons straining at all the usual places on his too-small shirt. He hadn't changed a bit.

He briefly filled in the gaps for his favorite professor from graduation to the part-time interim library job. There really wasn't much to tell.

Trivialities aside, the professor smiled and said rather grandly, "So to what do I owe the pleasure of your presence today, Mr. Siracke?"

Seth smiled, both with pleasure that Cantor remembered him and also because of his familiar and likable nature. He felt at ease and glad he'd come. "I wanted to talk to you about something… something kind of personal…well, it isn't about me. It's about a friend. You always have good advice, and you said if I ever needed anything, I should stop in, so here I am."

"Okay. Shoot. What's up?" said Cantor directly but with curiosity.

Seth faltered. *Why didn't I think this through? Where to begin?*

"Well, my friend has this recurring dream." Seth paused, unsure how to continue.

"Dream?" said Cantor, looking confused. "I'm no psychologist. I don't know anything about dreams. Unless—wait—is it a math dream?" he asked, chuckling.

"No," stammered Seth. Just then, a couple of other professors walked in and sat at desks nearby. Seth watched them, chewing his lower lip nervously.

Cantor picked up on Seth's uneasiness and said, "Hey, I haven't had my coffee yet. Do you wanna walk to the student union with me? We can finish our conversation there."

"Sure." Relief flooded Seth's body.

As they walked down the hall, the professor responded to greetings from many students who now filled the corridors. The emerging crowd made it difficult to talk, so Seth used the time to collect his thoughts. *How to ask Cantor such bizarre and personal questions?* Finally, Seth thought of an "in."

Cantor bought his coffee at the student union, which was bursting at the seams with people, and suggested they sit on a bench outside. The chilly morning air lured the students inside, leaving the outside benches free. They sat gingerly on the cold metal, trying to warm the seats with their bodies. Cantor slurped gratefully on the steaming hot coffee.

"Ahh, that's nice. Okay, Seth, tell me. What's up with this dream? You do have my curiosity aroused." He laughed with a genuine belly laugh.

Seth smiled apprehensively. "Well, you told me if I ever needed anything, I should come see you. And well, you probably remember that my dad moved away when I was young, and I haven't seen him in years. I don't have brothers or sisters, so there's not a lot of people to talk to about stuff." Seth examined Cantor's face, trying to read his expression.

Cantor smiled gently and said, "Yes, I remember. And I meant it. Shoot."

"Well, like I said, I have this friend who keeps having this dream."

"About what?" Cantor gulped down more coffee.

"He wrote it down." Seth once again dug the folded paper out of his jeans pocket and handed it to the professor.

Professor Cantor sat his coffee down on the bench, unfolded the paper, and began reading. When he finished, he folded the paper back up. Seth noticed Cantor's hands shaking slightly.

"That's intense," Cantor said quietly.

"Yes, it definitely is."

"So how often has your friend had this dream?"

Seth had his response ready since he was getting used to telling people now. "He has the dream a couple of nights a week for the past year."

"Whoa! That's a lot. So what's your friend done about it? That's a long time to suffer. Has he talked to anyone?"

"He's tried. He tried to talk to his girlfriend, but she wouldn't listen. She broke up with him a couple weeks ago. He went to see a psychologist a couple times. And he talked to Prof Whitman too," said Seth matter-of-factly. Just talking to someone who actually seemed to care *and* listen felt good…therapeutic.

"What happened with the psychologist? And Professor Whitman? Could they help?"

"He didn't think they helped. And the dream hasn't stopped."

"I think something like this might take a while. He probably needs to give them more time," suggested Professor Cantor kindly.

"My friend believes the direction they took wasn't what he needed." Seth shifted on the bench then blurted, "What do you think about God? And abortion? And what do you think about this dream?"

"It's not in my place to offer advice and especially not to someone I don't even know—as in third-party advice—and about such controversial and personal things," said a flustered Cantor.

Seth sighed. "We talked about all kinds of controversial things, and in math class of all places. Surely, you can at least give me your opinions about God and abortion. You don't have to comment on the dream. Just tell me your views," pleaded Seth.

Cantor inhaled a deep breath and closed his eyes. Clearly, this was not a good start to his day. He gulped the last of his coffee, threw the cup in the garbage can, and rubbed his hands on his pants.

"Okay, abortion first. I was pro-life when I first came here to teach. My wife's still pro-life. But I don't know, I guess I was naïve before, or, as my wife would say, I've been 'indoctrinated' into the pro-choice world. I used to argue for life with other professors on campus, but I could never win. I finally gave up. I'm now pro-choice. End of story. I'm not a fighter. Whatever people want, it should be their right to do. I just don't want to get into these fruitless moral arguments," said Cantor, shrugging his shoulders resignedly.

Seth chewed his lip. *I guess I can see that, Cantor. You're too nice to fight.* "What about God?"

"God's another area where I just gave in to the pressure. I guess I'm a fence-sitter on a bunch of important issues. Not sure if God 'is' or 'isn't.' To be honest, these questions are a painful bone of contention between my wife and I. I stopped going to church. I only go on Easter and Christmas now. My wife says this place—this 'bastion of elite intellectualism'—has messed with my head. She's right, I guess. I don't know. I just go with the flow. I have to, here at work, or I end up in all kinds of battles I don't want to be in. I'm a *math professor*, for heaven's sake. I just want to do math," said Professor Cantor, sounding tired.

Seth chewed his lip some more.

This isn't going as planned. He's not helping. I really thought this man could solve all the world's problems.

Seth rubbed his forehead, clearly distressed.

Cantor noticed.

"Look, Seth. I wish I had more to offer, but I don't." He paused, shifting his weight on the bench as he gathered his thoughts. "First, let me say, I recognize your handwriting, so I know this isn't about some mysterious friend. Clearly, this is troubling you, so I urge you to get the right kind of help. I hate to see you torturing yourself, and this isn't something to brush under the rug. I'm honored you came to me, so I'll do right by insisting you get professional help. Please go back to the psychologist, or please go see Professor Whitman again."

Now Cantor chewed on his own lip, pondering his next words. "Here's an idea. I'm trying to process what you told me. You didn't like how things went with the psychologist, and you have questions about God. So why don't you go see a pastor?"

"I guess I could talk to my mom's pastor, but I haven't been there for a long time. I don't even know if the guy's still there. Um… hey, Prof Cantor, who's your wife's pastor? Just in case my mom isn't going to church anymore."

"Oh, sure, yea, let me write it down for you." Cantor reached for a small tablet and pen in his shirt pocket. Seth smiled as he realized how much he idolized this man; he had started carrying his own pocket tablet and pen after he saw Professor Cantor doing it.

Professor Cantor jotted a few words, ripped a sheet from the tablet, and handed it to Seth. The note read as follows:

Pastor Frank
Word of Life Community Church

"I don't know the address. It's up on Clifton Street, near the end of town on the right. I'm sure you can find it on the Internet or in the phone book," said Professor Cantor, rising and reaching to shake Seth's hand.

Seth stood and shook his favorite professor's hand, feeling disappointed.

"I'm sorry, but I gotta run. I still have prep for today's classes. Good to see you, Seth. I hope the dream stops. Let me know how this works out. If I think of anything else, I'll let you know. Many people have gone through what you've been through. There's hope, and there's help. All the best to you. Keep in touch." And with that, Cantor disappeared into the growing crowd of students.

Familiarity marked the rest of Seth's day. He performed his duties at the library with mechanical motions. Even his conversations with Harold had settled into the mundane; each of them seemed to purposefully avoid talking about their earlier—strangely confrontational—conversation about Seth's dream. Both seemed relieved to put that uncomfortable situation behind them.

Life was so ordinary today and, in fact, somewhat pleasant even that Seth whistled a bright tune as he walked home from work. When only a block away from his apartment, his cell phone's quirky ring tone went off in his jeans pocket.

Hmm. My friends only text. Probably Mom.

Not feeling like talking to his mom, he ignored it, pressing the silence button inside his pocket. His mom only ever had doom and gloom to share about friends and distant relatives he barely knew or often didn't know. Seth didn't want anything ruining his good mood. *A conversation with Mom will only depress me.*

Just as Seth jogged up the stairs to his apartment, the cell phone rang again. This time, he pulled out both the phone and his keys, noticing a bunch of missed calls. He looked at the caller while inserting the key in the lock and pushing open the creaking, ancient door.

He paused with the door wide-open. *Katy's mom? What in the world could she want?* He hadn't heard from Katy in weeks. He looked curiously at the phone displaying multiple missed calls from Katy's mom. The ringing stopped as he closed the door and turned on the lights. Just as he considered calling her back, the phone rang again. *Typical.* Katy clearly inherited her lack of patience from her mother.

"Hello?" Seth pretended he didn't know the caller's identity but the implied question mark at the end of his greeting was sincere. He truly wondered why Katy's mom called him.

"Seth! I've been trying to reach you. Something terrible has happened to Katy!" Katy's mother sobbed without identifying herself. "Please come to Community General right away, the fifth floor waiting room on the east side. It's urgent."

"What happened?" asked Seth, both surprise and concern evident in his voice.

"She was in an accident. Please come now. I'll tell you more when you arrive." And she promptly hung up.

Seth stared dumbly at the phone now silent in his hand.

His mind didn't work. *What does it feel like to be in shock?* he wondered since he couldn't think what to do next.

Seth finally shook himself from the daze, walked to the closet, and pulled out a hoodie. The sun had gone down. With the calendar announcing the arrival of fall, the weather obligingly turned cooler. He appreciated the fact that he lived in the center of town where he could walk to nearly everything. Seth pulled up his hood and walked right back out the door he'd just walked into, locking the door behind him.

So much for a peaceful evening.

Seth arrived at Community General just fifteen minutes later. Completely unfamiliar with the hospital, he spotted a reception desk with, thankfully, an actual person sitting behind it. Seth asked the bespectacled gray-haired woman, hunched over a pile of papers, where to find the elevators. She rolled her eyes with exasperation and motioned to his left while munching loudly on an apple.

And right there they were. Directly in front of him, no more than a couple feet away.

Wow. Snap out of it.

Everything felt dreamlike. *Maybe a new recurring dream is beginning. Maybe I'll have two recurring dreams, and I'll never ever sleep again.*

"Stop," Seth said aloud to himself as he stepped into the empty elevator. Thankfully, no one heard him having a conversation with himself as he pressed the number 5.

He disembarked, wondering which way was east. As he tried to sort out the direction in his foggy mind, he noticed a sign directly in front of him: "East Waiting Room" with an arrow pointing right and "West Waiting Room" with an arrow pointing left.

Seth turned right and walked tentatively down the hall. He heard Katy's mom crying before he actually saw her. His heart pounded wildly in his chest, and he nearly stopped walking as fear took over. Just then Katy's mom walked out of a room and into the hallway. They stood face-to-face.

"Seth! Oh Seth!" She cried loudly, brokenhearted, as she hugged him. "Katy was in a horrible accident. It's not good. Please come in and sit down."

Clearly shaken, her features made no secret of the fact that she'd been crying for a while. Her blotchy red face; her puffy, bloodshot, swollen eyes; and her wildly unkempt hair looking as though she'd repeatedly run her fingers through it all spoke volumes. She blew her nose loudly into a tissue with visibly shaky hands while tears ran non-stop down her face. All makeup had long been wiped away with tears and tissues. Katy's mother, normally meticulous about her appearance, looked extremely out of character. Just seeing this distraught woman shook Seth even more, making him realize the gravity of the situation.

Katy's dad walked over and silently shook Seth's hand in greeting, his eyes also red with tears. Merin, Katy's sister, sat cross-legged on a stained, old chair nearby, crying quietly. She gave a little wave when she saw him. Seth had wildly conflicting and confusing emotions as he tried to piece together what he saw and heard.

"What do you mean it's not good?" Seth's voice quivered.

He and Katy may not be together anymore, but they'd been a thing for a long time. *You don't just stop caring about someone when they break up with you.* His thoughts gave validity to his emotional whirlwind.

"Oh, Seth," Katy's mom wailed. "She's in a coma. They just told us she's brain-dead! I don't believe it! I *won't* believe it. They haven't even given her a chance!" Katy's dad walked over and pulled her into a big bear hug, gripping her tightly. Clearly, she was about to lose it. Maybe Katy's dad was too. Seth couldn't tell. She sobbed loudly for a long time as her husband held her close. Eventually, he gently turned her toward the doorway. Katy's dad walked her mom out the door and down the hall, trying to calm them both.

Merin motioned to Seth to come sit beside her on one of the waiting room chairs. "I don't have the energy to get up," she squeaked.

"No problem. I understand."

"You don't seem that upset," said Merin, slightly accusingly.

"What? Of course, I'm upset. I'm just shocked. I haven't absorbed it yet. What happened, exactly?" asked Seth tentatively.

Merin relayed the details of the accident and of Katy's current condition. Finally, surprisingly to Seth, tears ran down his cheeks as he absorbed the enormity of the situation.

This can't be.

So many different emotions assaulted his senses, taking him on a maniacal ride in an alternate universe. Everything felt wrong. Evil. Dark. In his mind's eye, he saw a kind of carnival with distorted music and the most frightening clowns. Life suddenly got twisted, and he was powerless to make anything about it right.

"Merin," said Seth sadly after some time had gone by, both of them lost in their own painful thoughts. "I have to tell you something."

"What?" asked Merin without interest.

"Katy broke up with me a couple of weeks ago. I haven't seen her since. That doesn't mean I don't care about her just as much, because I do, but it seems like maybe you and your parents don't know we're broken up. I would feel weird if I didn't tell you," said Seth quietly.

"What? Oh my gosh, I didn't know." More tears poured down Merin's face. "Why did she break up with you?"

"I think we just grew apart. Both of us saw it. Not surprisingly, Katy took the obvious step. She's always been the one with initiative," said Seth in a half-hearted attempt at humor.

Merin laughed a little, then cried again. "You don't have to stay. We didn't know. This must be awkward for you."

"I'm not gonna just run out the door now that you know we broke up. I'm not that coldhearted. I care about Katy. This is horrible. I'm really sorry." And Seth meant it. He felt like a broken man. This night couldn't get worse.

He didn't know what else to say. No words seemed right.

Merin sobbed again, then blurted haltingly, "Katy and I had a fight. We never fight. What if our last words were angry…and hateful? How can I deal with knowing that the last thing I said to my sister—who I love more than life itself—made her mad!" she howled.

Her words shocked Seth. *Merin and Katy had a fight?*

Knowing Merin's personality, Seth realized Merin probably didn't start it. He didn't dare put his thoughts to words, though, because it wasn't appropriate in the situation and because he was confused. While Katy picked fights with just about everyone, he knew full well she never fought with her sister. They had a deep bond. Katy adored Merin, and somehow she just never got mad at her. *Never.*

"I know you and Katy don't fight much, so you can't beat yourself up about it. Everyone disagrees sometimes. I know how much Katy loved and adored you. Um, I mean I know how much Katy *loves* and *adores* you. Just think about those things." Seth did his best to muster up the right kind of support but failed miserably.

How does anyone deal with this kind of stuff? It's impossible to say the right words. I'm talking in the past tense as if she's already dead. God, help me. God, help Katy.

Wow, I must really be messed up. I just prayed. When's the last time I did that? Children's Bible school?

Just then, Merin stood to her feet and wiped the tears off her face with a tissue, pulling Seth from his thoughts. "I need to go see Katy. They probably won't let you back there since you're not immediate family. I could try to sneak you by the nurse's desk, though, if you want?"

"Um, no, I probably shouldn't then, if I'm not supposed to. Go ahead. Keep in touch and let me know how she's doing, okay?

I really do care, and I really do want to know," said Seth, surprised when tears started running down his face again. He couldn't make them stop.

Merin hugged him when she saw his tears and started sobbing again herself.

"I promise to keep you posted." Merin released him and turned to walk down the hall.

Seth's legs shook so badly that he had to sit back down.

God, please help Katy. Thank you. Amen.

He eventually got up, walked down the hall, and slowly back to his apartment on a dark, cold and very depressing night.

And of course, as a fitting end to a horrible day, Seth had the dream again. In fact, he had it *twice* during the course of a long and restless night.

CHAPTER 10

Seth's Mother

…If anybody is preaching to you a gospel other
than what you accepted, let them be under God's curse!
Am I now trying to win the approval of human beings,
or of God? Or am I trying to please people?
If I were still trying to please people,
I would not be a servant of Christ.

—Galatians 1:9–10 (NIV)

As streamers of sunlight announced the early morning through open blinds, Seth stretched and slowly pulled himself to a sitting position. *Man, last night must've been crazy.* His senses slowly took in the state of his room. Sheets torn off from the bed laid crumpled in a pile in the center of the mattress. Blankets and pillows strewn across the floor. *Brr.* Seth wrapped his arms around his torso and rubbed his biceps to warm himself.

He bellowed a long yawn and rubbed his eyes as he recalled the events of the last twenty-four hours. *So much happened. Professor Cantor. Work. The dream twice in one night. And Katy…the accident. Wow.* He put his head in his hands and tried to change directions with his thoughts. He couldn't think about Katy yet.

For the first time, Seth lamented not owning a car. Normally, he loved his earth-conscience ways, walking everywhere or taking public transportation. Katy and his friends thought he was nuts, but he was proud of not owning a car.

Today, though, a car would be helpful. Maybe I need to buy one after all.

Seth considered the day's activities. He had to work in the afternoon, but first, he had another project to take care of.

So he needed energy.

He had none. Zero. Nada.

He shifted to the edge of the now-bare mattress and pulled on a wrinkled shirt and pair of khakis he found lying within reach on the bedroom floor. He didn't bother to brush his hair or teeth.

Too tired.

After kicking his favorite worn Sperry's boat shoes aside—*too cold for those,* he thought—he dug around under the bed for cooler-weather footwear. Sneezing from the dust, he finally found both of his well-used Merrells, quickly brushing dust from each. *Better for cooler weather, but I definitely need some new shoes.* He pulled his last pair of clean socks from the dresser, realizing his clothing choices dwindled. *Now I have to do laundry too.* He yawned again as he slowly slipped on socks and shoes.

He slugged to the hall closet and reached into the back for a warmer coat, something that would break the wind better than last night's hoodie. In his poorly insulated apartment, he felt air blow through the edges of an ill-fitted window. *Definitely chilly outside.* A loose pane of glass rattled as a strong gust slammed into the side of the building. *And very windy.* A cold front had moved in.

He wasn't relishing this morning's foot journey.

First stop, a coffee shop, just a couple of buildings from his apartment. *I can make it.* Seth willed himself onward.

After zipping his coat, Seth dashed out the door with motivating thoughts of a large, steaming cup of black coffee. He didn't drink coffee much, only on desperate occasions. Like when he had to pull an all-nighter studying in college. And the rare times when he and his friends partied all night, and most unfortunately, he had a morning class. Most times, if he needed a boost, he drank an energy drink. But today's bitter cold morning and his lack of sleep evoked a craving for piping hot coffee.

Soon, he seated himself on an elevated, trendy stool in the coffee shop and warmed his hands around a tall, comforting cup of java.

Ah, yes, that's one thing energy drinks don't have—aroma.

He loved the smell and breathed it in deeply.

He felt better already.

Seth took his time. As he drank his coffee, his belly warmed, his mind cleared, and he considered how to tell his mom about Katy. Most people knew each other in this small town. News traveled fast.

She'll soon hear about the accident. Mom doesn't know we broke up. Neither one of us told our parents. Everything is too hard lately, even simple conversations.

Seth faced the truth of how isolated he'd become. Katy was right. He didn't hang out with friends. He didn't do anything except work at the library. He suddenly felt lonely and realized he wanted to see his mom.

He slid away from the table, the stool creaking along the floor. A couple of people looked his way at the distracting noise.

Time to do this.

Seth walked as quickly as he could the four blocks to his mom's house.

Along the way, he lost himself in memories; that way he didn't have to think about the cold, or Katy, so much.

His mom and dad divorced when he was twelve. It was for the best. They both drank too much and fought like crazy. Dad had an affair, Mom found out, and Dad left. He moved clear across the country with his girlfriend. Seth had only seen him a few times since. Mom grew bitter after Dad's affair and the divorce. She got so wrapped up in herself and her pain that it seemed as though she forgot Seth existed. She went through a string of low-life boyfriends over the years and made some poor decisions, but he still loved his mother.

Sometimes he wished he had a brother—even a sister would be nice. Especially lately. He needed someone to talk to. He never talked much with his mom, but he knew he had to tell her about Katy's accident.

A horn blew, jolting Seth's attention to the present. Surprisingly, he had arrived at his mom's house already. He walked up three cement stairs to the tiny porch of the brick building. A good find, her apartment was decent for its size. She had a first-rate landlord who kept the grounds in meticulous shape. She liked it here, and Seth had liked living here too, eventually. He preferred their bigger house, the one they lived in as a family. But Mom couldn't afford to stay after Dad left. Seth understood, but the adjustment was a difficult one. His heart ached for a warmer, happier time.

Was there one?

He tried to remember but couldn't think of any.

He stood at the front door, about to open it with his key and walk in, but realized she might not even be home yet. He glanced at his watch: 8:30 a.m. She worked the night shift at a bakery and loved it. Night shift paid better, and she slept in the afternoon. He craned his neck and leaned around the corner of the porch to look for her vehicle. He saw the aging but amazingly dependable, faded Chianti-red Honda Civic wagon parked in its usual spot.

Satisfied, Seth unlocked the door, opened it, stuck his head in, and yelled, "Mom? Hello!"

"Seth!" she yelled with warmth and surprise from the kitchen. "Hey, young man, hello. How are you? Ooh, it's so good to see you. Come in—come in—come in. What a treat! Ooh, I missed you," she gushed all at once, stringing her words together.

Seth smiled. Sometimes it felt really good to just go see your mom.

He relished the attention for a bit, and they shared small talk. He walked to the cupboard and pulled out an olive-colored 1970s-era plastic container. He popped off the lid and reached inside for the treasure: yellow crème-filled cookies. He grabbed a handful and munched. His mom laughed at the familiar sight of her son helping himself to his favorite snack.

After finishing off the delectable cookies, he turned to his mom with a serious expression. "I have some bad news. Well, I have two bad things, but one's worse than the other."

"Oh my god, Seth, what is it?" exclaimed his mom, worriedly clasping both hands over her mouth dramatically. While she braced for the bad news, Seth knew in some weird way she liked the drama of negative reports.

"A few weeks ago, Katy and I broke up."

"Oh no!" wailed his mom.

"But I'm okay with it. It doesn't bother me. I'm fine," he said reassuringly.

Seth paused just a beat and continued, "But the *really* bad news…Katy was in an accident. A bad one. She isn't doing good. They think she might die," blurted Seth, his voice shaking.

"Oh my god!" his mom sobbed. He didn't know how her emotions responded so quickly.

"What kind of accident?" she asked between sobs. "What happened? Is she at Community General? Oh my god! I should call her mom. I should go visit her today."

Seth relayed what little he knew about the actual car accident and Katy's condition. "Things aren't looking good. I couldn't get in to see her, only immediate family can. Merin said she'd keep me posted. I don't know what to do," he added and wondered why he said that.

"Oh my god, Seth! I'm going to the hospital to see Katy's mom right now. Do you want to go with me?" she asked in a panicked voice.

"No, I can't. I have to go to work. But call me and let me know if you find out anything more. If I don't answer, just leave a message."

Seth's mom dashed around the apartment, throwing on shoes and grabbing her coat, keys, and purse.

"Um, one more thing before you leave. Something else I wanted to ask you," said Seth haltingly.

"What's that, honey?" asked Seth's mom, stopping dead in her tracks, with concern in her voice as she waited for more bad news.

"Something else altogether. Nothing bad. Do you still go to that same church you went to awhile back. The one you liked so much?"

"The Temple of the Enlightened? On Broad Street? Oh yes, I love that place. I don't go all the time, you know me, but no one expects you to. They don't call it a church. It's a temple. I told you how they welcome me and don't judge me, right? They let everyone, how do they put it, 'define God for themselves.' Whatever seems right to me. No high and mighty, hypocritical, cranky churches for me! No way, no how." She paused her increasingly loud diatribe and then asked more calmly, "Why?"

"No reason, just wondered. I might check it out sometime."

"Oh, of course! You're going through such a hard time right now. Let me know when you wanna go. We'll go together. I'd love that so much!" she gushed.

"Okay. Well, I'll let you get going, and I gotta get to work. See ya." Seth walked toward the door. His mom followed him outside, locking the door behind her.

"See ya, honey. I'll give you an update on Katy later. Love you. Bye!" She waved as she jogged around the corner toward the car. Soon, she sprinted back around the corner again toward Seth. "Let me drive you to work. It's cold outside!"

Seth happily took her up on the offer, jogging quickly after her to the rusty Honda and plopping himself inside, pulling the door shut with a soft *whump*.

"Thanks." He chuckled as he rubbed his hands together to warm them and began twisting the radio knobs, trying to find a station to his liking. "What's the name of your pastor at that church, or I mean that…temple. I forgot his name."

"*Reverend*, Seth, and *her* name is Reverend Lucille Watts. Love her!"

Seth chortled, "Oh, like Lucille Ball."

"Yes, Lucille, like Lucille Ball," agreed his mom, dramatically drawing out the name. "She's young. You'll love her." Her attention turned to the traffic ahead of her.

Seth hummed to a familiar song playing on the radio. He didn't want to tell his mom that he had no intention of going with her to the temple. That isn't why he asked. He just wanted to talk to Lucille Watts and see what she thought about his dream. That was the next step in his plan.

When they arrived at the library, Seth climbed out, thanked his mom, and jogged inside to the warmth and familiarity of his favorite place. Peace enveloped him as he breathed in the comforting scent of the quiet house for books.

Seth noticed Harold in his usual spot, and the two exchanged a wave and a smile.

He had ten minutes before his shift started, so he looked up the Temple of the Enlightened on his smartphone. He walked downstairs to the conference room area so he wouldn't disturb anyone and dialed the number.

A busy-sounding receptionist answered, and Seth asked for Reverend Lucille Watts. In a few seconds, another friendly and energetic woman said briskly, "This is Reverend Watts. How can I help you?"

"Hi, I'm Seth. I know someone who goes to your church, and ah, I have this problem I need to talk to someone about and wondered if I could make an appointment with you?" asked Seth quickly, watching the clock.

"Sure," said Reverend Watts brightly. "When would you like to come?"

"I'm available tomorrow morning and any morning next week."

"How's nine tomorrow?"

"Sounds good. Ah, I can find the church, but where's your office?"

"Just come in the front door of the temple, and immediately on your right is a staircase leading down to the basement. Go downstairs, and my office is the first door on the left."

"Okay, thanks. I'll see you tomorrow at nine. Goodbye." Seth hung up and raced upstairs, still a couple minutes early for his shift.

At the end of his workday, Seth noticed his mom had left a message on his cell phone. He listened to it as he walked home. Katy's condition hadn't changed. His mom babbled on about the horrible state of affairs while crying, making it hard to understand what she said.

The message depressed him, so he didn't call her back. Instead, he lost himself in thought all the way home, not even noticing the chilled air.

Seth dreamed again, awakening more tired than usual the next morning. He gulped down an energy drink and readied himself for the morning's meeting with the reverend.

Finally, I'm going talk to someone who might actually be able to shed some light on this.

Seth grew excited about the possibility of his dream ending soon. Again, he didn't even notice the cold as he considered what to say to Reverend Watts. Arriving at the temple quickly, he discovered the building looked like any church he was used to seeing—not a temple—with its brick exterior and steeple. A pair of ornate wooden doors adorning the front entrance looked like most church doors. Following the reverend's instructions, he went directly to her downstairs office without a glitch, no other person in sight. He paused at the office door and knocked lightly.

"Come in," sang a friendly voice.

Seth opened the door and stuck his head around the corner cautiously. "Reverend Watts?"

"Yes, indeed. Please come in—Seth, it was, correct?"

"Yes," he replied tensely as he took in her cute and perky appearance. Like his mom said, she was young. Her shockingly bright orange-red hair looked a little like Lucille Ball's but much redder.

She motioned for him to have a seat next to her desk.

They talked pleasantries for a bit until Reverend Watts straightened a stack of papers on her desk and glanced impatiently at her watch. Evidently a doer and uncomfortable with casual chatter, she shifted in her chair and turned her gaze to Seth.

"So how can I help you? What would you like to talk about?" she asked kindly, but with purpose.

With no reason for half-truths, Seth dove right in. He didn't know Reverend Watts and had no intentions of revealing his mother's identity.

"I have this dream regularly. I hope you can give me some insight into its significance, because I think once I understand why I'm having the dream, it might stop."

"Oh." Reverend Watts clearly looked puzzled. "This is a new one for me. You're the first person who's come to see me about a dream." She chuckled. "What's it about?" she asked, again with purpose.

"Actually, I have it written down." Seth handed her the paper.

"Okay!" said Reverend Watts brightly, pleased at such efficiency. She read quickly, her expression not revealing her thoughts.

"Interesting," she said when finished, a bit too curtly, thought Seth. *Maybe I'm getting paranoid now too.* He chastised himself for reading more into a single word than he should.

"What do you think is the significance of your dream?" she asked, handing him the paper and leaning back in her chair, with a thoughtful look on her face.

"Well, obviously, I think it says something about God and abortion. And I think God's trying to say something to me about abortion. I hope you can tell me what God thinks about abortion," said Seth quickly, but haltingly.

She took a deep breath and seemed to choose her words carefully.

"I don't think any of us knows exactly what God thinks about abortion. Here at the temple—and we are universalist in our beliefs—we offer support to all people in their search for truth, and that search is unique for each person. We accept all who come, and we support you in your choices. So what God thinks about abortion is something you will need to determine for yourself in your spiritual journey." She leaned forward in her chair and folded her hands on the desk. "In general, we believe that women have a right to choose to have an abortion or not. Abortion is a legal right in this country, and we support that right and have made public statements to that effect," explained Reverend Watts, somewhat coolly and mechanically as though she recited her spiel from memorization.

"Uh, okay. But what about the Bible? What does the Bible say about abortion?"

"The Bible is only one possible source for answers. We don't believe it is the only source of truth, and we keep many religious texts here for study. We have the Bible, the Talmud, the Koran, the Dao de Jing, Dianetics, the *Book of Mormon*, various sutras, the pyramid texts, various Vedas, Book of the Zodiac, Darwin's *Origin of Species*, and I could go on," she said, ticking off the books on her fingers which held long, well-groomed nails, painted bright red to match her lipstick.

"Oh yes, I almost forgot, Freud wrote a book or two on dreams, I think. You might want to check those out. We have all of Freud's work. Oh, and Jung wrote about dreams too. We have work from all the premier psychologists here. You're welcome to spend time researching truth at our enormous library, just down the hall," she said, smiling and sweeping her arms toward the collection room while sounding somewhat sympathetic. "It's bigger than the college library, and many professors use it and attend our services here at the temple," she added with pride.

"Well, okay, maybe. But what does the Bible say about abortion?" Seth asked again, falling back to his only reference point for the conversation.

"The Bible has no scriptures directly referencing abortion. I explained our views. If you're having trouble coming to terms with an abortion, which I'm assuming that's what this is really about, then you could consider seeing a psychologist in addition to exploring various spiritual truths. I've had two abortions myself, and I freely and unashamedly share my abortion stories in my sermons. In fact, I think I can find a CD where I talk about them somewhere for you," she explained as she began flipping through pages of a CD notebook filled to the brim with CDs on her desk. "My sermons are on our website too. You could download them," she explained as she searched.

She paused. "There's no *shame* in abortion," she said emphatically, looking directly at Seth. "But unfortunately, some antiquated and intolerant religious views dominate our culture and cause unnecessary guilt for people. These views have probably tainted your thinking, and that's why you're feeling guilty and having the dream. I believe it's very important for you to get the right kind of help. While spirituality is important, there is much a psychologist can do to help. I have some names I can recommend, if you like," said Reverend Watts with exaggerated sympathy, as she opened a rolodex and flipped through. Her lengthy crimson nails easily picked through each card. She seemed to have trouble sitting still as her attention turned from the CDs to Seth to the rolodex.

Seth stood. "No thanks, been there done that. Thanks for your time." Anger stirred just below the surface, but Seth didn't know why. He walked out the door, quickly closing it behind him. He didn't care if he appeared rude. Nothing about the visit felt right. He didn't like that his mom came here. It felt…what was it? Too loose? Too anything goes? Whatever it was, Seth couldn't put his finger on it. Something just didn't feel right. And Seth always trusted his gut. He practically jogged up the stairs, out the door, and down the street toward the library. He desperately needed to put distance between himself and The Temple of the Enlightened.

Can't anyone help me? This is my life! My peace! Doesn't anyone care?

Seth wanted to scream in frustration, but instead, he just choked back tears—an all-too-familiar sensation. After a few deep breaths, he whistled in an attempt to calm himself as he approached the library for another workday.

* * *

Katy felt cold. She tried to talk to the voices around her but could not. She wanted to tell them she needed a blanket. She tried to move again. She tried to open her eyes. Nothing. She remained a prisoner in her own body. She heard the voices of her parents. They sounded worried. Sad. Crying.

They talked about her.

She heard someone, a voice she didn't know, say the words, "Brain-dead." Her mother wailed. Katy felt desperate to communicate with her.

What are they talking about? I'm not dead!

She could hear them, all of them. She comprehended their words.

I'm here! I'm not dead! She screamed as loudly as she could inside her head.

No one listened.

Katy heard someone say the words, "Organ donation," and once again, she heard her mother sobbing.

Eventually, Katy pieced together enough of the conversations to understand. They thought she was dead—*brain-dead*—and they wanted her parents to donate her organs.

Thoughts flooded Katy's mind.

Is this what death is like? Will I know what everyone is doing around me forever? Will I feel them cut out my organs? Will I know when they embalm my body for my funeral? Will I be aware of people as they come to my funeral and look into my casket? Will I hear them close the lid? Will I sense the darkness? Will I know when they shovel dirt on top? Is this death?

Katy heard every word spoken around her.

I can't be dead. I know what you're saying! I can hear you! I'm right here!

But she didn't feel any pain. She didn't feel anything.

She blacked out again.

CHAPTER 11

A Growing Friendship

...Do not grieve, for the joy of the Lord is your strength.
—Nehemiah 8:10 (NIV)

Seth and Harold's friendship deepened with time. Harold's kind nature and quick wit did Seth's heavy heart good. He found himself laughing whenever Harold was near, sometimes at the simplest of things. Harold had a knack for pulling fun out of anything, finding clever humor in places Seth never would've considered in all his seriousness.

Harold invited Seth to dinner. Over and over. But Seth always brushed him off. He told Seth he'd wither away to nothing if he didn't put some meat on his bones. Once, when a patron opened the front library door and a breeze blew in, Harold hurried, as best he could, to Seth's side and grabbed his arm.

Startled, Seth asked, "What's wrong?"

Harold, smirking at his own cleverness, said, "I didn't want you to blow away! That's a big wind for such a skinny sprite!" He chuckled as he walked away.

Seth couldn't help but laugh. He knew the comedy was dated and cliché, but Harold could pull it off. He just knew how to deliver a punch line. Even though Harold was just as skinny as Seth, Seth was never able to properly turn the tables on Harold's abrupt cleverness.

Seth envied Harold for that and realized that Seth James Siracke had no knack for humor—a stand-up comedian he was not.

Finally, Seth agreed to go to Harold's for dinner one evening when he worked the closing shift. Harold sensed that late-work nights didn't produce anything edible from Seth's cupboards. Usually too tired to cook, Seth just crashed for the evening and ate junk food or nothing at all.

Since 7:00 pm was later than Harold normally visited the library, he said he'd come back to get Seth after his shift ended.

Sure enough, Harold shuffled in the front doors of the library at 6:55 p.m., waving and motioning that he'd wait outside.

Seth did one more walk through of the library. He called out the usual closing mantra in the quiet building as he examined every inch of space, asking anyone to answer if still present. As predicted, no one replied from the rows of stacks in the now-clearly vacant structure. He locked the office door and turned off the lights, except for those left on at night for security. He locked the front door, pulled it shut behind him, and tested the knob. Satisfied, Seth turned toward the road. Harold stood beside a colossal, pale yellow Ford Granada. *Ancient.* Pretty good shape for its age though. *Like Harold.*

"Nice car. What year?"

"1981."

"1981?!" hooted Seth, laughing incredulously. "It's in great shape! And it's a classic. Worth money."

"Don't drive it much. Hmm. Guess it could be a classic, but doubt it's worth much," said Harold absently. He opened the front passenger door and stated firmly, "Rudy. Come. You need to get in the back."

He pulled out a gigantic yellow Lab, the same color as the car, by the collar. The dog's enormous wagging tail clunked against the outside frame of the vehicle as Harold led him around to the back door. He opened the rear car door and guided him into the back seat. The brute of a dog leaped, scraped, and plopped noisily onto the seat.

Harold closed the door carefully once the fair-haired beast had moved to the center and wouldn't get his unwieldy tail caught in the door.

"You have a dog?!" laughed Seth, pleasantly surprised. Harold never mentioned a dog. Seth wasn't allowed to have one growing up. His friend Mark had two. He loved going to Mark's house to play with the dogs when they were kids.

Seth felt more lighthearted already. A friendly dog. A cool classic car.

"Hi, Ruuudyyyy," Seth enthusiastically drawled the dog's name as he plopped into the front seat while simultaneously reaching around to pet the overly excited Labrador. Rudy whined and wiggled with pure happiness, licking Seth's face and putting a paw up on the back of Seth's seat while trying to thrust himself into the front of the car.

"Rudy!" said Harold sternly. "Sit!"

Rudy reluctantly obeyed his master, letting out a disappointed whine but compliantly settling himself on the long rear bench seat, putting his head down on his paws with a sigh. His position didn't last long.

As soon as Harold put the car in gear, Rudy immediately sat back up and put his head next to Harold's head, licking his ear. Harold chuckled and reached behind, fondly petting the dog while inching the Ford slowly toward the stop sign.

They drove only a couple of blocks behind the library to a row of older, small, square-shaped homes in a patchwork of colors—pink, blue, yellow, green, and more. They stopped in front of one of the few white-only houses. At a snail's pace, Harold pulled the boxy car into a short driveway and under a tiny carport that barely covered the boat of a car they drove. Situated directly beside the miniature dwelling, the carport's quarters were so tight that Harold couldn't even open his car door all the way without hitting the side of his house.

"This is it. Home sweet home. It isn't much, but it's home to me, and I like it." Rudy whined excitedly. "See Rudy likes it here too." Harold chuckled as he opened the rear passenger door just wide enough for Rudy to squeeze through.

Seth got out of the car and noticed a seemingly endless countryside stretched beyond the small, fenced-in backyard. In the darkness, he couldn't tell what kind of plants grew in the field behind the yard's boundary.

Must be a farm nearby. Nice. Kinda like living in the country, but you still live in town.

Rudy ran into the small backyard and did his business, then Harold opened the side door to his house—directly beside the car—and Rudy burst inside the small dwelling with renewed zeal. Harold chuckled. "You'd think he's been gone for days, as excited as he gets to come home."

Seth followed Harold into his quaint house.

Welcoming, just like Harold. Not fancy but comfortable. And genuine.

Harold had prepared for Seth's visit.

The table was set pleasantly, though plainly, and a bubbling crockpot, plugged into an electrical outlet on the counter, wafted a pleasant aroma. Harold walked over to the crockpot, lifted the lid, and stirred the contents.

"Smells *great!*" said Seth enthusiastically as his stomach rumbled and his mouth salivated in response to the agreeable smell. "What is it?"

"Homemade vegetable soup. I learned how to make it from my wife. She'd make big batches and freeze it for us. Now that it's just me, I do the same but freeze it in smaller batches. I unfroze a couple batches, enough for us both tonight. It's nice to have company." Harold smiled as he turned and looked pointedly at Seth.

"It's good to be here," said Seth awkwardly as he walked over and looked at the soup, "and it really looks and smells great."

Seth wasn't used to going to old people's houses for dinner. He couldn't recall ever doing it. Unless it was Mark's parents, but they weren't *that* old.

After they washed their hands, they sat down to enjoy dinner. Harold bowed his head, folded his hands, and said a short prayer of thanks. Seth watched with interest since it had been awhile since he'd seen anyone pray before a meal—not since he'd been to Mark's house a long time ago.

Harold and Seth enjoyed the soup and each other's company. After eating, he helped Harold load the dishwasher and clean up the kitchen. He remembered how much he hated doing that kind of thing himself, so he wanted to help. Plus, Seth imagined older people got more tired.

After cleaning up, they went into the living room to relax and unwind. Harold sat on a well-worn recliner, and Seth sat on the nearby couch. Rudy hopped up onto the couch next to Seth and whined and wiggled as though he met him for the first time again. He covered Seth's face with dog kisses. Seth laughed and ruffled the Lab's soft ears while wiping dog saliva off his face with his shirt sleeves. Rudy soon settled down next to Seth, laying his head on Seth's lap, tail wagging now and then as he and Harold talked easily.

"He likes you. Of course, he likes pretty near *everyone*." Harold snorted as he rolled his eyes.

"Oh sure, way to let a guy down. And here I thought I was special," joked Seth as he turned to ruffle the soft fur around Rudy's neck. "Ruuuuudddyyyyyy," teased Seth, causing the dog to whimper and wiggle his body with excitement.

"You're getting him all riled up again," warned Harold with a chuckle.

Time passed comfortably and quickly.

A chime from the clock on the wall brought Seth's attention to the hour—nine o'clock! He jumped up and apologized for staying so late, noticing Harold's stifled yawn and the tired redness of his normally flickering, light-filled eyes.

Harold eschewed his concerns, saying he could stay as long as he liked.

"Nope, I need to go. It's late. Thanks so much for a great dinner. I *loved* the soup. You're quite a chef. I'll see you tomorrow at the library." Seth rose and walked to the door.

"Just you wait, young man. I'm driving you home."

"No, you don't have to. I walk home all the time from all over the place. I love to walk, and my apartment isn't far," explained Seth with finality.

"Sure, just go and walk off all those calories I tried to pour into those skinny bones tonight. All that slaving away at the stove for nothing," harrumphed Harold, feigning annoyance but with a smirk on his face.

"Ha! My body's used to the walk, but it isn't used to good home-made vegetable soup, so it wasn't a waste at all. See ya tomorrow." Seth laughed.

"Good night, Seth. See you tomorrow."

Harold turned on the porch light and watched Seth walk into the night, praying for his new young comrade until his shadowy silhouette disappeared down the hill.

Seth savored the quiet walk home in the cold night air. He breathed deeply and watched frosty breath expel into the atmosphere as he reminisced about the visit with his unlikely new friend.

A peaceful smile formed on Seth's lips.

When he arrived at his apartment, he softly whistled a few tunes as he drowsily undressed. Climbing tiredly into bed, he fell promptly asleep.

Unfortunately, the rest of the night lacked the same serenity. The dream once again invaded his life, erasing the evening's pleasantness.

In the morning, Seth went through the motions of getting ready for work in a stupor, all the while feeling burned out. Extremely.

No happiness allowed anymore.

The dream would not permit it.

* * *

This time pain woke Katy. She hurt everywhere. The voices still droned. She felt her mom holding her hand, squeezing her fingers. She heard her mom speak. It sounded like she said *goodbye*. With finality.

No! screamed Katy inside her head. *I'm here!*

With everything she could muster, every ounce of strength, she focused all her energy into opening her eyes. She *willed* her eyes to open, over and over. Finally, success! Katy felt her eyelids flutter.

She heard her mom catch her breath as she stopped her whispered, teary goodbyes and squeezed her fingers tightly in a vice grip.

"Katy!" bellowed her mother. "Katy! Open your eyes, Katy!" And she kept shouting it over and over. Her mom patted Katy's cheeks and squeezed her arms and clapped her hand against Katy's hand in an obvious attempt to generate a response.

Katy heard a blend of voices grow louder near her, and many footsteps hurried close. A great deal of clanging and screeching and all sorts of commotion crescendoed.

One. More. Time. Katy forced her eyes open and said hoarsely, "Mom," then fell promptly asleep again.

The hospital room erupted in a flurry of activity. Katy's mom turned angrily to hospital workers who hovered nearby, waiting for her to say her final goodbye so they could wheel her daughter away and take her organs. "Leave!" she shouted to them while pointing at the door. They scurried out. "My daughter is alive," she screamed hysterically at everyone remaining in the room. "Do what is necessary to save her life!"

The room burst into activity with a rising swell of doctors and nurses, all visibly shaken by what had just occurred, or almost occurred. Katy's organ donation had been imminent.

At the library that morning, Harold noticed Seth's change in demeanor from the previous evening with concern. He thought he'd broken through whatever troubled this young man. But that didn't seem to be the case.

Harold stroked his chin and devised a new plan. He set out to hound Seth to come to his house for lunch that day.

"How long do you work today?"

"Until one," replied Seth shortly. He hated to hear annoyance creep into his voice. Harold didn't deserve that.

"I'm waiting here until you get off work, and we're walking together to my house at one, and we're having my famous meatloaf sandwiches for lunch today," announced Harold with authority and a tight smile. He felt it was time to get a little pushy.

Seth looked quizzically at Harold as he pondered the invitation. Finally, he gave a slight nod. Harold's satisfied smile lit up his face. Seth couldn't help grinning back.

Maybe it's time to tell Harold about the dream. He's seen a lot in his lifetime. Maybe he can help.

The short day went quickly. Seth worked all sorts of hours, but just part-time, so some days were short like this one.

He and Harold walked slowly to Harold's house. Seth wrapped his arms around his waist, guarding himself against the chilled air. Normally, he walked fast to stay warm; his jacket didn't exactly pass for a winter coat, so he put a lot of effort into slowing his pace to match Harold's. Advancing at the speed of an inchworm frustrated Seth's already frayed nerves, but he stuffed his impatience.

What's wrong with me? I want to lash out at everybody about everything, or rather, about nothing.

When they arrived at Harold's house, Rudy whined, wagged, and even barked a bit when he saw Seth walk through the door, leaping at him with such force that Seth nearly lost his balance. Seth laughed and ruffled the dog's ears as Rudy placed one paw on each of his shoulders. Dog saliva dripped from Rudy's tongue onto Seth's shirt. *Ew.* He pushed Rudy off and petted him as he stood by his side. Harold hadn't seen the rambunctious greeting by Rudy since he'd gone to hang up his coat in the hallway closet.

Harold returned to the kitchen and told Seth to hang his coat up, wash up in the restroom, and make himself at home while he got lunch ready.

In no time flat, Harold had a meal prepared, which consisted of cold meatloaf sandwiches with mustard on white bread, potato chips, and dill pickles.

Again, Seth noticed his stomach growling and his mouth salivating. Normally, he didn't think so much about food, but Harold's food always seemed appetizing.

They sat down to eat. Harold once again bowed his head and prayed out loud, and again, Seth just watched. Rudy even waited to eat until Harold's prayer ended. After Harold said, "Amen," Rudy ran to his own dishes in the corner of the dining room floor. Harold had filled them to the brim with dry dog food and water.

Harold wrinkled up his nose as he ate the meatloaf sandwich. "Oh. Darn. Sorry about that," he said gruffly.

"Sorry about what?" Seth's brows furrowed in confusion.

"The freezer burnt meatloaf. Darn!"

"Tastes great to me," said Seth honestly, then with surprise, "I never ate a cold meatloaf sandwich before. It's good with mustard."

Harold frowned and groaned in disappointment. "Ah. It's nothing like it should be…one of my specialties, but you can't even appreciate the goodness."

"Get outta here, Harold! This is the *best* meatloaf sandwich I've ever eaten!" Seth laughed.

"You just told me you never ate a cold meatloaf sandwich before."

"Exactly. That's what I mean. It's the *best* meatloaf sandwich I've ever eaten." He laughed again, somewhat giddily.

Harold laughed too.

They were back to feeling at ease with one another. Seth's peace returned.

They cleaned up and went into the living room again, just like last night.

This time, they sat at a little table in the corner and played checkers. While they played, Harold shared a lot of his life with Seth.

Captivated by Harold's stories, Seth entered a whole new world. Harold, a master storyteller, shared about the navy, growing up as a child, his marriage, and his career with the local electric company.

After a comfortable pause in the conversation, Harold looked at Seth and said, "I've been like a little old lady talking too much. Now you know all about me, but I don't know anything about you. Tell me about yourself." Harold leaned toward Seth with interest.

Seth gave a few minor, generic details about his life and stopped. An awkward silence ensued.

Harold frowned momentarily, then asked bluntly, "So why do you always look like a ghost is haunting you?"

Startled by Harold's incisive words, Seth's heart skipped a beat. *A ghost? I guess it might be.*

Surprisingly, Seth spilled his guts. Completely. But he told Harold the story in a different order than he'd told the others. Instead of starting with the dream, he started at the beginning. He told Harold about his childhood and his parents' divorce. He told him about his relationship with Katy. He even told Harold about the abortion. He told him about Katy's accident and that they had broken up. Then he told Harold about the dream.

At the end of Seth's description of the dream, Harold wept openly. Sobs wracked his body. Seth feared for the elderly man's frail heart in his obvious distress.

What if he has a heart attack? The man's in his nineties. What am I thinking dumping on him like this?

"I'm sorry I upset you. Can I get you something? Let's change the subject. Are you okay?" asked Seth in a bit of a panic.

Harold started laughing even as he wept, wiping his eyes with a handkerchief. Rudy had walked over and laid his head on Harold's lap, whining as Harold cried. Clearly, the dog tuned into his master's moods and felt sad along with Harold.

"Seth, I'm sorry for upsetting you, and you too, Rudy," he said as he looked down and patted the dog's head. "I have to think about how to say this so it'll make sense." Harold paused a moment to gather his thoughts while wiping his eyes and blowing his nose.

"You see, I'm a Christian. I told you that before. So as I've gotten to know Jesus, I got kind of softhearted over the years, I guess you could say. I think, maybe, I learned to be sad when God's sad. My heart breaks for you and Katy and for your aborted baby. And I bet God's heart breaks for you all too. And obviously, or maybe not obviously to you." Harold chuckled as he waved his arm in Seth's direction. "But I'm crying because what you just told me confirms God *is* speaking to me. Remember when I told you in the library to write down the dream? The dream about the winged babies and the room with pounding rain? I had no idea what it meant. I worried you'd think I was crazy. And you did! So I told God I listened to Him, but it didn't go too good, so I didn't understand why he told me to do that. So I guess I'm crying about a lot of things." He blew his nose loudly. Rudy whined and wagged his tail. It thumped against the side of the little table, making it shake.

Harold patted Rudy's head and laughed again. "But I'm laughing because God is good. He always knows what he's doing even when I don't." Harold stared at the table and shook his head incredulously. Then he directed his light-inflected blue eyes piercingly at Seth. "Now I know a lot more about how to pray for you."

Seth squirmed in his chair. All this God talk made him uncomfortable. His friend Mark was a Christian and talked like this, but he hadn't seen him in a long time.

"I guess that's good, because I could use some prayer," responded Seth haltingly, unsure of what else to say.

"I'll pray for Katy too," added Harold with a frown. "I'm worried about her."

"Thanks, I appreciate it," replied Seth soberly.

Harold yawned just as the clock chimed in the next room, announcing the late hour. Seth pushed himself to his feet. "I'm gonna head home. It's been a long day, and I'm kinda tired. Thanks again for the food. You're spoiling me with all these good eats."

"See you tomorrow at the library," replied Harold with fatigue in his voice. He didn't get up to walk Seth to the door this time.

Seth mentally kicked himself again.

I have got to remember this man's in his nineties. What am I thinking?

CHAPTER 12

Katy's Recovery

Give all your worries and cares to God, for he cares about you.

—1 Peter 5:7 (NLT)

Seth shoved his hands deep into his coat pockets to stay warm on the walk to his apartment, and just as he did so, he felt his phone vibrate. He'd missed a call while at Harold's. With his coat tucked away in the hall closet and with the phone in the coat pocket, he never heard it vibrate.

He looked at the caller: Merin.

Seth's heart raced.

She left a message, so he quickly punched into voice mail to listen.

"Hi, Seth, this is Merin. I have good news! Give me a call. Bye."

Seth immediately dialed Merin's number, and she answered as soon as it rang.

"Seth! Guess what?" she asked happily.

"What?" said Seth a little impatiently.

"Katy woke up!" she shouted into the phone, laughing and crying at the same time. Merin's voice shook. "Last week, the hospital wanted us to remove life support and donate Katy's organs. I couldn't bear the thought—none of us could—so we waited. But this morning, she's awake!"

"Whoa!" responded Seth breathlessly. He didn't know what he'd expected, but it wasn't this. "Totally awake? Talking? Walking?" asked Seth disbelievingly.

"She said a few words. She's still in bad shape. She can move her fingers and toes but can't walk because she has a lot of broken bones, so she still has a lot of healing to do. But I'm so thankful she's alive and awake." Merin signed with relief. She paused, and her tone changed as she growled, "She's definitely not brain-dead."

"Wow, they really said that she was? Are you sure?"

"Yes. They told us over and over again and pressured us not to keep her alive artificially since she was gone. I am so glad we didn't listen." Merin sobbed, her emotions all over the place.

"Me too," agreed Seth. Tears welled, and his heart raced at the painful thought. "Am I allowed to see her? Or should I?" he asked tentatively.

"She's in intensive care, so it's still just immediate family. But I heard them talk about moving her soon. After that, she can have other visitors. I know she'd be glad to see you."

"When did she wake up?" Happy but shocked by the news, Seth tried to process the information.

"This morning. Today was supposed to be the day we officially accepted her death, and her organs would be donated. Me and Dad said goodbye first. Then Mom held Katy's hand like she always did—she never left her side—but this time, she said goodbye. But then she heard Katy say, 'Mom.' I didn't hear it because I wasn't as close. After that, all 'you-know-what' broke loose because…well, you know my mom!" Merin laughed uneasily. "Things have bustled in there ever since. And Katy said a few words that I even heard later."

"Wow, that's really great." Seth's voice shook with emotion, and he paused briefly to compose himself as he struggled for words. Finally, he added, "Hey, keep me posted. Let me know when it's okay to visit."

"I will. See ya," answered Merin happily.

Just as the conversation ended, Seth arrived home. Despite the early hour, he fell immediately into bed with utter emotional exhaustion.

And of course, he dreamed.

The next day at the library, Seth told Harold about Katy. Thrilled, Harold whooped quietly in congratulations and playfully slapped Seth on the back, assuring Seth he continued to pray for them both.

Seth awkwardly thanked him again, still not sure what to say about all this praying stuff. He appreciated that Harold prayed for him, but he still didn't have the conversation with Harold that he'd wanted to have. Harold's emotional reaction to his dream had sidetracked things.

Seth wanted to know how to stop the dream. Still no closer to that goal than when he first started meeting with Dr. Westnar, he considered his next steps since, so far, no one and nothing helped.

During his morning break, he pulled the list that he'd written a while ago out of his wallet.

That's the problem. I've just gotten off track from my plan.

Number one: Professor Whitman. *Did that, no luck.*

Number two: Professor Cantor. *Did that, no luck. But Cantor gave me the name of his pastor. Where'd he put it?* Seth dug through his wallet some more and found the note Cantor jotted: *Pastor Frank, Word of Life Community Church.*

Hmm. Will Pastor Frank have something different to say than Reverend Watts at the Temple of the Enlightened?

What's next.

Number 3: Research dreams.

Aha!

Now that was something he hadn't done. After work, he'd find out what kinds of books this library had about dreams and borrow them. He'd also hole up in his apartment and do some Internet research.

After his shift ended, Seth looked up books about dreams. The library didn't have many in stock. He borrowed the few they had in the building. He could've had other books transferred in but decided he'd start with these.

Before going home, he stopped at the coffee shop on the corner below his apartment to get warm coffee and a sandwich to eat while he researched.

Just as he paid the cashier and gathered his 'to go' bag, someone slapped him on the back and said loudly, "Seth Siracke! Man how are you dude? Haven't seen you in ages!"

Seth turned to see his old friend Mark. Recognizable still, but different in appearance. Taller, thinner, new glasses, more grown up. Wow, it'd been a while.

"Mark!" Seth smiled broadly and matched Mark's enthusiasm. "I'm good! How are you?"

"Fantastic!" Mark smiled large, with the ever-present optimism Seth remembered. "Are you still in college?"

"No…graduated this past spring."

"Really? Wow, time flies. What was your major? Where do you work?" asked Mark, throwing out questions.

"I majored in journalism and work at the library part-time for now. I'd like to get a job as an investigative reporter."

Mark used to be his best friend. *How had they lost touch?* He tried to remember. "What about you?" Seth couldn't recall if he even knew at some point in time what Mark's future plans had been. The fact that Mark remembered his college plans amazed Seth.

"Hey, have a seat?" suggested Mark questioningly while pointing at a chair as he took a seat nearby. "I went to Twinhearts Bible College and earned a theology degree with a concentration in youth leadership. I'm a youth pastor at my church and plan to continue my degrees to some higher levels."

"That's cool." Seth felt awkward that the conversation shifted in a God direction again. Trying to be friendly, but also because of his own questions, he asked, "What church do you go to again? The same one you used to go to? I forget where?"

"Yep, it's the same church, the one you came to now and then with me—Word of Life Community Church."

Seth jumped. "Wait…did you say Word of Life Community Church?

"Yea, why?" asked Mark, confused by Seth's reaction.

"Oh, no reason. I'd forgotten the name. That's all." Seth quickly tried to cover his surprise. *That's the church Cantor gave me.* "Listen, I've got a project I'm working on, so I gotta get moving. Good seeing you, Mark."

"Yea, Great to see you. Hey, maybe we can get together sometime, hang out, catch up? What's your phone number?" asked Mark as he whipped out his cell phone, ready to enter the number.

Seth gave Mark the number. He guessed it'd be fun to hang out. He needed some cheering up.

They said goodbye, and Seth jogged the remaining feet to his apartment.

Time to do some research.

Several hours later, Seth closed his laptop. He'd skimmed the library books and scanned tons of websites without finding anything particularly useful about his dream. His findings simply echoed Professor Whitman's brief observations.

Maybe my research tactics are too generalized. That must be the problem. I have to get more specific.

Again, he dug out his list. *Number 4: Research the Bible.*

Seth wasn't ready for that one. He had to chew on that for a while, unsure why he felt so apprehensive. Maybe he was just tired.

He went to bed.

And dreamed the dream again.

A few days later, Seth's phone vibrated while he was re-shelving library books. He glanced at the caller: Merin. Anxious to know what was up, Seth went to the restroom and called her back.

"Hi, Seth," she said brightly.

"Hey, Merin. What's up? How's Katy?" he replied quickly.

"You won't believe it, but the hospital plans to move her out of intensive care in a week! She's still in lots of pain. Oh, she looks terrible but so much better than before. She can sit up and talk now. They're planning surgery for some less serious complications. Her right leg is broken, so she can't walk yet, but she's making so much good progress." Merin sighed with relief.

"That's great…really good news."

"Yep. Mom drives the doctors and nurses crazy. Since their wrong diagnosis, she watches them like a hawk. She insists they inform her of everything they're doing and why they're doing it. But really, without her, we may not have Katy." Merin's voice broke as she choked back tears.

"That's intense." Seth paused, unsure what else to say, then added, "But it's awesome news about Katy. Let me know when she's out of intensive care."

"Absolutely! As soon as she's out, you'll know, and then you can come see her."

"Okay, I gotta run 'cause I'm at work," said Seth a bit sheepishly. He hated breaking the rules by making a personal phone call, but he worried about Katy too. He determined he'd work a few minutes after quitting time to make up for the time he stole just now, or maybe he wouldn't take a break later. That'd work too.

"Oh, no problem. Thanks for calling back. I'll keep you posted."

The next day, Seth told Harold the good news about Katy. Harold grinned with pleasure and reminded Seth that he still prayed for them both.

Seth awkwardly mumbled his now standard, self-conscious *thank you.*

The next week flew by with nothing much out of the ordinary. Seth still had the dream. Not every night, but most nights. Enough to keep him constantly sleep-deprived.

His mom called to tell him about Katy. He didn't bother to inform her that he already knew. He left her talk because she so enjoyed the drama. She actually had more details than he did, so he let his mom fill him in.

On his way home from the library one evening, Merin called.

"Hey, Merin," he answered.

"Hi, guess what? Katy's out of intensive care! They moved her this morning. Now she can have regular visitors, and she's asking to see you. *A lot.* She keeps insisting she needs to talk to you, so hopefully you can stop in and see her?"

"Uh, sure. When are visiting hours?"

"Noon to eight o'clock every day."

"Okay, ah…I can't tomorrow 'cause I work in the afternoon, but I can get there around two on Thursday since I work in the morning."

"Okay, I'll tell her you're coming. Her body isn't quite Katy yet, but her personality's spiffier than ever. She'll be thrilled," gushed Merin.

"Thanks, see ya," replied Seth abruptly. He didn't like long conversations, and as tired as he's been lately, he really didn't like them.

Wow. He rubbed the back of his neck in exhaustion as he slowly walked up the creaking steps to his apartment.

So much happened in the past few weeks, so many ups and downs. I do want to see her, and I'm glad she's getting better, but I hope Katy doesn't want to get back together. I don't think I have anything left in me for that. Last time we talked, she didn't want to see me anymore. With all she's been through, I don't want to upset her, so I hope she doesn't want us to be a couple again. Maybe I'll ask Harold to pray about it.

The next day at the library, Seth made a beeline for Harold when he saw him. He filled Harold in about Katy and then gave him his prayer request—his hope that Katy doesn't want to get back together again. Harold looked surprised, chuckled a bit, and said "Okay. If that's what you want me to pray about, I guess I can pray about that for you."

"Thanks," Seth answered with more enthusiasm than he ever had when discussing prayer. Despite his enthusiastic reply, he turned to make an awkward exit, just as he did every time the conversation turned toward God.

"Hey, wait a minute," called Harold. "I have a chicken in the freezer, for a while now. Hopefully, it isn't freezer burnt yet," he added sheepishly, "but anyway, I wanna stuff it and bake it, but I don't want to do all that just for myself. Would you like to come for dinner Sunday? I know you don't work Sundays, and I can put it in the oven in the afternoon after I get home from church. Can you come, say around six?"

"Sunday? Six? Stuffed chicken? *Sure!*" Seth laughed enthusiastically. He liked eating with Harold.

"All right then." Harold chuckled in reply, his eyes sparkling. He turned back to the rack with today's newspapers.

Seth finished out his late library shift, walked home, and crawled into bed without eating supper. Fatigue overruled hunger.

The dream haunted his sleep yet again.

Thursday morning's work shift flew by. Though he'd gulped down a pop tart and a glass of milk before work, his stomach grumbled loudly and painfully after the morning work shift, demanding sustenance from its deprivation the previous evening.

He decided to eat lunch at a nearby diner, The Chinook, a rare treat. Plus, he had some time to kill before he visited Katy at two.

Seth walked into the bright, noisy, bustling diner and glanced around the crowded room for an empty seat. Yellowing photographs and paintings of the Rockies and other Colorado scenes adorned the walls that surrounded the diners. The owner of the diner was originally from Boulder where he experienced firsthand the warm, dry chinook winds.

He chose the closest available swivel stool along the metallic lined bar. Air swished out of the torn padding of the stud-lined blue plastic coating as he plopped himself onto the retro seat. He didn't want to hog a booth for himself.

He placed his elbows on the Rocky Mountain-adorned paper placemat and pulled the matching menu from the metal holder in front of him.

He recalled how he and his college friends visited this diner and overstuffed the booths and annoyed the waitresses with outlandish pranks. He hoped the waitresses had long forgotten him.

As Seth enjoyed his home-cooked meal of hot roast beef and steaming, buttery mashed potatoes, thick gravy, and sweet corn, someone came up behind him, slapped him on the back, and plopped down noisily next to him. Seth nearly choked on the food he'd been swallowing and grabbed a napkin just in case.

He looked around to see Mark. *Again?* He hadn't seen Mark in years, and in the space of a week or so, he sees him twice.

"Seth! Fancy seeing you here—again. Haven't seen you in years, and now I see you twice in one week. Weird, huh?" Mark echoed his very thoughts.

"Hey, I've been meaning to call you…this saves me the trouble. How'd you like to come over Saturday night? I still live at home with my parents. You remember where they live, right? And we still have our game room, but it's upgraded. We have the old favorites—pool, ice hockey, foosball, chess, checkers, board games. But now we have a big screen TV and video games too. I'll get some pizza, and we can catch up. I'll whoop your butt in foosball, just like old times. Whatya say?"

"Saturday night? Um, I don't know. What time?" Seth stalled. He wasn't sure he wanted to hang out, and he hasn't been the best company lately.

"I don't know. Six? If that's not good, tell me what time's better for you. I'm flexible." When Seth didn't respond immediately, he enthusiastically added, "It'll be fun, whatya think? You're coming? Yes?"

"All right," answered Seth reluctantly as he rubbed the back of his neck. Resigning himself and shifting gears, he added, slightly more upbeat, "Six on Saturday. And if I recall correctly, *I* always whooped *your* butt with foosball. So I will be certain to bring that to the forefront of your memory again." Seth laughed as he poked Mark's chest.

Mark slapped him on the back, got up from his seat, and said "Hmmm. We'll have to work that out on the foosball court. All right then, see you Saturday night."

"See ya Saturday," replied Seth as Mark waved, turned, and walked toward the diner door.

My life's gotten busy. Two o'clock today with Katy. Six Saturday with Mark. Six Sunday with Harold. Maybe I'm coming out of my zombie state after all. Well, not really…the dream hasn't stopped.

Seth rubbed his neck again.

Refreshed and contentedly full from the comforting meal, Seth walked slowly to the hospital, enjoying the mild weather. It was a fairly warm day for fall in the northeast; he didn't even need a jacket. Seth whistled a tune while he walked, feeling light on his toes, perhaps due to the sunshine, or maybe because he felt a little more normal since he'd actually had some human contact other than at work.

As he approached the hospital, he realized he didn't know where to go. He didn't know the floor or room number since Katy changed rooms. He stopped at the registration desk and asked for Katy's room number. He slowly made his way to her room, feeling less confident and exuberant as he did so. He didn't like hospitals. Sick people. Death. And that *smell*. Medicine or something. Seth wrinkled his nose.

And now Katy was hurt, badly. He never knew how to act around hurt or sick people. As he approached her door, he nearly stopped and turned the other way. Panic swelled.

Hospitals had that affect on him.

But he soldiered on.

He tapped lightly on the open door, not sure if he should just walk in or not. He softly said her name and then hesitantly walked through the doorway.

"Seth," she said happily. "Oh, I'm such a mess. I'm sorry. But I look a lot better than before. And I feel better too, every day a little more. Thanks for coming," she strung her words together without breathing, in typical Katy fashion.

No one else was in the room.

"Hello, Katy. Wow, you *are* all bruised up, aren't you?"

Katy smiled ruefully, her face and arms all shades of yellow and brown with visible cuts and scrapes in various stages of healing. She fixed a strand of unruly auburn hair sticking out from a bandage wrapped snugly about her head and self-consciously covered her right leg with a blanket. A myriad of metal screws and rods protruded, seemingly serving the purpose of holding her leg firmly in place. Tubes, poles with bags, and a couple of monitors announced the seriousness of her condition. Yet somehow, an alert Katy sat upright with the support of strategically placed pillows and a raised bed.

Seth tentatively walked closer, sitting lightly in the only nearby chair and narrowing his eyes with concern. "Looks painful."

"They give me good medicine, but yes, it's painful." She chuckled lightly, then winced from the pain of the small movement of laughter.

Katy went on in a serious tone: "Hey, listen. I really need to talk to you. I'm sorry the last time we talked was when we broke up, and I was pretty crazy—screaming and yelling like I do too much of the time. Weeks went by, and you didn't hear from me. And then, the car accident. They tell me I've been here for a while, so I guess we're practically strangers…it's been so long since we talked."

She paused to gather her thoughts with a sad look on her face, then continued: "But I need to talk to you about something. It's important," she said as her eyes welled with tears. "I never let you talk about the dream, or the abortion, even though it obviously bothered you. I thought I—we—made the right decision. It didn't distress me like it did you, or at least I didn't think so. Later, it did bother me, but I didn't know why. I was 100 percent pro-choice. I directed women to abortion clinics all the time, but suddenly, I got angry when other people talked about babies. I got mad—actually I got *enraged*—at a client who said her child was a gift, and she didn't want to abort it," explained Katy as her voice quivered. "I even got mad at my sister Merin, who I never get mad at, when she talked about having a baby." Tears ran down Katy's cheeks.

"Could you hand me the tissues?" she asked, pointing at a box on a table nearby.

Seth jumped up and grabbed the box of tissues, nearly knocking over a cup of water, and then handed her the whole box. His hands shook.

"Thanks," she said, trying to regain her composure. She wiped her eyes and blew her nose.

Seth sat silently, in amazement. How often he'd wanted to have this conversation with Katy!

He waited for her to continue, at the edge of the seat, wondering what she'd say next.

"I also realize how mean I got every time you brought it up. Obviously, I had some issues. I just didn't want to admit it to myself or you." She sniffed. "Then the accident. And I thought I was dying, or would be dead, because they were going to take my organs because they believed I was dead. But I wasn't dead! I was here! I am here!" Katy repeated with emphasis, slapping the bed with her hand to emphasize every word.

As Katy slapped the bed, wires jiggled and pulled on metal monitoring boxes, which creaked when they moved. Startled, Seth lunged to her side, afraid she'd torn out an IV.

Katy brushed him aside and shook her head to indicate she was fine. She wanted to tell her story. Seth sat back down. "But I couldn't get them to hear me. I kept falling asleep and waking back up. And I had weird dreams, and often, they were the same, so I can relate to your dream now. I dreamed about a baby in the womb—maybe the baby was me? The baby heard conversations around her. The baby knew the people were going to abort her. She was scared. She tried to tell them she was there, that she was alive, that she wanted to live. But she was too little, too tiny. She couldn't talk yet. They couldn't hear her thoughts."

Tears ran down Katy's cheeks. She grabbed another tissue and dabbed at them. "Soon, this lovely, comfortable, warm, soft, safe place that I—or the baby—was in…had an intruder. This big, shiny metal thing appeared. I tried desperately to get away, my heart raced, and the fear was so real, but there was no place to go. I thought I was going to die from a heart attack or from panic. Eventually, something grabbed me by the leg, tearing it off, then the arm, tearing it off, and I was pulled apart into tiny pieces. It was horrific. It was excruciating. It was hopeless. It was death." Katy sobbed, her hands and body both visibly shaking now with each sob.

Seth once again hurried to her side, his heart racing at the vivid and alarming description of her dream. Once again, she brushed him away and continued, "And then I would wake up from the dream, and I would hear people here talking about me being dead and needing to take my organs, and *it was the same as my dream*. They couldn't hear my thoughts, and I couldn't talk. Just like the baby in the womb. My nightmare didn't stop."

She paused to blow her nose noisily, then continued, "When I was *asleep*, I dreamed about a baby torn into pieces during an abortion. When I was *awake*, I could hear others saying that I was gone, and they wanted to cut my organs out of my body. It was *horrible!*" Katy wailed.

Seth jumped up and ran to her side once again, grabbing her hand to hold it this time, tenderly pushing sweaty entangled hairs off her forehead. He choked back tears. "Everything's okay now. The nightmare's over. You're awake. You made it through." His words calmed her, and they stayed like that for a while until she cried herself out.

When she relaxed, Seth gently removed his hand, walked to the chair, picked it up, and carried it next to her bed so he'd be closer and hopefully she'd feel comforted. He didn't know what else to do. He couldn't swallow the lump in his throat, and he couldn't make himself speak. He'd cry if he tried.

"But the nightmare isn't over," said Katy sadly. "The accident damaged my uterus. I'll never be able to have children." She sobbed again, even louder than before.

Again, Seth grabbed her hand, and this time, he reached over and rubbed her shoulder too, trying to comfort the inconsolable.

"My son, the one I aborted, is the only child I will ever have. And I killed him. I killed my son!" wailed Katy.

This time, Seth broke down too. They both cried for a long time, just holding each other's hand and allowing the intense pain of the moment to spend itself.

Finally, Seth spoke.

"You said you killed your son. You knew he was a boy?" asked Seth with pain in his voice.

"Yes, but I never told you. I'm so sorry. I never told anyone. But when you told me your dream, and you said you saw our aborted *son* in your dream in heaven, I freaked out. I could not take that. I could not face that. I could not, I would not."

Katy closed her eyes and covered her face with her hands. After a few seconds, she sighed deeply and continued, "I've changed a lot in the last couple of weeks. My mom thought I had brain damage since I didn't even ask about my 'precious' car...totaled by the way, but I don't even care. A car doesn't seem important anymore. You know I'm not a religious person. I *don't* think God's trying to talk to me like you do. Maybe it's my subconscious teaching me something. I don't know. But I do know that I'm sorry I didn't listen to you before. Please forgive me." Her emotions raw, Katy cried again.

"I do forgive you. And I'm sorry you had to go through all this." Seth waved his arm across the hospital room. "This is all real intense. And now, well, I'm just feeling overwhelmed. I really believe I've met our son in my dream." The tears streamed down his face as he broke down and wept again; he grabbed some tissues.

"Seth," said Katy earnestly, "what does he look like?" she asked breathlessly as the tears just didn't seem to have a way of stopping. They flooded over and dripped onto her hospital gown as her lip quivered uncontrollably.

"He's beautiful," whispered Seth honestly, realizing he'd never taken the time to really think about this fact before. "At the end of the dream, where he grows a little, he has brown curly hair like mine." Seth smiled, choking on his words as he also couldn't control the torrent of tears. "But he has your green eyes," he whispered softly.

Katy wailed loudly. Her body shook violently with each mournful sob and clenched fists covered her face as she gasped to breathe.

Seth slipped his shoes off and gently crawled into the hospital bed next to her, careful to maneuver around the tubes and to stay far away from her leg rods. He cradled her torso in his arms.

They stayed like that, crying in each other's arms for a very long time.

No one else came into the room the entire time Seth visited, allowing privacy to grieve. No other person could possibly understand their profound sorrow.

When they had both calmed, and Seth thought Katy might actually have fallen asleep, he gently removed himself from her embrace. He gingerly crawled off of the bed, trying not to wake her, but without luck.

"Seth," she whispered hoarsely.

"Yes?"

"Are we going to be okay?"

"Yea, I think we're gonna be okay," he answered. "For now, you need to sleep. You just had an exhausting experience, but it was probably good to grieve. We both needed it."

"Yes, our son at least deserves that," answered Katy sadly. "Good night. Thanks for coming. Please come see me again. Please. I don't know if there's anything more for us to say or not. I have to think about things. I'm glad we talked." Katy breathed, exhaustion evident in her voice.

"Good night, Katy. I'll be in touch. See ya," he said gently, but when he looked back, she'd already fallen asleep.

As he walked out the door, he nearly ran into a hospital worker bringing in a dinner tray. He looked at the time—6:00 p.m. He'd been here four hours!

Poor Katy, she's so exhausted she'll miss dinner.

The walk home went quickly. Emotionally and physically drained, Seth didn't feel like doing anything except sleep. He crawled into bed wearily, but with a glimmer of hope.

Maybe now that Katy and I have finally had a heart-to-heart about our aborted son, this nightmare will end.

Unfortunately, it wasn't to be.

Seth had the dream.

CHAPTER 13

Mark

So don't make judgments about anyone ahead of time—
before the Lord returns. For he will bring our darkest
secrets to light and will reveal our private motives. Then
God will give to each one whatever praise is due.

—1 Corinthians 4:5 (NLT)

Saturday came quickly. Seth looked forward to heading to Mark's house and getting his mind off things for a while. He needed some distraction.

He walked to Mark's house, a longer walk than he normally traversed, but he enjoyed the challenge.

Seth rang the familiar doorbell, and a dog immediately yipped in the background. He took in the surroundings as he waited. The pleasant, medium-sized house with beige vinyl siding had a well-kept lawn. Normally, the home's outline burst with a profusion of flowers and interesting plants, but not so much today with winter closing in. His destination—an addition on the back of the house nearly as big as the house itself—contained the game room. A glimpse of the huge backyard brought back a flood of memories. *Good times.* He and Mark played Frisbee, football, and catch back there. A small stream offered plenty of muddy adventures, and the towering maple tree provided endless climbing opportunities for a couple of rambunctious kids.

Mark opened the door, interrupting Seth's reminiscence, and a little black and white fox terrier ran directly to Seth and hopped up on his pant legs, his tail wagging furiously. Seth chuckled and bent to pet the short, energetic dog.

"Scooter! Down!" said Mark sternly. "Hey, man, come in!" Mark's tone changed to his typical enthusiasm.

The little terrier ran back into the house as Mark opened the door wider, and Seth followed. "You have a new dog."

"Yea. We've had Scooter for a couple years now." The little dog had already lost interest in his guest and wandered into another room. "Mom and Dad aren't home, but they said to tell you they're sorry they missed you, and they'll see you next time."

The interior was different than Seth remembered. New carpet maybe? New paint? A little nicer than before.

Mark noticed Seth looking around curiously.

"Mom and Dad fixed things up a little since my brother and sister moved out. Now it's just me here. They know I'm old enough not to mess the place up anymore. And they figure I'll move out soon too, so they can remodel without fear of kids destroying things."

"It's nice," replied Seth awkwardly. The conversation wasn't really guy territory. He wanted to get to the game room, and Mark read his thoughts. They finally stepped down three carpeted stairs and into one of the favorite rooms of his childhood.

Just like Mark said, a big screen TV now dominated the room, and a new overstuffed teal-colored corner couch looked particularly inviting for playing video games.

"This place is even more awesome than I remember." Seth laughed.

Soon it was like old times. Seth was like a kid in a candy store. He tried everything—the old and familiar, and the new too. Mark had pizza and soda delivered, and eventually famished from the activity, they sat down to enjoy the munchies.

When finished, bursting at the seams from eating the whole pizza, they sat back on the couch while their stomachs digested the feast.

"You look awful, and I do mean *seriously awful*. What's up with that?" asked Mark bluntly.

"Well, probably because I just ate way too much pizza and drank way too much soda. You don't look so good yourself," he joked.

"No, I'm serious man. Not just now, but when I saw you at the deli and the diner. You're pale, with like dark circles under your eyes, and much thinner than before, and you were already skinny when we were young," said Mark, more serious this time. "Are you sick or something?"

"What? No, I'm not sick. That's just weird that you'd say that," answered Seth with annoyance.

"Sorry, but you just don't look good. So I guess maybe I'm worried about you. You aren't doing drugs, are you?" he asked with concern.

"What? Man, have you turned into my mom or what? No! I'm not doing drugs. I'm not saying I never did any. I partied in college but haven't touched the stuff since I graduated. No drugs, seriously," said Seth, perturbed.

"Okay, but just sayin' you don't look good. Maybe you should go see a doctor."

"I don't need a doctor. I'm fine!" growled Seth. He didn't know why he got so upset. Not wanting to ruin the night, he calmed his voice and said resignedly, "I'm just not getting enough sleep."

"Why not?" asked Mark, leaning forward and cocking his head to one side as his eyes narrowed and brows furrowed in genuine curiosity.

Seth looked down at his hands folded tightly in his lap. *Man, I'm just too tired for all this intensity lately*. He rubbed his eyes, then the back of his neck, taking a deep breath.

"I've been having this dream. A lot. For about a year, and it just won't stop. I tried talking to people about it—a psychologist, a couple of professors, some friends, even my mom's pastor. Nothing's helped. I'm sleep-deprived because it's kind of like a nightmare," he said quietly.

Mark moved to the edge of the seat, interested and concerned at the same time. "Tell me about the dream."

"Aw, man. Seriously. Do you know how many times I've told this thing?" asked Seth with exasperation.

"Come on, give me a try. What could it hurt? Maybe I can help in some way, at least I'll try. I'd like to hear about it."

Seth appreciated Mark's genuine concern. If there was one thing he knew, Mark was for real and cared about him. Mark cared about everyone. He just had that knack. He loved people in a way most others didn't.

"Okay." Seth shrugged his shoulders. *What's one more time?* He recited the dream in its entirety from start to finish.

"Wow, that's heavy," said Mark honestly. Seth could see the wheels turning in his friend's mind. "And how often do you have the dream? I know you said you had it for about a year, but how often during the past year?"

"Almost every night now. It's getting more frequent."

"Whoa. So tell me, and I'm not prying, I'm just trying to understand, but…did you have a girlfriend who got pregnant and then had an abortion?" he asked without any trace of judgment.

"Yes."

"Tell me about it. About her. What happened? Are you still dating? Does she know about your dream?"

"I think you should be the investigative reporter, not me," answered Seth, trying to lighten up the conversation. But he did as Mark requested. He filled him in on his life for the past year, up to and including the visit with Katy this past Thursday.

"Wow, man, you've had a rough year," replied Mark compassionately. He sat back in his seat and looked at Seth thoughtfully. "You do know that God loves you, right?"

"Yes, I remember that from when I came to church with you," said Seth with a hint of sarcasm as he rolled his eyes. "So what does that have to do with the dream?" Mark always tried to get people to love God as much as he did. It amused Seth to discover Mark's passion for evangelism still thrived.

"I'm not sure exactly what role the dream plays in what I'm trying to say, but you know that a relationship with Jesus Christ is not the same as going to church, right?"

"I don't know. I guess I know that. I'm not sure."

Mark launched into an explanation about salvation and coming to Christ, something Seth had heard too many times when they were younger. His attention drifted, and his eyes glazed and grew heavy. Mark noticed and abruptly stopped talking.

"Sorry. I get so single focused. Let's try this. Have you ever asked God to forgive you for aborting your child?" asked Mark gently.

"I don't know…no. I never felt I had to. Everyone told me it was a good choice, the right choice, before and after too. Well, almost everyone." Seth's voice changed as he remembered Harold's different reaction. Harold had cried. He said he cried about things that broke God's heart.

Have I broken God's heart? wondered Seth for the first time.

"I don't want to talk about this anymore. There's been too much talking lately, and I need to go home," said Seth grumpily as he got up and walked dejectedly toward the back door, his whole body heavy with exhaustion.

Mark jumped up from his chair. "No problem. Wait, listen, can I pray for you first?"

Seth turned. "All right…I guess." Seth shrugged his shoulders reluctantly. He couldn't remember the last time anyone prayed directly for him one-on-one before. Maybe never. He didn't even remember Mark doing that when they were younger. *Oh yea, that's right, he's a youth pastor now.*

Mark walked toward Seth, put his hand on Seth's shoulder, and closed his eyes. Seth watched Mark carefully as Mark talked with his other hand, waving it around expressively as he prayed out loud.

"Father God, I thank you for my friend Seth Siracke. I thank you for bringing him back into my life. What a blessing he is to me, Lord. I am fortunate to call him my friend. Lord, I pray you would ease the burden he carries. Open his eyes to see and his ears to hear what you want him to know and learn from this experience. I pray you would draw him nearer to you and that he would feel your presence in his life, guiding and directing him. Give him wisdom and guide him to the solution that will end the haunting dream and enable peaceful sleep. May he come to feel, know, and truly experience your love and come to an understanding of what it means to have a relationship with you. I pray for the salvation of his soul. Call him to you, Lord. Show him your ways. In Jesus's precious name, I pray. Amen." Mark opened his eyes.

Tears streamed down Seth's cheeks, and he hurriedly wiped them away with his shirt sleeve in embarrassment. Confused by his lack of control over his emotions, his face turned red. Mark grabbed a napkin from the table where the empty pizza box sprawled and handed it to him.

"Thanks," said Seth awkwardly, looking away as he discretely wiped the tears and blew his nose.

"No problem, man. I cry when people pray for me too. It just happens sometimes." Mark slapped him on the back and squeezed his shoulder in his familiar way.

Recognizing his friend's awkwardness, Mark changed the subject. "I'm gonna drive you home. Hold on till I grab the keys," he said with finality.

Seth waited for Mark to retrieve the car keys from the kitchen, too tired to argue.

Other than Seth's occasional offering of directions since Mark didn't know where he lived, neither man spoke on the short drive home, each lost in thought.

After saying goodbye, Seth tiredly climbed the steps to his apartment as Mark pulled away from the curb in his older model Hyundai Elantra. It suddenly bothered Seth that he needed other people to drive him around.

I need to ask Mark how much he paid for his car and where he got it.

He dreamed again.

But something was different this time.

After waking, Seth hurriedly turned on the light at the nightstand and rummaged through his wallet for the piece of paper where he'd written his dream. He unfolded it, grabbed a pen from the nightstand drawer, and began to quickly write down what had changed before he forgot anything.

He wrote the date and then added the change to the dream. The dream had gotten longer.

At the end of the dream, when I see my son grow into a several-month-old child, and my son looks deep into my eyes, this time, something different happened. After looking into my eyes, the child looks toward someone to his right. I notice then that someone is holding my son. It's Jesus, and he smiles with pure love at my son, and my son smiles the biggest and most beautiful smile back at Jesus.

Then Jesus looks at me, smiling in the same way, and lifts his free arm (the other one that he isn't using to hold my son) toward me. The arm seems to beckon me to come toward him—toward Jesus. And light envelopes me from all sides. I can feel the love of my son and also God's love. I feel the love into the core of my being. Light and love surround and fill me completely. I'm drawn in, like I'm losing myself.

Seth had awakened at this point, again distressed.

Am I going to die?

CHAPTER 14

Chicken at Harold's

And do not bring sorrow to God's Holy Spirit
by the way you live...

—Ephesians 4:30 (NLT)

Seth napped a couple of times on Sunday before getting ready to go to Harold's, hoping to catch up on sleep. His stomach growled as he showered and dressed. He'd only eaten toast and a banana all day, so he happily looked forward to chicken and stuffing, salivating as he anticipated the meal.

He walked quickly, wearing his winter jacket and a hat because the weather had definitely turned colder. Harold must have been watching for him from the window because Rudy came bounding out the side door and leaped, throwing the full force of his hefty blond body against Seth just as he stepped onto the driveway. Not anticipating the strength of the dog's momentum, Seth fell to the ground, laughing loudly as Rudy stomped his chest and licked his face and ears, whining and wagging his tail with pure doggy delight. "Ruuudddddyyyyyy." Seth laughed as he ruffled the soft, thick fur around the dog's ears. Harold walked outside and chuckled when he heard Seth's belly laughs.

"That dog sure has a way of making people happy." Harold decided against calling Rudy off and left them to their fun. He went back inside to tend dinner.

Seth sat up beside Rudy and continued petting him, relishing the feel of the giant dog's incredibly soft and comforting fur beneath his fingers. Rudy plopped down beside Seth, clearly enjoying himself as he relaxed and leaned against his visitor.

Soon, Seth's butt got cold, so he jumped up and walked toward the house with Rudy in tow. Rudy bounded ahead and lunged toward the entrance, raking his nails across the metal storm door.

"Rudy!" said Harold sternly in warning from inside the kitchen. "Come on in, you two hooligans."

Seth opened the door, and Rudy sped past him with such vigor that he nearly knocked Seth to the floor again. Seth laughed. "That dog's such a bruiser. Hey, Harold, how ya doin? How's that chicken comin?" asked Seth, rubbing his hands together in anticipation.

"Hello, Seth. I'm good, thank you. The chicken smells fantastic, so I hope it tastes as good as it smells. Hopefully, no freezer burn this time," he answered ruefully. "Rudy's been crazy all day. I'm gonna give him some chicken soon, and he knows it. He gets to eat people food on Sundays. It's his favorite day."

Harold had the table set already. Just before he began to mash the potatoes, Seth asked politely, "Can I help with something?"

"You can pour us some water. And then you can get the chicken, stuffing, and corn out of the oven and put them on the table," answered Harold over his shoulder. He'd already put the food in serving bowls and placed them in the warm oven until Seth arrived.

"Can I use your bathroom to wash up first? Me and Rudy spent some time together." Seth winked, holding up both hands, wiggling his fingers, and opening his eyes extra wide for effect.

"Of course. Ya can't have stinky dog hands when you're cookin'." Harold waved in the direction of the bathroom.

After washing up, Seth busily completed his assignments as Harold finished the mashed potatoes and carried them to the table.

So hungry he could hardly contain himself, Seth forced himself to wait patiently while Harold prayed a short prayer of thanks and then gave Rudy his Sunday treat of people food. In no time, Harold and Seth enjoyed the fine meal.

"Oh, man, Harold. You're an excellent cook. What an awesome meal! The best I've eaten! No kiddin'!" Seth savored every last bite.

Harold grinned from ear to ear.

They settled into an after meal cleanup routine. Seth now knew the process well, including where Harold kept things, so he went to work. Soon, the cleared dining room table, kitchen sink, and counters gleamed.

We make a good team, thought Seth, and he told Harold so.

"Yes, we do. Never thought of it that way, but I like it."

Once again, they retired to Harold's worn but comfortable living room.

Anxious to talk this time, Seth directed the conversation, "Hey, I've been meaning to talk to you. Remember when I told you about my dream? You told me that the things that break God's heart break your heart?"

"Yes, I remember."

"What breaks God's heart?" asked Seth quietly.

"Oh *my*, let me think a minute how to answer." He paused for what seemed like an eternity, but Seth didn't rush him, letting him sort out his thoughts. "The first thing that comes to mind...Jesus said the most important thing is to 'love the Lord your God with all your heart, soul, and mind, and to love your neighbor as yourself.'"

Harold stroked his chin thoughtfully and gazed into space. "So I think, probably, the number one thing that breaks God's heart is when people don't know Him. He created every single person, He loves each one more than anybody can possibly understand, and He wants us all to know Him...to talk to Him...to just be with Him. When people live their lives as though he doesn't exist, I think that breaks His heart. And those who refuse him and his offer of eternal life through Jesus...that's what breaks His heart the most. At least that's what I think."

Seth thought about that for a bit. But it wasn't the answer he wanted, so he tried again.

"Does *abortion* break God's heart?" Seth's voice shook this time.

Harold looked surprised. "Oh, I should've realized what you were asking. Any sin breaks God's heart because sin separates us from

God. I don't pretend to speak for God, believe me, but I think anytime we hurt someone intentionally, we break God's heart. Cause... like I said a little bit ago...in addition to loving God, we should love our *neighbor* as ourselves. Abortion isn't loving toward the unborn child. It's intentional harm, and not just harm but death, committed against the most innocent neighbor of all. If we loved the baby in the womb as ourselves, then no baby would be killed because we sure wouldn't abort ourselves, would we? We'd say, 'Wait, give me a chance, please!'"

Seth tried to take in the words. *A baby killed.* Those words shook him. He pushed the unpleasant thoughts away and wiped his sweaty palms on his pants.

Harold paused a few seconds as he reached for his Bible, then continued, "One of the ten commandments is 'Thou Shalt Not Kill.' I'm sure you've heard of it. So that's a big reason not to abort a baby right there. But there's so much more. Let me see if I can find something to show you what I'm tryin' to say. Oh...I wish my wife was here." Harold sighed wistfully. "She knew more about this abortion stuff than I do." His voice trembled with emotion.

Harold was lost in his own thoughts and didn't notice the blood drain from Seth's face. Emotions swirled as Seth processed Harold's words, *Thou Shalt Not Kill.* He couldn't handle the direction his thoughts were going, so he refocused his attention to safer things.

Harold still misses his wife. The realization surprised Seth since she'd passed away a long time ago.

Harold glanced up and noticed how pale he had become. "Oh, Seth, please forgive me for not being more careful with my words. I didn't mean to upset you."

Seth wondered how he could read his thoughts so easily but answered honestly with a quivering voice. "Please continue to be direct. I want you to."

Harold looked uncertain. "Hmmm. Okay. Lord, help me, guide me, give me wisdom," whispered Harold as he thumbed through his Bible.

"Ah, here's one. Let me read it." Harold's sparkling blue eyes glowed with excitement.

"For you created my inmost being; you knit me together in my mother's womb. I praise you because I am fearfully and wonderfully made; your works are wonderful, I know that full well. My frame was not hidden from you when I was made in the secret place, when I was woven together in the depths of the earth. Your eyes saw my unformed body; all the days ordained for me were written in your book before one of them came to be."

"That's from the book of Psalm, chapter 139, verses 13–16. Have you ever read that?"

"Uh, no, I haven't," answered Seth awkwardly. The words *You knit me together in my mother's womb* and *Your eyes saw my unformed body; all the days ordained for me were written in your book before one of them came to be* hammered in Seth's chest as his guts twisted in a knot.

This feels…important.

"Do you have a Bible?" Harold's eyes twinkled.

"Ah, yes, as a matter of fact, I do."

"Then you should write down the chapter and verse so you can look it up later." Harold rummaged around on the slightly cluttered lampstand for a tablet and pen.

"That's okay. I have a pen and paper." Seth pulled out his trusty mini notebook and pen. "What was it again?" He flipped open the tablet and clicked the pen, poised to write.

"Psalm 139:13–16."

"Um, what page number?" asked Seth seriously.

"Your page numbers won't be the same as mine unless you have exactly the same Bible published in the same year. Do you have the NIV Bible? Does it look like this?" asked Harold as he closed the cover so Seth could see it.

"What's NIV? I don't think my Bible's the same as yours," answered Seth honestly as he examined the cover. "So how do I find, ah, what was that you said again?"

"Psalm 139:13–16," answered Harold patiently. "Here, I'll show you."

Harold proceeded to give Seth a lesson on Bible layout—Old and New Testaments, book, chapter and verse. He showed Seth how to look at the table of contents to find Psalms.

Seth jotted a few notes to himself. "Okay, got it."

"But that's just one verse, Seth. The Bible's loaded with verses that can help answer your two questions—What breaks God's heart? And does abortion break God's heart? Let me try to find another," said Harold eagerly.

Again, it seemed to take him a while, and again, Harold muttered a prayer for help under his breath.

"Here!" he said triumphantly.

"The Word of the LORD came to me, saying, 'Before I formed you in the womb I knew you, before you were born I set you apart; I appointed you as a prophet to the nations.'"

"This one comes from the book of Jeremiah, chapter 1, verses 4 to 5. You should write that one down too," said Harold, eagerly pointing at Seth's tablet.

Seth carefully wrote down the scripture after Harold repeated it a couple more times for him and again, patiently, showed him how to find the book of Jeremiah.

"I thought of this verse in Jeremiah when you told me the part in your dream where you realized the purpose or identity of the aborted babies. How did you say, mothers…and fathers…and poets…and I forget what all you said exactly."

Seth pulled out his wallet where he had folded and shoved the written dream. He lifted the paper out, unfolded it, and shook it to remove the wrinkles. "Hmmm. I should type this up since it's getting beat up from being jammed in my wallet." He laid the wrinkled paper in front of Harold where they could both see it.

Harold slowly moved his finger down the sheet of paper as he skimmed the contents of Seth's dream. His finger paused, going over and over one of the sections a few times.

"Here!" exclaimed Harold with success. And he pointed at each word as he read it aloud:

> *So many random words, thoughts, sensations, and visions explode at me at once, jumbling, overlapping. It's confusing. Some things make sense; some don't:*

Political leaders, affection, cures for diseases, tenderness, ample social security resources, smiles, green-energy solutions, optimism, mothers, bliss, fathers, cheerfulness, siblings, inventions, beautiful music, poverty solutions, laughter, peace makers, beauty, job creators, hope inspirers, love, purpose, art, doctors, transportation solutions, value, new technologies, joy, uncles, belief, aunts, trust, foster parents, courage, pastors, camaraderie, teachers, anticipation, professors, companionship, educational innovations, delight, nutrition solutions, friends, poetry, vibrant colors, health, beautiful sounds, prosperity, architects, nurses, authors, cousins, farmers, dependability, harmony, police, and so many other things.

My mind cannot take it all in. Overwhelming purposes, sounds, expressions, and rainbows of colors reverberate in my head. It is hard to comprehend, let alone try to document in writing.

Each baby had a purpose, set aside before they were even conceived, and these were some of the purposes. The unbearable weight of the weeping and mourning consumes me. So much greater than a mere human can conceive of, or imagine, mankind has no idea of the eternal consequences of abortion. Precise awareness of such deeply unfathomable loss is incomprehensible, even as it is shared with me. I cannot fully grasp the profound deprivation.

Again, tears streamed down Harold's face, so he had to pause and collect himself.

A few minutes went by before Harold said, "God knew Jeremiah before he formed him in his mother's womb. Like your dream, God created Jeremiah specifically for a purpose."

"God creates each one of us for a purpose. If we abort a baby in the womb, we don't allow that child to live out their purpose. We cut it short. We try to *overrule* God, deciding that somehow we can decide better when someone's life should begin or end, and so we snuff out a life that God has created for our own selfish reasons."

Seth shifted uncomfortably, feeling overwhelmed. "Yea. Wow. This is pretty intense." Seth's voice shook as he rubbed his eyes tiredly. "Are there more scriptures like these two?" he asked after a few moments of reflection.

"Oh yes. Let me spend some time thinking, and I'll write some down for you."

"Okay, thanks." Seth realized the late hour again, but he still had so much more he wanted to talk about. "I need to ask something else," he added a bit fearfully. "There was a new part to the dream last time I had it, which never happened before. My dream never changes." Seth shifted nervously in the chair.

"Oh? What new part?"

Seth turned the written dream over to the back where he'd written the addition and pointed. Harold read:

"At the end of the dream, when I see my son grow into a several-month-old child, and my son looks deep into my eyes, this time, something different happened. After looking into my eyes, the child looks toward someone to his right. I notice then that someone is holding my son. It's Jesus, and he smiles with pure love at my son, and my son smiles the biggest and most beautiful smile back at Jesus.

"Then Jesus looks at me, smiling in the same way, and lifts his free arm (the other one that he isn't using to hold my son) toward me. The arm seems to beckon me to come toward him—toward Jesus. And light envelopes me from all sides. I can feel the love of my son and also God's love. I feel the love into the core of my being. Light and love surround and fill me completely. I'm drawn in, like I'm losing myself."

Harold finished reading and glanced up. Seth's pale face registered wide-eyed fear. "What's wrong?" Harold put a concerned hand on Seth's shoulder and squeezed reassuringly.

"After I dreamt that, I woke up wondering if I'm going to die soon." Seth trembled.

"What? No, oh, goodness no. I don't think this new part of your dream has anything to do with you dying. Why do you think that?"

"I'm not so sure. I think God's telling me I'm going to die for aborting my son." Seth swallowed hard and strained to choke back tears.

"Where'd you get that idea? Your dream is about *love* and *life*, not death. Listen here, we're all sinners. Some Christians like to think their sin isn't as bad as the sin of others, and they point their fingers and criticize. That's judging, and it's wrong. Sin is sin, and we all do it. That's why we need a Savior. We can't get it right no matter how hard we try on our own. Not one of us deserves to go to heaven. And yes, the wages of sin is death, but there's a solution—Jesus! Jesus paid the price for our sins on the cross and offers a way to heaven for those who believe in Him. When you saw Jesus beckoning you, it's because he wants to have a relationship with you. By giving your heart and life to Jesus, you'll be able to meet your son face-to-face someday in heaven—that would be wonderful, Seth. That's the invitation Jesus gave you—salvation…eternal life. He's inviting you to come and get to know him." Harold coughed. "Excuse me, I need a drink of water. Do you want one?"

"No thanks." *Tired, bone-tired.* Seth's head spun.

Harold came back a few minutes later with a glass of water. He settled back into his chair, setting the glass on the small table next to him.

"Here's what I think," explained Harold, leaning forward with hands folded in his lap. "I think Jesus wants you to ask Him to forgive all your sins—not just the abortion, but all your sins. And tell Him you believe He is who He says He is—your Lord and Savior. Ask Him to come into your heart and guide your life." Harold smiled reassuringly. "Would you like to pray and ask him now?"

"I don't know." Seth hesitated, shook his head, and put his hand up as though to say "stop." "Let me think about it," he added.

A lot to take in.

"That's good. Only you can come to the point of salvation. It's between you and Jesus. Ask Him to show you, and I think the truth you're seeking will be found soon."

Seth didn't respond for a few beats, then his mind went back to his dream. "One more quick question. Does the Bible say anything about dreams?"

"Oh, dreams. Yes, let me think. I'll try to find some scriptures," he said and began searching again.

"That's okay. It's getting late. I'll get those another time."

"Here, let me at least get you started. Look in Genesis, Judges, and Daniel. I can't remember where off the top of my head. Oh, and read the second chapter of Matthew too. At least I can narrow that one down to a chapter." Harold chuckled. "I guess that'll do for now."

"Gee whiz, I feel like I'm in school again. Why don't you just tell me to read the whole Bible?" asked Seth sarcastically.

"That's a great idea. You should do that."

"Oh, brother." Seth rolled his eyes. "I'll just start with this... might take me a while."

"Just dig in. I love to read God's Word. It energizes me. I think you'll like it too, the more you read. Give it a chance."

"I will. I'm on a mission, you know, trying to make this dream stop."

"You'll find resolution. I'm praying for you."

"Thanks, and thanks for the awesome dinner, *Chef Harold*," joked Seth as he walked to the hallway and grabbed his coat and hat. "I have to get going. It's almost ten, sheesh! You should have chased me out of here a while ago," Seth scolded.

"Oh, no, not at all. I like when you visit. Come again soon." Harold yawned.

"All right. See ya." Seth closed the door gently behind him.

Once again, Harold turned on the carport light and watched Seth walk into the night and out of sight. Seth didn't know, but Harold busily prayed.

Seth didn't notice the biting cold of the night as he considered the evening's conversation. For the first time, he sensed he was on the right track. His dream was obviously about God and obviously about his aborted son. Harold had a good grasp of the Bible. He'd be a welcome resource if he had questions.

I need to dig into these scriptures, but not tonight. My brain's fried.

Seth thought he might try talking to God a little as he walked, but it felt foreign. Though he'd bowed his head in church with Mark as a kid, he never paid attention to the words people said when they prayed. He wasn't sure how to talk to God. Mark and Harold had no trouble doing it. Seth gave it a shot.

God, I don't know how to talk to you. If you're there, show me whatever you're trying to show me. Help me get this, whatever I'm not getting. I know I'm thickheaded sometimes, but I need this dream to stop. Please. If you're real—really real—I want to know.

CHAPTER 15

Word of Life Community Church

Keep on asking, and you will receive what you ask
for. Keep on seeking, and you will find. Keep on
knocking, and the door will be opened to you.

—Matthew 7:7 (NLT)

Seth slept like a baby Sunday night and woke up feeling refreshed
for the first time in what seemed like ages. To make things even
better, he got to sleep in since he worked the afternoon shift.

A grin stretched across his face as he finally opened his eyes to
luxuriously warm sun rays beating on his skin through open blinds.
He lay there for a couple minutes, quietly watching dust particles
float in the sunbeams. Such a strange sensation to wake up feeling
this good. He took his time getting ready for work, enjoying momentary
peace.

Just before walking out the door, Seth's cell phone buzzed with
a text message. Mark invited him to hang out Tuesday evening.
His church had a recreation room with basketball, a pool table, air
hockey, a lounge, and even a small bowling alley. The church opened
the facility to the public Tuesday nights. Seth felt so good that he
immediately sent off a text accepting Mark's offer.

Sounds fun.

Then, just as he pulled his apartment door closed, wiggling the knob to make sure it locked, his cell phone vibrated again, this time with a ring. He glanced at caller ID before answering.

"Hey, Katy."

"Hi, Seth."

"How are you?" He hadn't talked with her since his visit on Thursday.

"I'm good. I'm glad we talked."

"Me too," Seth responded candidly, wishing they'd done it a long time ago. His heart had softened toward Katy in just a few short days. He missed her.

"And I've been thinking about everything."

"Me too," he repeated his earlier response. His heart hammered. For the first time in a while, he realized he might want to spend more time with her.

"And…this is hard for me." She paused, laughing, sort of, but Seth thought she could've been crying too. He couldn't tell.

"Me too," he said once again, encouragingly, not sure where she was going.

"But I think…what I'm trying to say is…I can't see you anymore. I know we broke up, but we kind of left things open when we talked. And…I can't. I can't see you…because it's too painful. If I see you, even as friends, I'll be reminded of things I don't want to be reminded of. It hurts—there's too much history. So I called to tell you that I can't be friends with you, and I can't see you. I'm sorry. I think it's what I need to do, so I don't go crazy thinking about stuff," she explained, softly sighing.

Seth choked back tears. For some reason, her words stung this time. He smothered the pain.

"Okay. I understand. It is painful…for both of us. I get it. Take care of yourself. I hope you recover—completely. And I hope you have a great life. Really, I wish you all the best." Seth's voice broke and a tear ran down his cheek. "Goodbye, Katy," he added with finality, glad she couldn't see his tears.

Katy said goodbye and hung up. And just like that, it was all over between them.

Seth wiped his eyes with his coat sleeves. He had walked while talking to Katy and found himself at the front door of the library already. He leaned back against the building, taking a couple of deep breaths to regain his composure.

A few beats later, a composed Seth pulled open the library door.

At least work would distract his thoughts for now.

Tuesday evening arrived quickly since Seth worked late Monday and most of Tuesday.

He walked to Mark's church. Though it'd been a while, he remembered the route.

The fun evening soothed Seth's wounded soul. Just like old times, he and Mark played hard—competing heavily on the basketball court and eventually tying at air hockey; their friendship was unaffected by its long hiatus.

Mark introduced Seth to people from his church. The friendly gang invited him to church on Sunday with such exuberance that Seth found himself accepting the offer.

The rest of the week flew by. He hadn't gotten around to reading the scripture verses Harold gave him, and Harold didn't ask. Seth didn't want to disappoint him, but for some reason, he found himself dragging his feet again.

He had the dream several times this week. With lack of sleep, frustration about the never-ending dream, and now the final conversation with Katy too, Seth felt miserable.

As she normally did, his mom called and invited Seth to Thanksgiving the following week. She always made a fuss and baked a small half turkey with all the trimmings for the two of them.

But he didn't feel thankful about much these days.

Sunday morning arrived in a blink.

Butterflies fluttered in Seth's stomach. He'd never gone to church on his own before; he'd only ever gone with Mark and his parents. And it felt weird.

What do I wear? Where do I sit? What if I have to sit by myself?

Seth examined his limited wardrobe options. Digging through the closet, he found a pair of khakis and one white button-up dress shirt he'd worn to both his high school and college graduations. He didn't bother looking for a tie. This would have to do. He sniffed the shirt's armpits and sighed with relief. Apparently, he remembered to wash it after graduation.

Forgetting how long it had taken to walk to church on Tuesday, Seth left extra early. He stopped at The Chinook for breakfast on the way, suddenly regretting his decision to attend the service. He didn't feel like going to church at all. He almost went home but remembered he'd told a bunch of people he'd come today. A man of his word, Seth resolutely continued his trek after eating.

Stepping inside the church's front door, Seth saw several people he'd met Tuesday evening. They greeted him enthusiastically and seemed genuinely glad to see him. Their caring demeanor reminded him of Mark. And Harold.

Why are these people always happy? They must not have any real problems. They just live in their goody-two-shoes bubbles and don't know what real life is like.

The sudden angry thoughts surprised Seth, and he pushed them out of his head.

Soon, he saw Mark, and they shot the breeze for a couple minutes. Mark and some others invited Seth to sit with them. He noticed people dressed pretty much any way they wanted. Some wore jeans, some khakis like him, and some wore suits.

The service was a little different from what he remembered as a kid. More people, and modern music—they had drums and guitars now. Seth liked the music part and the sermon too. The pastor grabbed his attention from the beginning, seeming to speak directly to him. The pastor's words even affected Seth's emotions. A couple times, he choked back tears, gritted his teeth, and dug his fingers into coolly crossed arms to maintain composure. Sometimes the pastor's words made him think about something specific, and his mind wandered—but in a good way—as he related to what the pastor said.

Time flew by. Near the end of the service, the pastor invited people to "give their testimonies," as he called it, about what God was doing in their lives. The stories captivated Seth. Many spoke of some kind of triumph over tragedy. Clearly, these people didn't have easy lives after all. He blushed as he remembered his earlier thoughts.

At the end of the service as Seth worked his way to the door, Mark invited him to the church's game room again on Tuesday. He cheerfully accepted.

Tuesday arrived quickly.

By practically running to church that evening, Seth arrived promptly when it opened. He didn't realize few people arrived early. Most sauntered in as the evening wore on. He didn't see any familiar faces yet, but he did recognize the pastor. When Seth glanced in the pastor's direction, their eyes met, and the pastor walked over to greet him.

"Hello! I think I saw you here last week, and I saw you on Sunday too. Is that right? I'm Pastor Frank," he said graciously as he extended his arm to shake Seth's hand.

Seth shook the pastor's hand. "Hi. Seth Siracke. I'm a friend of Mark's. Yea, I was here last Tuesday and on Sunday." He felt nervous for some reason.

"Do you live around here?"

"Yea." Seth explained where he lived, that he'd lived in town his whole life, and occasionally visited this church with Mark as a kid.

"Do you know the Lord?" asked Pastor Frank bluntly.

Seth didn't understand how people talked about God so easily, like it was the most natural thing in the world, because it seemed pretty weird to him.

"Um, probably not in the way that you mean, I guess," replied Seth uncomfortably. "Though I'm learning—a lot of people are trying to teach me." He chuckled nervously.

"Really? Tell me about it." He gestured toward a couple of modern, brightly colored, living-room-style chairs in the lounge. "I'd love to hear more," he added with a smile.

Seth found himself relaxing in Pastor Frank's easy-going presence. His focused listening and gentle sense of humor kept Seth engaged and talking.

He told Pastor Frank everything. He couldn't believe how his life story spilled out so easily. He told him about Katy and the abortion and the dream and her accident and recovery and even her phone call this week…about Harold and their friendship, about Mark and their friendship, about his visits with the psychologist, Professor Whitman, Professor Cantor, and Reverend Watts. By then, the game room had filled up, and their conversation became less private. When Seth reached for his wallet to pull out the written dream, Pastor Frank suggested they continue the conversation in his office.

Seth followed him, and the pastor assumed the role of a tour guide, explaining the functions of different rooms and sections of the building, along with the history of Word of Life Community Church.

When they arrived at his office, Pastor Frank gestured toward a deep-burgundy studded leather chair while he settled into a similar chair. A well-polished antique mahogany coffee table sat between them. Rather than behind a desk, Pastor Frank sat in a chair next to Seth, like two friends chatting. Seth liked the feeling.

He settled into the comfortable chair and unfolded the paper with the dream onto the table for Pastor Frank to read, which he did in an attentive manner. He leaned forward and toward Seth, resting his elbows on his knees as he read.

"This is interesting, Seth," he said when finished. "So in all these journeys you've described to me, what conclusions have you come to about your dream?"

"Well, obviously the dream's about God and my aborted son. And God's trying to tell me something, but so far, I must be missing whatever he's saying because the dream hasn't stopped. Once I understand what God's telling me, then the dream will stop. At least that's what I believe."

"And what do you think God is trying to tell you?" asked Pastor Frank gently.

Seth wept. Not expecting such an instantaneous emotional response, an embarrassed flush crept up his face.

Pastor Frank immediately moved his chair closer, alongside Seth's, and put his hand on Seth's shoulder. "It's okay. Sometimes when we feel God's presence, we can't help but weep. It's normal." Pastor Frank grabbed a box of tissues and handed them to Seth as he tried to regain his composure.

"Let's have another go," said Pastor Frank when Seth had calmed down. "What do you think God is trying to tell you?" He moved his chair slightly away to put some more comfortable distance between them again.

"I think…God wants me to ask for forgiveness for aborting my son…and that he wants to have a relationship with me," Seth said softly and hesitatingly.

"I think the Lord has given you wisdom," said Pastor Frank kindly, "So have you asked for forgiveness? And have you asked to have a relationship with Jesus?"

"No," said Seth, an almost child-like frustration creeping into his voice.

"Why not?"

"I don't know. I just don't know. I'm confused. I'm not ready," replied Seth angrily.

"So you'd rather suffer with the dream?" asked Pastor Frank, trying to understand.

"Maybe I'm having a battle of wills with God," said Seth boldly.

"Ah, you're wrestling with God. We all do that sometimes. Especially as realization dawns about the thing God wants us to let go of and give to him, allowing Him full reign over our lives. Sometimes we just don't want to let go of our stuff—of ourselves," said Pastor Frank honestly.

"Sounds weak to me, like a bunch of wussies. *Submission. Give your life to Christ.* Why would anybody want to do that?" asked Seth unflinchingly.

"Good question. But when we're weak, we're made strong by the author of our lives. It takes strength of conviction and courage of decision to give one's life to Christ. And the more you submit to God, the stronger you become, and the better your life gets. And that's no lie. I don't mean you won't have problems. We all have problems because we live in a sinful world. But life is good with God in it because the one who has your very best interests in mind is in control of your life. It's a great way to live. By all means, keep wrestling. He wants you to wrestle with Him if you need to. You'll learn about Him that way," said Pastor Frank with a gleam in his eye.

Seth and the Pastor continued talking for a while longer. Pastor Frank shared wisdom from the Bible and encouraged Seth to spend some time on his own searching God and the scriptures.

Pastor Frank sent Seth off with a prayer. "Father God, thank you for bringing this intelligent and inquisitive young man, Seth Siracke, into my life. What a blessing he is to me. He may not realize it yet, but he is a man after your own heart. I pray, Father God, that you would grant him wisdom in his search. Lord, teach him your truth and your ways. Draw him near. Open his eyes to see. Give him ears to hear. May he feel your love and know your presence, and may he come to a place of shouting your goodness from the mountain-tops. Bless him and keep him and minister to him now and in the coming weeks, months, and years. May he learn to hear your voice and walk in your ways, knowing you as the *author* of his life in the depths of his heart. In Jesus's precious name, I pray. Amen."

"Thanks," said Seth, maybe a little less awkwardly than usual. He was starting to get used to the God stuff.

Pastor Frank led him back to the game room, and Seth saw Mark and his friends. Mark joined them. "Hey, Pastor Frank, are you hiding Seth from us?" he joked.

"No, not at all. Just showing him around. He's all yours. Hope to see you soon, Seth. Take care now." Pastor Frank waved and began making his rounds in the crowded room.

Seth didn't feel like playing games anymore. He had too much on his mind and needed to be by himself. *And maybe with God?*

"Hey, listen, Mark, I gotta run. I have some things I need to take care of."

"Okay," said Mark with surprise. "No problem. Are you coming to church on Sunday?"

"Um, not sure, maybe. Later," said Seth hastily over his shoulder as he made his way to the door. As he walked through the gymnasium door, he gulped a big breath of cold November air to clear his head. He walked slowly home, trying to sort through his thoughts.

By the time Seth arrived at his apartment, he'd decided to look up the scriptures Harold gave him. Pastor Frank had offered suggestions too. Seth pulled the Bible off the bookshelf and blew the dust off. Though dusty on the outside, the crisp interior showcased its mint condition. The black leather cover felt smooth in his hand when he opened it, and the white pages glistened. A new leather scent filled Seth's nostrils, making him realize how little the book had been used in the past.

Seth carefully combed through each scripture, methodically checking each one off. He even read the entire books that had been suggested. He used the Internet to search references to scripture and abortion. Surprisingly, Seth found himself randomly reading here and there as well in the Bible. Many times, tears streamed down his face.

Seth kept asking God to show him.

Something about Seth's conversation with Pastor Frank nagged at him. Pastor Frank called God the *author* of his life. As an aspiring journalist, the word *author* hit a nerve. An author creates writings from scratch, out of nothing, but the author has clear and distinct intentions for writing. The author has considered the purpose of his writing before he begins writing. An author desires to create a masterpiece, so great care, effort, and thought go into his writing.

As Seth pondered these insights, along with the scripture readings, he realized—to the core of his being—that God was the author of life, of all life…of his life, and of his aborted son's life.

As truth sank in, Seth fell to his knees, passionately crying out to God in a way he'd never done before. Though new and strange at the same time, the behavior felt right and wonderful. Seth asked Jesus to forgive all his sins, including the abortion. Remembering Mark's instructions when they were kids, he asked Jesus to come into his heart and teach him His ways.

Spent and broken on the living room floor, his life changed in an instant. He just didn't realize it yet.

Seth slept all night curled up on the living room rug. He didn't dream. When he awoke to find himself still on the floor, adrenaline surged and he lurched to his feet, afraid he was late for work. A quick glance at the quietly ticking hands of the kitchen wall clock revealed the early hour, so Seth breathed a sigh of relief.

He'd slept through the whole night without dreaming.

Thank you, Lord! he thought happily.

CHAPTER 16

The Fire

I have told you all this so that you may have peace in
me. Here on earth you will have many trials and sorrows.
But take heart, because I have overcome the world.

—John 16:33 (NLT)

The library bustled, and Seth whistled as he worked. Anticipation of his mom's Thanksgiving turkey and filling lightened his demeanor and gave rise to a spring in his step. Tomorrow couldn't come soon enough.

Seth saw Harold come in, and though they waved at one another, Seth didn't have time to talk. It seemed as though everyone who had the day off work visited the library for books to read over the long holiday weekend.

Things bustled outside the library too. A couple of fire trucks raced past, sirens blaring. A bunch of people gathered about the windows to get a glimpse of the rare, heart-thumping scene. Seth wondered where the fire was.

Harold stayed in his reading chair longer than usual today, fully engrossed in a new World War II book. Eventually, near the end of Seth's shift, Harold checked out the book to take along home. Seth waved again as Harold left.

About thirty minutes later, Seth readied to leave too since his shift ended.

Time to start looking for a journalist job.

The thought surprised Seth. It'd been a long time since he'd even considered job hunting. Depression and fatigue had prevented forward motion. But now Seth felt as though a new day had dawned. He could start over.

He whistled softly again as he planned to buy a local newspaper at the convenience store on the way home to look at job postings. He walked toward the exit when his coworker Jenny called his name. Seth turned, wondering what she could want. Jenny pointed at the phone in her hand.

He walked back to the desk, his brows furrowed curiously.

"You have a phone call," she said and dismissively handed him the phone.

Bewildered, Seth hesitantly took the phone.

Who would call me at the library? Everyone has my cell number.

"Hello?"

"Seth Siracke?" said a booming, take-charge male voice on the other end.

"Yes?" answered Seth questioningly.

"This is Police Officer John Grant. I'm here with Harold Connar. His house is on fire, and he's asking for you. Can you come to the scene?"

What? Harold Connar? Who's that?

"Um, are you sure you have the right person? I don't know any Harold Connar. Wait! Is he an older man? Where's his house?" asked Seth, suddenly realizing he'd never even known Harold's last name.

Officer Grant gave Seth the address and replied in the affirmative about Harold's age.

"Oh! Yes, I know him. Oh my gosh, his house is on fire? Is he okay?" asked Seth breathlessly, his heart hammering wildly in his chest.

"He's physically okay. He wasn't home when the fire started, but he's asking if you'll come to the site so he can talk to you," said the officer matter-of-factly.

"I'm on my way. I'll be there in a couple minutes." Seth ran out the door and up the street—at full speed. His adrenaline surged, helping him race to Harold's house in record time. He feared for his friend.

As Seth crested the hill to Harold's house, he couldn't believe the scene. Three fire trucks, an ambulance, and a police car, all with lights flashing, blocked the roadway. Bystanders crowded the streets. And Harold's house! Seth's heart leapt into his throat, and he choked as he inhaled smoke-filled air. The home no longer existed. Gray smoke poured from a pile of black embers—the only haunting remains of an old man's lifetime dwelling.

Seth's eyes scanned the crowded scene for Harold. He found him sitting on a gurney in the back of the open ambulance. He jogged toward the ambulance.

"Harold!" he yelled as he got close, choking again on the smoke-filled air.

Harold turned to look. He had an oxygen mask on his face. He motioned for Seth to come.

Seth climbed into the back of the ambulance with Harold. The ambulance workers moved aside. They were expecting him.

"Are you okay?" Great concern etched Seth's face. He sat next to Harold and put his hand on his shoulder.

Harold pulled the mask off. "Rudy's gone," he said, crying now. "That dog was so good to me. Rudy was in the house. Now he's dead. He's all I had." Tears ran down both cheeks and dripped onto his shirt. "He burned up," choked Harold as he bent over, sobs wracking his frail body.

"I'm so sorry, Harold." Seth's voice broke as he awkwardly hugged the traumatized man.

"You're Seth?" interrupted an ambulance worker quietly.

"Yes," Seth's voice quivered from the unfolding trauma.

The ambulance crew member, concern evident on his face, continued speaking as he gently placed the oxygen mask back onto Harold's face, "We're going to take Harold to the hospital. His heart rate and blood pressure are very high, and he passed out a few minutes ago. We need to get him calmed down, start an IV, and examine him further."

"I don't need to go to the hospital," interrupted Harold stubbornly.

"I think it's for the best. I can ride along if you want. Right?" asked Seth, turning to face the ambulance crew.

"Yes, you can ride along," answered a crew member.

"Okay. Um, let me run over there quick," said Seth as he pointed to the crowd, "to the police officer to tell him I'm here. I'll be right back."

He wanted to tell Officer Grant he'd arrived, since the officer had taken the time and effort to call him at Harold's request. The officer thanked Seth for coming, gave Seth his business card, and told him to call later because he had questions before filing his report.

Seth ran back to the ambulance and climbed inside. The crew showed him where to sit.

Harold calmed down when he realized Seth intended to ride along, but he just lay on his side, crying.

The crew shut the doors, and soon, the ambulance weaved slowly among the chaos of vehicles and bystanders. Once they cleared the crowd, they picked up speed.

Seth didn't know what to say.

This is horrible.

He tried not to cry about Rudy. He couldn't imagine how Harold felt in the face of so much loss.

I can't abandon him. I need to be here for him. He has no one.

Seth said a silent prayer for Harold as he squeezed his shoulder. Awkward and short, but still a prayer.

Harold kept crying, oblivious to everything around him.

Seth hated to see this gentle old man in so much emotional pain.

Soon, they arrived at the hospital, and the crew whisked Harold inside. Seth stayed in the waiting room while hospital staff examined Harold. Before long, a doctor informed Seth they admitted Harold for observation, and Seth could visit after he received a room assignment.

Seth waited again until a nurse finally gave him directions to Harold's newly assigned hospital room.

As Seth traversed the hallways and elevators of the same hospital where Katy had been, he wondered if she was still here. Harold's room occupied a different floor, so he probably wouldn't find out.

Harold's room looked a lot like Katy's. He had an IV but looked comfortable in the bed.

"Hey, buddy. How are you doing?" asked Seth kindly.

"Not good." Tears still streamed from his bloodshot eyes. "My home's gone and all my memories. My dog's gone. My wife's gone. So I'm not doing good. I wanna go home now too—to be with the Lord. Nothin' left for me here," he said with fatigue.

"I'm here, aren't I? Hey, I don't want you to go home with the Lord yet. I'm just getting to know you, friend." Seth paused. "I can't imagine how you're feeling. You lost a lot. I'm sorry, so sorry." Seth's voice broke as he tried to find the right words of comfort.

"Thank you," said Harold, and with that, he fell promptly sound asleep, a slight snore escaping his gaping mouth.

Concerned that Harold had fallen asleep practically in the middle of a sentence, he went to find a nurse. He explained to the nurse's station attendant what had happened, and she checked Harold's chart.

"He's been given a sedative to help him calm down and rest. The medication makes people very drowsy. He's likely going to sleep through the night because the sedative will be readministered in a few hours. They really want him to get some rest," she explained with a gentle smile.

"Okay, thanks," said Seth, still worried.

He looked in at Harold one last time. After watching him for a bit, Seth was satisfied that he would likely sleep awhile, so he went home.

As he considered the events of the past few hours, he practically ran to his apartment. He had work to do.

As soon as he got home, Seth called the police officer to answer any questions he had. Seth also tried to glean as much information as he could about what had happened. Seth asked the officer if he could look through the wreckage of Harold's house for anything salvageable. That's when Officer Grant directed him to the town's fire chief.

Seth called the fire chief to learn more. Fire personnel had already traced the source of the fire to an electrical short in the wall outlet where Harold plugged in his Crock-Pot to warm the evening meal. The fire chief explained it was a pretty cut-and-dry case. Fires weren't uncommon in old houses with faulty wiring like that of Harold's home. Seth asked if he could take a work crew to the house to sort through anything recoverable. The fire chief agreed as long as a member of the fire department accompanied them for safety, but he doubted much could be saved.

Next, Seth called Mark to share what happened and ask for prayers for Harold. He asked if Mark thought they could get a work crew together to sort through the home's remains for anything that can be salvaged. Seth also explained that the fire chief wanted someone from the fire department to come along to help for safety reasons.

Excited to help, Mark asked when Seth wanted to get together.

"Well, tomorrow's Thanksgiving. The library's closed, so I'm available, but I'm sure most of you aren't. I go to my mom's for lunch, but I'm not there long usually. I'm supposed to work Friday and Saturday, but I can take off. I have a little bit of leave earned, and this could count as an emergency. I'm sure they'd let me have off. So I'm available anytime from tomorrow afternoon through Sunday."

"Good. I'm on it. I'll get back to you."

Seth called Pastor Frank next. He had a lot to tell him—both good and bad. First, he told the pastor about the prayer he said the night before.

"Praise God! The angels are rejoicing in heaven! You're saved!"

Seth didn't even respond to Pastor Frank's excitement. "Now for the bad news." He told the pastor about Harold's home and dog and that Mark worked on gathering a crew to salvage the remainder of Harold's belongings.

"My next request's a big one, but I'm gonna be bold and ask," said Seth, pausing uncertainly.

"Go on, what is it?"

Seth asked the pastor if their church ever built a home for anyone in need. He explained he hoped Word of Life Community Church could rebuild, or sponsor, or organize the rebuilding of Harold's home. He added, a bit desperately as he realized his request seemed vague and outlandish at the same time, that the house only needed to be very small and modest like the original home.

"Did Harold have homeowner's insurance?"

"I'll find out," answered Seth. *Hmm, should've thought of that.* "I know I'm not a member of your church, and maybe this is way over the top. If it is, just say so. But I thought I'd ask since I know Harold's a senior citizen living on his own with a fixed income. And he loved his home. Even if he has insurance, he could probably use help coordinating everything," explained Seth apprehensively.

"Your request is not over the top. A church is supposed to be here for the community. Let me see what can be done. I'm one of four pastors at our church, and we have a leadership team that also needs consulted. I'll have to take it before a couple of committees too so it might take a while to get an answer. We've never done anything like this before, but we must be ready to respond to needs as they arise. I can't promise anything. Even if the home is small and modest, it's still a huge responsibility. And I'll need an answer on the insurance."

"Yes, I agree. I'm trying not to get overwhelmed just thinking about it. I understand completely. Thanks for taking it under consideration and talking with the committees. If the answer's no, that's fine. I just needed to ask. If you have any questions, let me know," said Seth graciously.

They said their goodbyes.

Seth sat back in the chair, inhaled an exhausted, deep breath, and rubbed his eyes wearily. He realized his clothes reeked of smoke. He pulled off his shirt tiredly and ran his fingers through his unruly mass of curly brown hair, which also stank. Deep fatigue set in.

He felt very uncertain about what he'd started. How did he think he could accomplish all this? He pulled out his mini notebook and began jotting notes. With so much going on, he needed to put some of this down on paper. Things were going to get complicated.

Satisfied that he'd written down enough of the details to take some pressure off his mind, Seth stretched and rose. He walked slowly through his apartment, examining each room intently as though seeing it for the first time. He stood in the doorway of each room, his arms crossed, and his fingers massaging his chin, deep in thought.

Plenty of room here for Harold. Katy was gonna move in. If there's enough room for Katy, there's definitely enough room for Harold.

Just before stepping into the shower, his cell buzzed. It was Mark.

"Hey."

"Seth, how's tomorrow at two?"

"Wow, you wasted no time. Thanks. Tomorrow at two is perfect!" replied Seth enthusiastically.

"Okay, we'll all meet at Harold's house at two. There's a fire department member who attends our church coming along. He's a friend of my parents. Bring heat-retardant gloves and boots, garbage bags, a mask, and goggles," said Mark. "My parents reminded me that it'll be messy—and perhaps dangerous, smoky, and hot—trying to sort through everything so soon. But we wanted to try to get started tomorrow and then come back Friday morning if we have to, cause it's supposed to rain…maybe snow… Friday afternoon and all weekend."

"Thanks for thinking of the weather and goggles and stuff. I'll make sure I have everything. See you at two, and thanks again. This really means a lot to me," added Seth sincerely.

And he meant it.

Harold meant a lot to him. He wanted to help, and Seth knew he couldn't help Harold on his own.

Seth prayed for Harold as he showered off the day's smoky residue.

And then he slept like a baby.

CHAPTER 17

Thanksgiving

Be thankful in all circumstances, for this is God's
will for you who belong to Christ Jesus.

—1 Thessalonians 5:18 (NLT)

Refreshed and energized, Seth awoke early, his mind buzzing about the tasks ahead. He donned the only pair of boots he owned. They used to be his dad's, and although they were old, they were pretty good quality. He hoped they were at least somewhat heat-resistant because he couldn't afford to buy any.

Once again, he lamented not owning a car. With so many stops to make all over town, he'd have to jog to get everything done. To ensure stamina for the day, he ate a hearty breakfast even though he'd have a big Thanksgiving lunch at his mom's. He gulped down oatmeal, toast, scrambled eggs, and even grabbed a banana on the way out the door.

He remembered to jam a couple of garbage bags into his winter coat pocket. *It's good these pockets are deep. They'll be packed full of stuff today.*

Seth ran to the large local retail store. Finding it open this Thanksgiving morning, he whispered a little prayer of thanks and walked quickly through the store, looking for the items he needed. He bought a pair of heat-resistant work gloves, a dust mask, and a cheap pair of dust goggles. On his way out the door, he shoved the purchased items, fortunately all fairly soft and flexible, into his other deep pocket.

Next, he went to check on Harold. He jogged to the hospital but stopped outside the building to catch his breath before going inside. After calming his breathing, Seth made a beeline for Harold's room.

Glancing at his watch, Seth noted the time: 10:45 a.m. He could visit about half an hour.

He rounded the corner into Harold's room but stopped dead in his tracks. Harold already had a visitor. A slightly chubby middle-aged woman with graying blonde hair and gold-rimmed glasses sat in the chair next to Harold's bed. She wasn't a nurse. She wore stylish jeans and a green sweater with a gold necklace and earrings. She and Harold seemed engrossed in a serious conversation because they both had frowns on their faces. Seth turned to leave, not wanting to interrupt, when Harold called out to him.

"Seth, come in. I want you to meet my daughter." Harold waved his arm toward the woman.

Seth turned slowly at Harold's words, his eyes wide, mouth agape.

He didn't know Harold had a daughter. How could he not have known this? He just told the police officer that Harold had no family!

A daughter!

"I didn't…know you had a daughter." Seth stammered, glued to the spot where he stood.

The woman rose and walked toward Seth, heels clanking heavily on the tiled floor, her hand outstretched in greeting. "I'm Jillian," she said with a stern expression.

"I'm, I'm Seth, a friend of Harold's, ah I mean, a friend of your dad." Seth shook her hand in greeting.

Jillian quickly returned to her chair, her smartly tailored clothes swishing with the sharp speed of her movements.

"Jillian lives in California. I asked the nurses to call her and tell her about the fire after we got to the hospital yesterday."

"I caught the first flight here…arrived about a half hour ago. I haven't had an opportunity to check into my hotel yet," she explained in an efficient manner.

"You have a place to stay then?" asked Seth, not sure what to say.

"Yes. I'm at the hotel on North Street, within walking distance," she answered brusquely, pointing up the street and then pushing her fashionable gold-rimmed glasses back on her nose.

"Okay. This is a surprise. Well, I'll let you two catch up. I'm heading to my mom's for Thanksgiving. Enjoy yourselves," said Seth awkwardly.

"Wait. Let me give you my card in case you need to reach me. My cell number's on here, so you can contact me anytime," explained Jillian, handing him a business card. A business card in any other similar situation might have seemed bizarre, but here it was perfectly appropriate, considering the tone of her voice. She talked as if she sat at a corporate desk in a boardroom conducting a business transaction.

"Okay, thanks," said Seth, clumsily taking the card and waving goodbye to them both.

Weird, he thought as he walked slowly down the hospital corridor, whistling quietly.

He read the card:

Jillian Connar
Physical Therapist
Children's Hospital of Sacramento

Seth felt sorry for the children at that hospital. She seemed kind of scary, like a drill sergeant or something. The card listed an address and several phone numbers. He found Jillian's cell number on the card, just as she'd announced. He carefully placed the card inside his wallet.

I wonder why Harold never mentioned her.

At least I don't have to run to my mom's now. There's one thing to be thankful for.

Seth took his time walking, trying to sort out his next moves.

He'd call Jillian later to tell her about his idea of Harold temporarily moving in with him. *Maybe she'd already made other plans?*

Seth stopped walking as his heart skipped a beat. *Whoa.* He wondered if he might have stepped *way* out of bounds by contacting the church about rebuilding Harold's house.

He didn't know Harold had a daughter.

He didn't know Harold had any living relatives, and he didn't want to step on Jillian's toes. These were her decisions to make, not his. He really needed to talk to her and decided he'd call as soon as he finished visiting his mom, after Jillian and Harold had a chance to visit.

Wow, I might've seriously messed up.

Soon, he arrived at his mom's. She greeted him as he opened the front door, calling his name from the kitchen when she saw him pop his head inside.

"Hey, Mom! How are you?" he yelled over the drone of the TV. His mom had the Thanksgiving Day Parade tuned in. She never missed it.

He caught the aroma of turkey and filling as soon as he entered, and his taste buds salivated.

"I'm good! Come in!" she said happily. "You're early, but I like it! What's new with you?" she asked while bustling around the kitchen doing food prep.

"Well, a lot, actually," laughed Seth.

"Oh really? What?" she gushed with interest.

Seth usually didn't have a lot to say, so he knew he'd grabbed her attention. He told her all about Harold, his house burning, and his plans for the afternoon as he munched celery sticks.

"Mark? I didn't know you and Mark hung out anymore. That's nice he's helping like that," she responded as she carried rolls to the table. Seth grabbed one.

"We've hung out a few times. He's a good guy," replied Seth, automatically helping his mom bring the rest of the food to the table.

"Oh, he *is*. I've always liked him," added his mom absently as she brought the last of the bowls to the table. "Time to eat!" she announced, lavishly bowing and waving her arms simultaneously over the table of delicacies.

"I'm starving. It looks so good!" said Seth with relish, pulling out an old, worn wooden kitchen chair, plopping down quickly and digging in.

"Yes, eat, boy, *eat!* You're way too skinny." She furrowed her brows with concern.

"That's why I'm here, Momma," he teased.

"Ha! Don't remind me you only come by to eat. I'll just get depressed."

"Oh, you know that's not true."

"Hmm." She shrugged her shoulders and changed the subject. "So I'm sure you heard about Katy's miraculous recovery, right?"

"Yes, I did, that's really great," said Seth happily.

She then launched into a long-winded presentation about Katy, filled with the minutest details. Seth let her talk uninterrupted, because as usual, he learned things he didn't know before. Such as the fact that Katy had fulfilled her maid-of-honor role at Merin's wedding in a wheelchair. Seth also found out Katy had been discharged from the hospital a while ago and was undergoing physical therapy for her leg—making good progress. He was glad, and he wondered again if he still had feelings for her.

When they finished eating, Seth helped his mom clean up.

Afterward, she offered to drive him to Harold's burned house so he wouldn't have so far to walk.

Seth happily took her up on the offer, showing his mom the gloves, mask, goggles, and garbage bags while explaining the purpose of each.

"Good thinking," she said proudly.

"Actually, these were all Mark's ideas."

"Oh. What about a box?"

"A box?"

"Yea, you're going to need boxes to put the stuff in you're salvaging," she said with exasperation. "Honestly, Seth, I don't know how you live day-to-day sometimes."

Seth didn't like the comment but stayed silent.

She opened the creaky cellar door and climbed down the narrow steps into the basement. He heard her rummaging around, and soon, she came up with two sturdy boxes.

"Here, take these. We'd better get going if I'm going to have you there by two."

Seth's mom drove to Harold's house. Puddles from the previous night's rain splashed noisily as the car's tires plowed through.

Ugh, not only is everything burned, but now it's wet too.

As they crested the hill, Seth saw Mark and the crew already standing in a circle in the driveway. Harold's car sat parked in a neighbor's driveway where he must have left it last night after discovering his house had been the destination of yesterday's screaming fire trucks.

The charred devastation struck Seth anew. Emotions swirled to the surface, but he quickly stuffed them.

I'm glad to help Harold. How hard would it be for someone to go through this with no one to help?

But he has a daughter! Maybe he doesn't need my help after all.

Confusion washed over him, but Seth realized he couldn't let on his uncertainty to this dedicated crew. He swallowed a lump in his throat as he gazed at the crowd of people awaiting his arrival—at 2:00 pm on Thanksgiving Day—when they could be home eating pumpkin pie in a warm house and watching football with their families.

He retrieved the boxes from his mom's trunk, thanked her for the ride, and turned to his group of new friends.

"Hey, Seth." As Seth set the boxes on the driveway, Mark greeted him with a high five—something they did a lot as kids and naturally fell back into.

Everyone greeted one another briefly, then Mark said somberly, "Over there, under that blue tarp, are the charred remains of a dog. I guess that's Rudy?"

"*Aw* man." Seth rubbed the back of his neck, not sure what to say. He didn't want to see Rudy's dead, burned body.

"Yea, it sucks. Kevin drove back to his house a couple minutes ago to get a shovel. We thought we'd dig a hole in the corner of the backyard and bury him. Sound okay?"

"Yea, that's a good idea. You don't mind doing that, do you? I don't think I can."

"No problem. I didn't know the dog. Neither did Kevin. We'll bury him."

One worker asked if the house had a cellar. Seth said he didn't think so but wasn't sure. A member of the group, also a volunteer member of the fire department, explained he'd already checked, and there was none. The fire department worker took over at that point. He gave safety instructions to everyone in the group, and the search began.

The group worked carefully and tirelessly until the sun began to set. Everyone agreed to come back early the next morning to finish up before bad weather rolled in.

Amazed at the generous, compassionate nature of these people, Seth felt a lump in his throat.

He'd never known anyone like this before.

Mark offered to drive Seth home, and he gladly accepted. He now had two big boxes, though only one had a couple of items in it. Nevertheless, Seth wondered how he'd get the stuff home, so once again, he thanked Mark for his foresight. Mark suggested they just leave the boxes in the car overnight.

Once Seth settled into Mark's car, he had an idea as he watched the last of the sun's rays dip below the horizon. He'd visit Harold again to tell him what they were up to. He asked Mark to take him to the hospital instead, a shorter distance anyway. When they arrived, Mark said he'd pick him up at six forty-five the next morning.

Seth asked Mark to pop the trunk before leaving. He pulled out a clean garbage bag from his pocket and walked around to the back of the car. He put one of the items from the box into the garbage bag. He wanted to show it to Harold.

Seth shut the trunk and waved to Mark who pulled away. He jogged up the steps of the hospital's main entrance and made his way to Harold's room.

He heard the quiet drone of the television as he glanced into the room and noticed the absence of visitors. Harold lay on his side dejectedly, back to the door, paying no attention to the voices on the screen.

"Hey, Harold, how are you?" asked Seth quietly from the doorway, not wanting to startle him with his arrival.

Seth walked around the bed so he could see him. Harold's red and blotchy face gave away the fact that he'd been crying. His normally vibrant blue eyes held a dull, glazed stare. He didn't look in Seth's direction when he spoke in a hoarse whisper, "Hi, Seth."

"What're you watching?"

"Nothin'."

"How are you?" Seth tried again to engage Harold in conversation.

"I don't know. Tired."

"How was your Thanksgiving? Did they feed you turkey and stuffing?" Seth grinned.

"Yea, it was pretty good too," said Harold, brightening a bit, and then added, "Otherwise, it was a real crappy thanksgiving."

"I agree it is pretty crappy, but you still have lots to be thankful for."

"Humph."

"You have your life. You could've been at home when the house caught fire. I'm really glad you weren't. And you have your friends. You have me," added Seth sheepishly. "And your daughter," he added, still confused about why Harold hadn't mentioned her.

Harold ignored him, staring blankly at the wall.

"I have something for you." Seth held the garbage bag behind his back and rustled it. Harold finally turned and looked in his direction. Seth walked backwards toward the room's bathroom, making exaggerated efforts to hide the large, obvious, loudly rustling bag while glancing back at Harold and grinning mysteriously.

Harold simply harrumphed at Seth, not seeming to care much about what he was doing.

Seth closed the bathroom door behind him. Tucked inside the bag was a small black safe, covered in soot. Seth threw away the big black garbage bag and used paper towels, soap, and water to clean off the grime from the safe as best he could. After a few minutes of scrubbing, rinsing, and drying, he walked out with the safe, again hidden behind his back.

"I found this for you," explained Seth as he carefully brought the safe around to the front of his body so Harold could see it.

"What's that?" Harold said hoarsely. He didn't recognize the safe at first.

"Some friends and I went to your house. We looked for things that weren't damaged in the fire, and we found this safe. I'm assuming you'd like it back?" asked Seth tentatively, not sure what mysteries the container might hold.

Harold stirred and his eyes lit up in recognition. "Oh my goodness. Yes, oh, thank you. Do me a favor. Hand me my wallet, in the top dresser drawer over there." Harold pointed to a set of sterile-looking metal drawers built into the wall. Seth retrieved Harold's wallet and handed it to him.

He slowly sat up and opened the wallet with shaky hands. Harold dug around in a little compartment for a couple seconds, finally producing a small key.

"Here's the key to that safe. Here, you open it." Harold offered the key to Seth.

Seth put the safe carefully on a small table next to Harold and gingerly opened it, all the while hoping the contents inside weren't harmed from the fire. He breathed a sigh of relief. Inside, papers and a photo album—filled to overflowing with photos—appeared intact.

"Oh, thank you, Lord." Tears welled in Harold's eyes. "Hand me that photo album, will you?" Harold's voice quivered. "I thought I'd lost this. Thank you," said Harold again as he began looking at the photos with shaky hands. He told Seth stories about some of the photos. The overstuffed album contained precious photos of his wife, his daughter, navy pictures, and so much more.

The memories offered much needed soothing balm for Harold's wounded soul.

When he finally finished talking, they sat in comfortable silence for a few minutes. Seth spoke first. "I haven't told you something that's a pretty good thing for me to be thankful for."

"Oh? What's that?"

"I asked Jesus to come into my heart," explained Seth awkwardly, not sure how to tell Harold. He again relied on the descriptive words he remembered Mark using when they were kids.

Harold's eyes lit up, and a smile filled his face. He chuckled. "That's wonderful news! When did this happen?"

Seth gave Harold the details he craved, and his smile never faded as Seth talked.

After a bit, Seth asked the question that burned in his mind, "Harold, how come you never mentioned Jillian?"

Harold's smile faded, and he sighed deeply. He searched for his words for a few moments. "I messed up so much in my life." He sighed again and shook his head. "I didn't always know Jesus, and I wasn't a Christian when I raised Jillian. I was a mean SOB, and I drank too much. I wasn't a good dad." He adjusted his bed, so he was sitting up straighter. He looked at Seth and said sadly, "My daughter hates me." His shoulders sagged dejectedly. "She doesn't think someone can change. I keep praying that someday she'll see and believe that I'm different. She moved out after she turned eighteen and made her own life in California, far away from me."

Harold choked back sobs, sighed deeply again, and, after a moment, continued, "You see, I'm a sinner saved by grace, like you." He turned to Seth with sadness in his eyes. "There's so much I wish I could go back and change, but I can't. I do the best I can now, and I pray I'll see the day my daughter can forgive me."

Harold adjusted the bed to a leaning position again and shifted his body, trying to get comfortable. "I didn't tell you about Jillian because...how do I explain to you that my daughter hates me? I'd give anything to make things right between us." Tears rolled down Harold's cheeks again.

Silence lingered until Seth spoke. "Thanks for telling me. It must have been difficult to share. I'm sorry for bringing it up. I didn't know." Seth felt awful that he'd brought the mood down again. "I'll pray for you. Man, it feels weird to say that." Seth laughed, trying to lighten things up.

Harold chuckled in reply. "Weird? Maybe. But prayer is one of the greatest things you can do for someone. I would love if you prayed for me. I—well, Jillian and I both—need prayer."

They sat quietly for a few moments, and Seth leaned forward in his chair.

"I don't mean to change the subject, but I have something else to ask." Seth paused, wondering how to ask the next question and unsure of how Harold would react. "Would you like to move in with me till we can figure out other arrangements? I have plenty of room. Katy was going to move in, and if it was good enough for her, I know you'd like it too. In fact, I insist you move in with me for now until you figure out your next steps. I insist," Seth repeated emphatically.

Harold's eyes registered surprise. "You know what? You're an answer to prayer in many ways tonight, if you only knew."

Seth looked at Harold with a questioning gaze.

Harold chuckled. "Thank you, Lord. You see, they told me I'm being discharged tomorrow. But I didn't tell them I don't have any transportation, and I don't have any place to go. I just trusted God. He came through with you, so I'm not going to make you twist my arm. As an old man, I've learned to appreciate the Lord's blessings and his answered prayers."

"Oh!" Seth's adrenaline pumped as he realized *tomorrow* was sooner than expected.

"Did you tell Jillian you're getting discharged tomorrow?" Seth realized he still hadn't called her.

"No, I didn't tell her. I didn't want to burden her. I'm surprised she even came."

"What's your discharge time?" Seth calculated his schedule in his mind.

"They said probably around two."

"Here's what we can do." Seth's mind raced. "I'll get your car and drive it here at two so you can have your car back, and then we'll drive together to my apartment—your new home. I'm your new roommate." Seth smiled.

"Okay, but it's my *temporary* new home, and you're my *temporary* roommate until I get things figured out. But I do appreciate it. You have no idea. My car keys are in the same drawer where my wallet was. Go ahead and get them." Harold, again waved his hand at the dresser drawer.

"So you trust me with your car then?" Seth teased.

Harold chuckled again. It's not exactly the kind of car I'd picture a young man being interested in, so I can't imagine you're gonna run off with it. That creaky clunker's seen better days, just like this old body of mine."

"Okay, creaky." Seth grinned. "I'd better run. See you tomorrow at two." He pulled out the car keys and walked toward the door.

"Seth?"

"Yes?" Seth paused at the hospital room doorway.

"You're right. I do have a lot to be thankful for."

"Me too." Seth smiled. "Good night, Harold."

"Good night."

Seth whistled to calm his nerves and sort out his thoughts as he walked down the hospital corridors and out into the star-filled night.

So much had happened in the last couple of days. He needed to clean up his apartment tonight to get ready for Harold to move in tomorrow. And he needed to call Jillian.

He dug out Jillian's card and dialed her number while he walked. Just as he turned the corner, a brisk breeze slammed his body, causing a shiver. He leaned forward into the wind, pulling his jacket closer. She answered on the first ring, with a question in her voice, obviously not recognizing Seth's unfamiliar number.

Seth had a brief and difficult conversation with Jillian. She had no plans for what Harold would do next and seemed real unhappy about the need to consider it. With reluctance in her voice, she indicated she would perhaps try to buy a newspaper tomorrow to begin looking for an apartment. She then curtly added that she had to get back to California for work on Monday, so there wasn't exactly a lot of time.

Seth explained his ideas for next steps with Harold and that Harold was being discharged from the hospital tomorrow.

She seemed profusely relieved that Seth had taken the reins. Seth gave Jillian his address and asked her to stop in and visit them on Sunday before she left for California. She agreed, and they ended their conversation.

Harold's right. Jillian seems angry at him.

He prayed for both Harold and Jillian, ignoring the cold. The phone call and prayer time made the walk seem short, and soon, Seth was at his apartment.

He worked until midnight, cleaning each room and readying it for his new roommate. Then he collapsed into bed, exhausted, sleeping all the way through the night.

CHAPTER 18

Moving Day

But whoever has this world's goods, and sees his
brother in need, and shuts up his heart from him,
how does the love of God abide in him?

—1 John 3:17 (NKJV)

Though it felt like an ungodly hour to Seth, Mark picked him up promptly at 6:45 a.m., and they drove to the burn site to meet the others.

By the time they finished picking through the wreckage, they'd gathered only a meager collection of salvageable belongings. A couple of drinking glasses—miraculously unbroken—and a few clothing items that oddly didn't have a mark on them were among the paltry findings. The clothes needed a good washing because they reeked of smoke but otherwise seemed untouched by the destructive flames. A couple of dishes, silverware, knickknacks and tools rounded out the sum total of the discoveries, which didn't even fill two boxes.

They all tried not to feel too disappointed. So much work for very little reward.

Seth thanked them all profusely.

Mark offered to drive Seth, but Seth explained his plan to pick up Harold from the hospital and move him into his apartment, offering proof to Mark by dangling Harold's car keys in front of his face.

"Can you drive?" joked Mark.

"Duh. You know I can drive. I just don't have a car."

"Yea, but how long's it been since you've been behind a wheel?"

"Not long. I borrow my mom's car occasionally."

Mark and Seth loaded the boxes into the trunk of Harold's car.

"Okay, well, it's great that you're letting Harold move in with you. Keep in touch, man." Mark put his hand up to high-five Seth.

"Hey, wait. Something I forgot to mention. Do you remember when we were kids and you told me you asked Jesus into your heart…and after that, you always tried to get me to do it too, but I wouldn't cause I thought you were weird?"

"Yea." Mark chuckled.

"Well, I did it. I asked Jesus into my heart."

"You did? Whoa, no way! I mean, *yes* way! That's totally awesome. Praise God," whooped Mark. He high-fived Seth, and Seth laughed. "When?"

"A couple days before Thanksgiving."

"Aw man!" yelped Mark, embracing Seth in a giant bear hug, "You have no idea how many times I prayed this would happen."

Seth laughed again while awkwardly shoving Mark and pulling himself out of the embrace. Mark laughed at his friend's discomfort. "Yea, well, just wanted to let you know. I gotta go pick up Harold."

"Hey, maybe I can stop in and meet Harold after he gets settled in?"

"Yea, sounds good. Talk to you soon." Seth waved as he stepped into Harold's car. He turned the key in the ignition, and the old car started immediately. He gave himself a fair amount of time to get familiar with the controls inside Harold's ancient Ford Granada. Then he silently prayed a short request for protection as he pulled carefully out onto the road.

I really need to get myself a car, thought Seth for what seemed like the hundredth time in the past week as he soon pulled into the hospital's parking lot.

Before going in to get Harold, he called the library. Though scheduled to work this afternoon, he hoped they'd understand why he couldn't. He'd never called off before. He told his supervisor the whole story. Surprisingly supportive, she offered to help in any way she could. Seth breathed another sigh of relief.

He walked into the hospital at exactly two, but it took almost ten minutes to get to the room with the unbearably slow elevators stopping at every floor.

Harold sat on a chair in his room, all dressed and ready to go, a hospital-provided bag containing the precious safe lay next to his feet.

Hospital staff insisted he go out in a wheelchair, and a friendly nurse soon arrived pushing it. Harold mumbled ungratefully, wondering out loud why he had to get into such a contraption when he could walk perfectly fine. But he obliged. The cute, young nurse, a real charmer, had Harold laughing in no time as they rode the elevators and walked to the exit. They waited inside while Seth drove Harold's car to the curb beside the patient ramp.

Harold yelled to Seth when he jumped out of the driver's side, "You need to drive. I don't know where you live." The nurse helped him out of the wheelchair and to the car. He let himself slowly down onto the passenger seat. The friendly nurse wished him well, closed the car door, and waved goodbye as she turned back to the hospital.

Seth's heart raced nervously.

Driving Harold's car by myself? No problem. Driving Harold's car with Harold in it? An entirely different matter.

After they pulled out of the parking lot and onto the street, Harold said with surprise, "You drive like an old lady!"

"I haven't driven for a while. I'm a little rusty. You don't want me to wreck your car, do you?"

Harold sighed. "No, I don't want to lose my car too."

They pulled onto the side street where the entrance to Seth's apartment was located. "River Street," harrumphed Harold as he read the street sign. "Where's the river?" He chuckled.

"No river. I don't know why it's called that."

Harold began quietly singing an old hymn as he looked around questioningly. "As I went down to the river to pray, studying about that good old way."

"Over there." Seth pointed to the steps leading up to his second-floor apartment. Harold stopped singing to look where Seth pointed. "Keep singing. You sing good."

Harold rolled his eyes in response, then frowned. "Oh, you live upstairs. Hadn't thought of that."

"Can't you walk upstairs?" Seth mentally kicked himself for not thinking of this.

"I can, but I don't like to do it a lot. I get out of breath. Once I'm up there, I'll stay for a while." He laughed a little uncertainly.

"Okay." Seth felt terrible that he hadn't considered that his second-floor apartment might present a problem.

They walked slowly to the staircase, and Seth reached out to help Harold.

"I don't need help. I'm not crippled. Just slow," explained Harold. "You go ahead up awhile. I'll make my way there eventually."

Seth walked to the top of the stairs and unlocked and opened the door for Harold. He waited patiently for him at the top. When Harold got there, he said, "Let me just stand here a minute and catch my breath."

Seth closed the apartment door so he wouldn't let all the heat outside. The entryway had a small porch area, and the two just stood there with Harold leaning over the rail, supported by his folded arms. He curiously took in the view down the street. Seth realized he'd never done that before, so he leaned on the railing with Harold.

"Ya know, I never stood here like this before. Quite a nice view of the park from here, isn't it? Never even noticed."

"Amazing what you can see when you slow down a little and really look," mused Harold, more to himself then to Seth.

"I think I'm gonna get a chair or two to put out here. It'd be a good place to sit, wouldn't it?"

"Maybe when the weather warms up," suggested Harold. He turned and said, "Okay, I'm good. Just had to get my breath."

They went inside.

Seth showed him around, and Harold seemed to like things just fine. He sat down at one of the two kitchen chairs Seth had in his tiny kitchen.

"It'll do. It'll do just fine. Thank you for your hospitality. I promise not to be a burden. And I can cook, so I'll earn my keep." Harold winked.

"Yes, you *can* cook. You're a great cook," agreed Seth.

Seth joined him at the table, and they enjoyed a peaceful chat.

Since he only had one bedroom, Seth offered it to Harold, but he soundly refused, insisting he'd sleep on the couch. After some debate, it became clear Harold wasn't budging on the point, so Seth relented.

He demonstrated to Harold how the living room couch pulled out into a bed. Seth pulled out extra padding for the bed, which he stored in a closet, and gathered an extra pillow, sheets, and a blanket. He stacked everything next to the couch for now.

"Make yourself at home. *Mi casa es su casa.* Turn on the TV if you want." Seth nodded toward the small television in the corner and handed Harold the remote. Harold sat gingerly on the slightly lopsided, threadbare plaid recliner, turned on the television to a news station, and fell promptly asleep.

Seth used the time to unload the rest of Harold's belongings from the car, do some laundry, and clean up the few items they'd salvaged from the remains of Harold's home.

When Harold woke up, he flipped through his photo album again. At one point, Seth noticed Harold staring at a photo of Rudy, so he used the opportunity to tell him about burying the dog. Harold thanked him, adding sadly, "Maybe I can make him a grave marker sometime."

Seth nodded his agreement. "I'd be happy to help." Harold thanked him and continued his trip down memory lane as he poured over each photo, occasionally sharing a story with Seth. Seth settled onto the nearby couch to listen.

Soon, Seth's empty stomach growled ravenously so he excused himself to figure out what they could eat. He dug around in the fridge and pulled out some deli packages, sniffed them, and checked the dates. Satisfied, he made bologna and cheese sandwiches for supper.

Harold seemed to enjoy the simple meal, finishing it off quickly. "Tomorrow, I want to start thinking about what to do next," he said determinedly after finishing his sandwich. "But today, I just need some time to myself…to think and pray."

Seth left him to his thoughts for the rest of the day. Harold spent a lot of time reading Seth's Bible and praying. Seth tried to stay quiet and out of his way as much as possible while sending up a few silent prayers to God himself. He realized what Harold needed most, perhaps, was more of an emotional healing than a physical one.

Later, even with a visitor in the next room, Seth slept soundly all night long.

Seth had to work on Saturday, and Harold insisted he be left to his own devices for the day. Since he worked the morning shift, Seth promised to buy Harold a newspaper on his way home, along with a couple of warm platters from the local grocery store's deli.

Seth's supervisor surprised him by bringing in some clothing, which had belonged to her father. She knew Harold from his frequent library visits and felt certain the clothes would fit just fine.

When Seth arrived home with the clothes, Harold accepted them gratefully. He tried them on and discovered they fit pretty well. Always the gentleman, he immediately penned a thank-you note to Seth's supervisor.

After enjoying their platters, Harold immersed himself in the newspaper, looking closely at the advertisements for apartments, circling a few he wanted to check out the next week.

CHAPTER 19

Healing for the Soul

He heals the brokenhearted and binds up their wounds.

—Psalm 147:3 (NIV)

Noisily chirping birds feasting at a neighbor's birdfeeder and brilliant sunshine streaming through dusty living room windows woke Harold early Sunday morning. He folded his blankets and put them in the hall closet, closed up the creaky couch, and puttered about the kitchen making coffee and toast. Soon, the unusual rattles and clunks emanating from the room next door aroused Seth as well.

Harold and Seth chatted pleasantly over breakfast and took turns in the bathroom. Harold wanted to go to his church, and Seth planned to attend Word of Life Community Church, so they soon bid one another goodbye, each going their separate ways.

At Word of Life Community Church, Seth had long talks with both Pastor Frank and Mark about his newfound faith and next steps for Harold. Pastor Frank said a decision from the church about helping with the rebuilding of a house would take some time because he still had a lot of people to talk to. Seth also still needed to talk to Harold about whether or not he had insurance.

In the meantime, the same group that had met up to salvage items from Harold's home planned the final cleanup of the remaining wreckage, along with the local fire company. The residual junk posed a danger to anyone who might venture onto the property. One volunteer, a construction worker, had access to heavy equipment and agreed to clear the lot quickly. Seth appreciated their initiative.

When Seth finally arrived home from church, he found Harold bustling around his kitchen. The women from Harold's church had brought home cooked platters, and he had them steaming and ready to eat. Seth's stomach rumbled—how wonderful to come home to a hot, home-cooked meal!

Over the warm, satisfying lunch, Seth filled Harold in on the volunteer efforts to clean up his property. "How can I ever thank them for all of this?" Harold's eyes welled with tears.

As they cleaned up the kitchen, a knock sounded at the door. Wondering who it could be, Seth opened it slowly while curiously peering around the edge. There stood Jillian. He had forgotten she was coming.

So she's a woman of her word.

Seth swung the door wide. "Jillian, hello! Come in." He waved her inside.

Harold's face broke out into a huge smile, every wrinkle curving upward, his eyes sparkling merrily. He hugged her, but she barely returned the gesture, looking very stiff and awkward. He showed Jillian around the apartment, chattering on about how Seth's church would be cleaning up the burn site and that he and Seth were working on the next steps for finding a place to live.

Satisfied after the brief tour, Jillian abruptly turned to leave, stating she had to catch her flight. She waved as she mumbled good-bye and closed the door behind her.

She is so obviously uncomfortable around her dad.

After Jillian left, Seth asked Harold if he had homeowner's insurance. It turned out he had only a small amount, not nearly enough to cover the cost of building a house, even modestly. Seth explained how his church might help with construction. He emphasized it was purely speculation at this point but one possible option.

Seth also showed Harold the remaining items they'd salvaged from the burn wreckage. Harold cherished each piece, holding and examining each item with reverence.

Seth also loaned Harold some of his own clothes to wear temporarily until he could fully replenish his wardrobe. Though close to the same size, their styles could not be more different. Seth laughed until his stomach ached as Harold modeled the young man's clothes and pretended to walk and talk like Seth.

After the modeling fun, Seth handed Harold a roll of peppermint lifesavers he'd purchased at a mini-market on the walk home from church. Harold smiled in thanks.

Seth and Harold fell into a routine.

Seth taught Harold how to use his laptop. He especially focused on how to look up Bible verses on the Internet. Harold loved the feature and used it addictively.

And Harold frequently allowed Seth to use his car.

Harold changed his library routine to coincide with Seth's work hours, for the most part, at least on short work days. They rode together to the library, and Seth worked while Harold did his usual library thing. However, now that he had a new skill—computers—he began to use the library's technology, spending his library hours in new ways as he learned to enjoy web surfing.

Although things became more routine, Seth's past still troubled him. While the dream had seemingly stopped, his guilt about aborting his son had not abated. In fact, it had grown to the point where it constantly nagged and consumed Seth's thoughts.

Everywhere he went, he thought about his son. After Harold's house burned down, Seth wondered if his son would've grown up to be a firefighter. After the conversations with Officer Grant, he wondered if his son might've been a police officer. As he talked with Mark and Pastor Frank about possibly rebuilding Harold's home, Seth wondered if his son would have grown up to be an engineer. When Seth and Harold worked together to organize Harold's finances after losing his checkbook and other financial papers in the fire, Seth wondered if his son might have been an accountant. When Seth drove Harold's car and turned on the radio to listen to music, he wondered if his son might've been a musician. When Seth saw families at the park, he wondered if his son might have married and had children.

These thoughts never ended. One day, he saw a little boy with a full head of bushy brown curly hair and green eyes, and Seth's heart caught in his throat—he looked so much like his son had looked in the dream.

The abortion weighed heavily on his mind.

One day after church, Seth shared his concerns with Pastor Frank.

"I know you asked God to forgive you for the abortion, Seth, because you told me."

"Yes."

"Let's talk." Pastor Frank walked toward his office, waving for Seth to follow. He sat on the corner of his desk and picked up a Bible lying in the center. "The Bible says God forgets our sins after we confess and repent, even as far as the east is from the west." He motioned to a chair next to the desk. Seth sat.

Pastor Frank opened his Bible and flipped through. "Here. 1 John 1:9 says, 'If we confess our sins, he is faithful and just and will forgive us our sins and purify us from all unrighteousness.'"

He flipped through some pages again. "And another I'm thinking of is from Psalm 103:12. God has removed our sins as far as the east is from the west." He set down his Bible and walked to a bookcase, pulling a different Bible from the shelf. "Let me read this Psalm from the New Living Translation. It's so good." He stood next to the bookcase while he read aloud, "Verses 10–13 say, 'He does not punish us for all our sins; he does not deal harshly with us, as we deserve. For his unfailing love toward those who fear him is as great as the height of the heavens above the earth. He has removed our sins as far from us as the east is from the west. The LORD is like a father to his children, tender and compassionate to those who fear him,'" concluded Pastor Frank, closing the second Bible.

Seth shrugged his shoulders and shook his head. "Well, why don't I feel forgiven then? Why do I feel horrible all the time?"

Pastor Frank walked back to the desk and casually sat on the corner again.

"God has forgiven you, but you haven't forgiven yourself. Let go of it, just like your heavenly Father has. He's not constantly thinking about your sin like you are. It's in the past, and I pray you would begin to believe that God speaks the truth. You are purified from all unrighteousness. Allow Him to transform you into the likeness of His son. He wants you to 'go and sin no more,' and He's got a good future for you." He jumped off the desk and squeezed Seth's shoulder. "You're forgiven and free to be who God created you to be. Learn who that is by spending time with Him in prayer and by reading His Word," said Pastor Frank gently but earnestly.

"Thank you," replied Seth simply. He stood, and they both walked out of the office. Seth waved, turned, and started for home, pondering all he had said.

"Thank you, Jesus, for forgiving me. I forgive myself too. Teach me what you want me to know, Lord," said Seth quietly and sincerely in prayer.

Seth came home to an empty apartment after church. Harold hadn't returned yet from his service.

Hmm, I'm already late. Wonder what's keeping him?

Seth decided to read the Bible and pray since he had the apartment to himself. A while later, he heard the door creak open. Yawning, he glanced at his watch to discover it was four in the afternoon already.

"Hey, Harold, *man*, where've you been?" asked Seth curiously from the living room.

Harold walked into the living room with an oblong box tucked under his arm and a grin on his face.

"I was playin' checkers with a friend and look what he gave me." Harold pulled out a checker set. "My friend said there was no sense him having two sets, so he gave me one, seeing that mine burned up in the fire," said Harold, smiling.

He opened the box and showed Seth.

"We'll have to play sometime, but not now. I'm all played out for today."

"Harold, you're a man of mystery…always out gallivanting around. Soon, I'll hear you have a lady friend too," said Seth teasingly.

"Oh heavens no. Heavens no. One wife was enough. Her memory keeps me happy," insisted Harold.

Soon, he napped on the recliner.

Word of Life Community Church fully embraced the rebuilding of Harold's home.

Consequently, Seth and Harold found themselves immersed in a whirlwind of meetings and a myriad of details. The community came all out on Harold's behalf as well. The library held fundraisers. The local fire company held fundraisers. Every time a group scheduled a fundraiser, Harold was, understandably, asked to attend.

Seth noticed that it seemed to tire him out and asked Harold about it.

"It's not that I don't want to go, and it's not that I don't appreciate everything being done, because I do, but I want to contribute financially too. I have some money. I'm starting to feel like a beggar, and I don't like it," he said honestly. "I want to donate money to my own house," Harold said with frustration.

Seth called Pastor Frank and explained things, and the pastor invited them to come to the next building committee meeting so Harold could give his desired contribution. Harold seemed satisfied with the plan.

When the meeting day arrived, Harold grinned and hummed all the way to the church. He tapped his fingers on the faded steering wheel in beat to the tune he sung quietly.

"What are you so happy about?"

"Life's good. It's a great day. That's all." Harold smiled mischievously.

"Really?" Seth drawled. "I don't think I'm getting the whole story here."

Harold just smiled.

At the meeting, Seth soon discovered the source of Harold's cheerfulness. When Harold handed a committee member a check for ten thousand dollars, he shocked everyone, including Seth. Seth didn't realize he had that much money to donate. Everyone in the room clapped with surprised glee.

One member jogged over to the thermometer chart, where they tracked their fundraising progress, and dramatically and playfully filled the chart in nearly to the top with a red magic marker. With Harold's modest insurance as well as his ten-thousand-dollar cash donation, and the donations from the church and community, only a few thousand dollars remained to their goal. Therefore, at this point, they decided to stop fundraising efforts and focus solely on building the house.

Everyone agreed, and the meeting ended on a positive note.

As they walked to the car, Seth said, "I didn't realize you had that kind of money saved up. You inspire me."

"That's about all I had saved, but I hate taking charity when I don't have to. I was saving for a new car, but at my age, that's kind of silly, I guess. My car's just fine and will probably last me for however much time I have left."

"Oh," said Seth, feeling very uncomfortable as he considered the fact that Harold spoke about his death as though talking about the weather.

"When you get as old as me, you have to come to terms with these kinds of things," said Harold with a smile as though he'd read Seth's mind. "But *you* should save money for a car, young man," Harold reprimanded Seth. "And when are you going to start looking for that journalism job? You don't have the pesky dream anymore, so you don't have an excuse. And don't act like you have to babysit me, because you know darn well that isn't true either. I can take care of myself," Harold said sternly.

"I know. Yes, I know. Sorry. I do need a car and a job, and you're right, it's time." Seth gratefully patted Harold on the back.

Harold pulled into the mini-mart on the way home, pointed to the entrance and said authoritatively, "Go get yourself a newspaper so you can look at the job vacancies."

"Okay, but there are better ways now. There're more job postings online than in the newspaper."

"Then look at the newspaper *and* the Internet!"

CHAPTER 20

Christmas

For to us a child is born, to us a son is given, and the government
will be on his shoulders. And he will be called Wonderful
Counselor, Mighty God, Everlasting Father, Prince of Peace.

—Isaiah 9:6 (NIV)

Work crews from the church and the community moved full steam ahead on Harold's new house. Heavy equipment removed all remnants of the former house, and everything was rebuilt from scratch.

Immensely enjoying himself, Harold visited the work site daily, chatting and joking with workers and helping as much as he could. Everyone loved Harold. His joyful presence and positive attitude inspired the workers, making their efforts all the more meaningful. Local construction companies donated time and labor, generously allowing employees—experts in their fields—to work on the home a couple days each week, rotating employees to the site. Many volunteers from Word of Life Community Church, Harold's church, and from the community at large assisted. As a result, a concrete foundation was poured and an outer shell built in record time.

The weather cooperated beautifully. Other than a fizzle of a snowstorm just after Thanksgiving, no more snow fell, virtually no rain, and the region enjoyed warmer than normal temperatures. Now only a couple of weeks before Christmas, Seth couldn't believe the progress made in such a short amount of time.

But work crews reminded Seth and Harold that inside work would go much more slowly because they had less volunteers lined up due to the Christmas and New Year holidays. Extra effort had been expended to get the home's exterior shell finished quickly before bad weather hit. Completing the outer frame allowed crews to work inside throughout the winter, uninhibited by weather.

Regardless of the reasons or circumstances, Seth and Harold were greatly impressed and appreciative of everyone's earnest efforts.

Seth immersed himself into the activities of Word of Life Community Church. He went to every service, Bible study, and activity remotely relevant to a young, fresh out-of-college male.

As a result, he came to know some pro-lifers who regularly went to the local abortion clinic to pray. This active group prayed at the clinic during all open hours. The prayer vigil took the form of people actually standing across the street praying for any and all who entered the building—workers, clients, women, men. The group invited Seth to join them.

At first overwhelmed as he considered the request, Seth's heart raced, and his body shook. It wasn't where Katy had her abortion, so he was thankful for that. She had driven over an hour away so they wouldn't run into anyone they knew. But even though this was a different clinic, he remembered the day well, and though her abortion didn't bother him then, it certainly did now. He didn't know if he could be a part of the prayer vigil.

Maybe it's too soon? But God nudged him. *Maybe this was the very thing he needed to heal the wounds in his soul.*

If he went, he didn't want to go alone. Even though he wouldn't be alone, *per se*, he'd be more comfortable if Harold came along. Maybe because Harold knew Seth's history, and most of the others in this pro-life group did not. So Seth hedged on his answer, saying he'd get back to them. He didn't have a lot of time to consider because the prayer vigil started the next day at 9:00 a.m.

Seth rushed home from church to talk with Harold. He explained what the group did and asked Harold if he'd like to come along.

Harold looked surprised and said, "Oh yes, I'd love to come. I used to do that with my wife. She went to pray at the abortion clinic every Wednesday from nine to noon. I went along sometimes, not every week like she did. I'd very much like to go with you."

Seth called the contact person and informed her that he and Harold would take the nine-o'clock-to-noon shift on Monday. She explained a couple of others might help and profusely offered her thanks. She went on to enlighten Seth about the power of prayer and the difference prayer makes in the lives of those who enter the clinic.

Seth didn't doubt her words.

The next morning, Seth and Harold awoke early and bundled up, wearing lots of layers. Though not bitter cold, the winter-like temperature made three hours of standing outside difficult if unprepared for the elements.

Harold drove to the site. Upon arriving, as Seth turned to step out of the open car door, Harold said, "Hold up, I brought some things for us." He stepped out and walked around to the trunk. Seth joined him. Harold pulled out two folding chairs, a thermos of steaming, hot coffee, and a couple of cups. He smiled wryly and said, "I used to stand for three hours, but don't think I can do that anymore." He winked at Seth as he handed him a chair and a cup.

"Good thinking," said Seth appreciatively, realizing Harold had made a couple of trips up and down the outdoor apartment stairs early this morning without his knowledge. Once again, his appreciation for this kindhearted gentleman grew.

Seth and Harold carried their belongings to the assigned location, unfolded the chairs, sat down, and began praying silently. Soon, two other women—one in her twenties and one middle-aged—joined them in prayer, waving their greetings. The women had brought their own chairs and thermoses.

Seth quickly grew tired of sitting, so he got up and paced as he prayed. Harold took turns sitting and standing, as did the two women.

Maintaining a silent, respectful vigil, the prayer team said nothing to anyone who entered. Instead, when someone arrived at the clinic, they immediately arose and prayed for each person and continued prayers until those same people left. Each walked about as they prayed, sometimes gesturing, partly to keep warm and partly in earnest, sometimes even praying aloud but quietly to themselves. For some reason, out here at the clinic, it felt more sincere to stand and walk while praying, but understandably, Harold sat more than the others.

Around 10:00 a.m., a maroon sports car with a black racing stripe caught everyone's attention as it sped into the parking lot and squealed its tires when stopping. A man sat behind the wheel, his arms flailing wildly, as he and a woman in the passenger seat argued. The group stepped up its prayers.

Soon, an attractive, well-dressed woman got out of the car and walked slowly toward the clinic with her head lowered dejectedly. The man stayed in the car but appeared restless. He kept looking over at the prayer team, sometimes gesturing in a not-so-friendly manner.

Before long, he vaulted out of his car, angrily slammed the door and stomped across the street, walking purposefully toward Harold all the while screaming profanities and pointing directly at him.

He walked right up to Harold, waved his finger point-blank in his face, and yelled, 'I know you, man. I know you! I gave you ten dollars at the community fundraiser at the firehouse…for your house. I didn't know you were one of those religious *freaks*, those 'holier than thous' trying to tell me what to do. It's her *choice, old man*. I want my money back. I want my ten dollars!" If possible, his voice seemed to get even louder as he shouted. His body trembled, his face flushed red, the veins in his neck bulged, and the extremely volatile situation ratcheted up a notch as he thrust out his hand and wiggled his fingers in Harold's face, indicating he wanted the money now.

Concerned the irate man might harm Harold, Seth, who'd been frozen to his spot, finally shook himself free from momentary shock and started toward Harold. But Harold lifted an arm toward Seth, motioning him to stop.

The man turned to Seth and screamed, "You stay out of this, *nutjob*! This isn't your business!" As the irate man shouted, spittle flew from his mouth, and landed on Harold's face as he looked back in Harold's direction during his tirade.

Harold slowly reached into his pocket, retrieved his wallet, and handed the man ten dollars. He ripped it from Harold's hand, turned, and began walking away but whipped his middle finger at the group as he did so. He crossed the street and got back into his car, slamming the door loudly.

Everyone ran to Harold. Harold calmly pulled out his handkerchief and wiped the spittle off his face.

"Harold! Are you okay?" asked Seth with concern. "That guy's crazy! What the heck is up with him?" growled Seth angrily.

"Should we call the police?" asked the middle-aged woman, her hands shaking as she dug her cell phone out of her purse.

"No!" said Harold emphatically. "Don't call the cops. It isn't necessary. I gave the man his money back, and he left. End of story," he said evenly.

Seth's eyes narrowed, his face turned red, a deep scowl formed on his lips, and he shook from head to toe with rage at the way his gentle friend was just treated.

"You have to get rid of the anger, Seth. It doesn't help." Harold looked kindly into Seth's eyes. "Anger keeps you from thinking clearly and prevents God from moving. Let's just pray for him."

Seth sighed and rubbed the back of his neck, shaking his head in amazement at Harold's calm. Briefly, he wondered if he would have been angry like the man in the sports car if people would have been praying at the clinic where Katy had her abortion. He honestly didn't know but doubted it because he really didn't think much about the abortion or praying, one way or another, back then. He turned his attention back to the present.

The group prayed.

A while later, they all looked across the street as movement caught their eyes. The woman, who'd arrived with the irate man in the sports car, exited the clinic and walked slowly into the parking lot, her head still bowed. She gingerly lowered herself into the maroon car and closed the door behind her. As soon as the door clicked, the man revved the engine and sped out of the parking lot, screeching his tires all the way down the street.

A tear rolled down Harold's cheek. The group prayed again.

On Friday night, Jillian showed up at Seth's door. He couldn't believe his eyes.

An ecstatic Harold hugged her again, and she stiff-armed him with what might be called a hug in reply.

"I don't usually visit over holidays, but thought I should check in since you lost your home and ended up in the hospital," she said in a brisk, businesslike manner. Jillian awkwardly handed Harold a box wrapped in Christmas wrapping paper.

"Oh! It isn't Christmas yet, is it?" asked Seth, a bit panicky as he realized he hadn't bought anything for his mom or Harold yet.

"No. But I definitely don't travel on Christmas, so I came early. Airports are too crazy around holidays. Thanksgiving was enough holiday traveling for me."

"Oh my goodness, thank you, Jillian. I didn't know you were coming. I just mailed your gift yesterday so now I don't have anything to give you," answered Harold with concern.

"No big deal. I'll be home before it arrives. My flight leaves tomorrow afternoon. I just wanted to check in," she said brusquely.

"Oh! Thank you. I'd like to show you the house they're building for me, but it's too dark now. Can I show you tomorrow?"

"If we go in the morning," Jillian answered with reluctance.

"Yes, first thing. Should I open this now?" Harold turned the gift over in his hands.

"If you want," Jillian replied disinterestedly.

"Come in," said Harold, motioning for Jillian to follow him into the living room.

Seth stayed in the kitchen, thinking he should give them some alone time.

Harold sat on the recliner, and Jillian took a seat on the couch. He proceeded to open the gift: a new pair of pants, a button-up shirt, and a sweater vest. The kind of clothes Seth had always seen Harold wear to the library. Though he'd been given some donated clothes, had been wearing a few of Seth's, and had bought a couple pieces at the Salvation Army, his wardrobe remained meager since the fire.

"Oh, how nice!" Harold said, tears welling up in his eyes. "Thank you so much, Jillian. I need clothes badly. I appreciate this very much."

Jillian stood. "You're welcome. I figured you could do with some clothes. I'm heading to my hotel now. When should I be here tomorrow to see the house?" she asked sternly.

Harold looked toward Seth in the kitchen. "What time?"

"What time's good for you, Jillian? How early can you come?" asked Seth.

"Eight?"

"Eight, it is," answered Harold.

"All right." And with that, she walked out the door, closing it behind her.

What an enigma. She obviously cares about her dad, or she wouldn't have come, but when she's here, it's like she can't wait to get away. Strange.

Seth felt the tug of the Holy Spirit urging him to pray for Jillian, so he said a quick prayer for both Jillian and Harold.

The next morning, Jillian arrived promptly at eight, and the three of them drove in Harold's car to his house. No workers were present at such a bitter cold, early hour in December.

Harold proudly walked around the outside of the house, explaining everything to Jillian like an excited child, his warm breath coming out in clouds of condensation in the wintry air.

When he opened the front door to lead them inside, Harold stopped so abruptly that Jillian ran into the back of him. This ruffled her feathers, and she mumbled grumpily about stopping so quick.

Harold just stood there, not moving.

"What's wrong?" asked Seth from behind Jillian.

Harold didn't answer. He just swung the door wider and walked into the center of the room, turning in a circle with a pained expression on his face.

Jillian and Seth followed him in.

Red spray paint spewing vile words covered each inside wall. The vandals also wrote *Pro-Choice*, and the word *freak* appeared occasionally as well. The red paint, though dry by now, had dripped and run from each letter like blood. "Get out of my life," "Get out of my bedroom," and "It's my body" were boldly sprayed on the floor. A couple of upside-down crosses completed the morbid display.

The three of them stared in stunned silence, mouths agape.

Soon, Jillian said sternly, "I agree with the sentiments, but not the methods."

Harold simply looked defeated.

All of them turned their heads as they heard vehicles pull into the driveway and doors closing. Soon, a group of volunteers from Word of Life Community Church walked in the door. They greeted Seth and Harold, then they had the same stunned, silent reaction as they looked around.

Everyone remained silent for a very long time. Then someone finally said, "We need to call the police and maybe the newspaper."

"No!" said Harold sternly, then he corrected his voice, deliberately calming himself. "I don't think we should do that. Involving the police and the newspaper would give the person who did this more attention than they deserve. I think we should just cover it up with paint and ignore it and pray for them," he said quietly. "I just feel bad for all of you. You've all worked so hard," said Harold as he began sobbing.

Immediately, he found himself surrounded by a group of people hugging him. Jillian just stood in the background, observing.

One of the workers said, "They haven't ruined anything. These walls will be covered with insulation and drywall. And the floors will have flooring put down eventually—carpet and linoleum—depending on the room. Nothing was actually hurt, except maybe our feelings."

Another worker said, "I have an idea. Let's go buy some gold spray paint and cover up the writings with gold and gold crosses. And maybe some yellow paint too, so we can paint the sun (as in the son) and smiley faces. And maybe some blue paint, and we'll draw ocean scenes and lake scenes and streams, kind of like streams of living water. And while we're painting over this stuff, we can pray over the house, walls, and floors, covering the whole place in prayer. That way Jesus triumphs and any intended harm is transformed into good."

Everyone loved the idea, so the same group that just arrived now happily hopped back into their cars to go buy their own spray paint.

Seth and Harold looked at one another and chuckled.

These people are amazing.

"I need to leave now," said Jillian sternly from the corner of the room, her face white as a ghost. She had remained silent for most of the exchange.

They all climbed silently into Harold's car. Seth ranted all the way to his apartment about how the crazy guy in the maroon sports car at the pro-life prayer vigil had to be responsible for the vandalism.

Harold remained silent, allowing Seth to vent.

Jillian wouldn't even come into the apartment, saying she had to go catch her flight. She didn't allow Harold a chance to hug her. She just stiffly waved goodbye, with her back to everyone, and left.

Harold made his way slowly up the steps to Seth's apartment, and as usual, he rested at the top. Seth had bought a chair though, so this time, Harold sat on the tiny porch while catching his breath.

As their routine now dictated, Seth waited inside for Harold.

When Harold eventually came in, he said, "She's pro-choice. Vehemently pro-choice. She and my wife argued about it so much that it got to the point where we had to call a truce in the home. We decided we wouldn't talk about it anymore. It's a sore subject at our house," explained Harold.

Seth immediately felt guilty, smacking himself on the forehead. "Oh man!" he said but just as quickly changed his mind. "Well, I was pro-choice too, but now I'm not, so I'm not going to feel guilty about being pro-life or apologize because I'm pro-life, and Jillian isn't," he added with frustration.

"No one's asking you to apologize. I was just letting you know why she left, virtually without another word. That's all," said Harold with fatigue.

Something bothered Seth. There had to be more to the story with Jillian. He should pray about it but decided to do it later.

Seth's thoughts went back to the vandalism. "Like I said earlier, I'm pretty sure we know who did this…the guy at the clinic… sounded like the same stuff he said to you."

"Probably, but like I said earlier, we don't do anything more, just pray."

"If he pulls something like this again, then we do need to do more. I'll pray. But we can't let this go if he does it again," said Seth firmly.

"Okay, I agree. If he does more, then we'll do more. But I don't think he will," said Harold with finality.

Later that week, Seth went Christmas shopping for his mom and Harold. He thought about how he didn't see *his* dad either, kind of like Jillian and Harold, but worse. His dad lived in California too, like Jillian.

Why do people from the East run to California when running away from something?

At least Jillian and Harold saw each other sometimes. It'd been years since he'd heard from his dad, and even longer since he'd seen him. Seth tried not to think about the loneliness of missing his father and the pain of wondering why he didn't love him enough to check in, even just once in a while. Swallowing hard, Seth tried to get rid of the lump in his throat. *Stuff it, Seth.*

Harold allowed Seth to use his car to shop for Christmas gifts…a good thing since he came home with quite a haul.

He bought his mom some perfume, bubble bath, a scented candle, new gloves and a matching scarf, some socks, a stylish sweater, a set of drinking glasses (he had broken two in the past year), and a restaurant gift card.

To some, it might seem like a lot of stuff, but Seth liked to get his mom a bunch of gifts. She didn't have people buying for her, and she always bought him a pile of presents too.

To others, it might seem like a heap of cheap junk. To Seth's mom, though, she'd thankfully enjoy and use every single thing, cherishing each item since he picked it out for her. Always a special time in the Siracke home, Christmas brought out the best in both of them.

He bought Harold a new NIV Bible. He'd been borrowing Seth's and using the Internet to look up scripture, but Seth wanted to replace the one lost in the fire. He also bought peppermint lifesavers, a pair of pants, a shirt, and a sweater. Before shopping, Seth rummaged through the closet while Harold was away to look at the sizes and styles of clothes Jillian purchased. He wanted to be sure he got the right stuff.

Seth whistled Christmas carols all the way home.

Harold sat in the living room, reading the newspaper when he arrived with his purchases.

"No snooping!" Seth barked with mock sternness as he rushed to the bedroom to hide the bags in his closet.

Harold chuckled.

They'd split the cost of a mini artificial tree and several cheap decorations. A few brightly wrapped presents from Harold, carefully placed under the sparsely decorated Christmas tree, added to the joy and festiveness. Almost like a small child, Seth could barely contain his excitement about wrapping Harold's gifts and adding them to the pile of oddly shaped packages.

He grinned to himself. *My first Christmas in my own apartment.*

On Christmas Eve, Harold and Seth attended an enjoyable community Christmas Eve service at a church in town that neither of them attended. Afterward, they exchanged gifts. Seth instructed Harold to open his presents first, and he happily complied. Harold expressed pleasure with everything he opened, especially the Bible. Seth had written a note inside:

"Harold, Thanks for all you've taught me. You're a great friend. Seth."

Harold's eyes welled with tears, and he cleared his throat to keep them from spilling over. Okay, your turn now, open your gifts. Harold had bought Seth a journal and a classy pen set, as well as gift cards at a gas station and clothing store.

"For your new job—*if you ever get one*—and your new car *eventually!*" said Harold, rolling his eyes.

"Hey! I'm working on it." Seth had applied to a couple of places but didn't expect to hear back from anyone until after the holidays.

They listened to some Christmas music before going to bed and also read the Christmas story from the book of Luke.

For some reason, as Harold read, Seth wept. Grief for the loss of his own unborn son overwhelmed him as he thought of baby Jesus in the manger. Harold stopped reading when he noticed Seth's state of upset. "What's wrong?"

Seth wiped his tears away, blew his nose, and tried to gather himself together. Finally, he said, "I don't know. It just hit me. I started thinking about my son. I guess I'm still grieving his death."

"That's understandable. And it's good to grieve. I still cry sometimes when I think about my wife, friends that passed, and even my mother from time to time...and that was a long time ago. I cry about Rudy too. Grieving's normal. Don't let anyone tell you otherwise."

"Well, maybe. But this death is different. I caused his death. It wasn't natural. It isn't the same kind of grieving." Seth furrowed his brows in frustration.

"You didn't take his life."

"I might as well have," yelled Seth, the veins in his neck bulging, "cause I sure as heck did nothing to save him, and I went right along with it too. It was our choice. What a miserable choice! I wish I could go back and change it, but I can't."

Harold didn't react to Seth's anger. He calmly replied, "You're right. There's nothing you can do to change the fact that your son was aborted. You'll have to come to terms with it. But you already know God has forgiven you, so you need to forgive yourself too."

Seth visibly calmed from his sudden outburst as Harold continued, "I've done a lot of things I had to repent of—a lot of things I wish I could go back and change, believe me. But I have to look forward. I have to let God change me now, so I don't make the same mistakes again. Don't let what happened in the past make you bitter—allow it to make you better. Let God change you into something new. I think He already is, son. He already is," said Harold gently. "Can I pray for you?"

Seth nodded, a lump in his throat. Harold launched into a long, gentle, quiet prayer over Seth.

As he spoke, Seth fell sound asleep on the couch.

Harold let him sleep and reclined on the adjustable chair, deciding it was as good a place as any to settle in for the night.

On Christmas day, they both went to Seth's mom's house. She had happily invited Harold to attend, and they had a pleasant day, stretching late into the evening.

When they both came home, they played a lazy game of checkers while enjoying cups of steaming cocoa and buttered toast.

"Yum." Seth laughed. "It's been ages since I had this."

"Me too." Harold chuckled.

Snow fell lightly, and wind howled around the apartment, rattling loose window panes. Inside the warm and cozy residence, they both made their way to bed, sleeping peacefully through the night.

CHAPTER 21

Jillian

The time is coming when everything that is covered up will be revealed, and all that is secret will be made known to all.

—Luke 12:2 (NLT)

Seth worked the early shift the day after Christmas, and he tried to get ready quietly so as not to awaken Harold.

He noticed the photo album on the kitchen table lay open to a picture of Rudy.

Hmm.

Seth often caught Harold looking at photos of his dog and sometimes saw him looking at dogs on the Internet with the laptop. Harold missed Rudy.

Seth flipped through the photo album absentmindedly while he munched his banana, looking at several pictures of Jillian.

Now here was a confusing person.

She seemed happy as a little girl. Several pictures of Jillian and Harold showed them clearly enjoying one another's company. In one, Harold smiled proudly while supporting Jillian—grinning ear to ear—on a bicycle as she learned to ride. In another, an adoring Harold lifted a gleeful Jillian onto the back of a pony. Seth flipped through the album, noting other examples of a happy home. Jillian looked like a little girl who loved her Daddy. In fact, she seemed really cheerful.

What happened?

He decided at that moment to find out. He'd take it upon him-self to try to reconcile Jillian and Harold's relationship. Things didn't make sense. He dug out his wallet and quickly found her business card. He would call Jillian after work.

At the end of his shift, Seth jogged downstairs to one of the vacant rooms so he could make a private phone call. He dug out Jillian's card and dialed her number. His heart skipped a beat in his chest as nerves took over. He took a deep breath and wiped his sweaty palms on his pant legs while waiting for her to pick up.

When she answered, her voice sounded so chipper and friendly that Seth at first thought he might have dialed the wrong number.

"Hi! This is Jillian!" said the bright voice.

"Hi, Jillian. This is Seth Siracke, the person your father lives with right now."

Her voice turned deadpan. "Oh. What's up?" she said shortly.

"Um, do you have a couple minutes to talk?" Seth stammered, thinking maybe he'd made a mistake.

"Just a couple," she said with annoyance.

"Um, I was wondering. Your dad seems to really care about you. And um, it seems like you're mad at him or something? And I was, ah, wondering if maybe there's something I could do to rectify the situation?" sputtered Seth awkwardly.

"What? You called me at work because you think I am mad at my dad, and *you want to rectify the situation*! You have no idea what you are talking about, and you have no right to interfere in my life," she growled angrily.

"I'm sorry," Seth sputtered. "I don't want to upset you. It's just that Harold, um, your dad and I have gotten to be friends, and he doesn't seem to be the kind of person to me that you see him as, and I was wondering, what happened between you two?" asked Seth nervously.

"You have balls, kid, I'll give you that, but this conversation is over. Don't call me again. Goodbye." She hung up.

Well, that went well, thought Seth sarcastically, walking out the back door toward River Street while rubbing the back of his neck with fatigue and disappointment. He couldn't even whistle as he mulled over the troubling conversation.

When he got home, Seth decided to write Jillian a letter and mail it to the address on her business card.

He sat down on his bed with a paper and pen and began writing.

Harold was busying himself looking at pictures of dogs again on the laptop, so Seth took his time composing the letter. He rewrote it a couple of times.

He bared his soul. He explained how he'd met Harold at the library and how their relationship developed. He didn't tell Jillian about his son's abortion because he felt that fact wasn't important to Jillian and Harold's relationship.

He talked about Harold and how much Harold loved Jillian and how Seth didn't see his own dad and wished he could. He asked if there was anything he could do to fix whatever was broken in their relationship. He asked if she'd be willing to tell him what happened that made her so angry at her dad. Seth confessed he was pretty mad at his own dad too and explained why he felt that way. He shared Harold's regrets about being a mean, angry dad who drank too much and made lots of mistakes in life. He explained how Harold wished he could go back and change things, especially the kind of dad he'd been. He reminded Jillian there was no telling how many years Harold had left on earth, and he hoped he could help them reconcile before it was too late. He gave her all his contact info—his phone, email, mailing address.

Seth reread his letter carefully several times, then got an envelope and stamp, and raced down to the corner to mail it before he changed his mind.

When he got back upstairs, he had second thoughts.

I hope I'm not making things worse.

A few days later, Seth's heart raced with excitement when he saw an email from Jillian. This had to be good news. Maybe he really could help fix their relationship.

With shaking fingers, he clicked to open the message.

As he read, all the blood drained from his face. He felt faint.

Jillian seethed with anger. First, because Seth sent the letter to her work address, and second, for daring to send such a letter at all. She called him a meddling creep and told him not to ever call her or mail anything to her work address again.

Seth sat silently for a while chewing his lip and trying to calm his nerves.

Finally, he thought, *She had obviously misunderstood.*

Seth typed a reply, trying to keep his words as kind as possible and trying to clarify his previous boldness, hoping to better explain himself.

She just had the wrong impression of him. That's all. Seth wanted to do all he could to salvage his reputation with her.

After rereading the message several times and satisfied with his reply, he hit *send.*

He anxiously busied himself around the apartment, fretfully checking his email every few minutes. He whistled to calm frayed nerves.

Soon, a reply appeared in the inbox. Seth's heart raced.

He sat down, took a deep breath, and clicked open the email, nervously rubbing the back of his neck.

This one was worse.

This time, she told Seth that if he contacted her one more time, in *any* format, she would call the police and file harassment charges against him.

Seth steadied himself against the table, quickly slamming the laptop shut as though closing it would defy reality and make his panic disappear.

Man, I've really messed up. Panic and fear consumed Seth. His breath rasped loudly and quick. His heart pounded so intensely in his temples that he thought a vein would rupture.

He had to talk to someone, but not Harold, of course.

He yelled to Harold in the living room, interrupting his TV watching, to say he was going out for a while. "To Mark's house," he added impulsively. Then with a quivering voice, said "Hey, can I borrow your car?"

"Sure, go ahead. Have fun," answered Harold absently, obviously engrossed in what he was watching on the TV screen, not noticing Seth's distress.

Seth grabbed the keys, rushed out the door and down the steps. He pulled his phone out to call Mark but stopped. He shoved the phone back into his pocket. He needed to be alone. He needed to think.

He jumped in the car and started driving. He drove past Mark's house to the mountain at the edge of town. He pulled into a small dirt parking lot, shut off the engine, and pulled the keys from the ignition. He sat for a few minutes, taking in his surroundings. Years ago, Mark and his parents would hike up here, and he and Mark, and sometimes Mark's brother and sister and dogs, tagged along.

Seth stepped out of the car, locked the doors, and shoved the keys into a pocket with his cell phone. He scanned the edges of the empty parking lot for the trail. Soon, he spotted the path's entrance at the forest's edge and headed in that direction.

His heart rate had slowed but fear still gripped him. He prayed a short prayer for help with the situation with Jillian and began hiking the trail. It was good therapy. He stepped off the trail to walk toward a rocky ledge where he could look down on the town. The beautiful view brought a much-needed peace to Seth's thoughts. He breathed deeply of the fresh air and sat down on a rock for a few minutes to rest. At this lower vantage point, when he scanned the forest behind him, he noticed something from his childhood he had forgotten about. *Teaberries!* They covered the forest floor.

He remembered Mark's dad showing him how to find teaberries as a young boy. He told him to look closely for hidden treasure, and it wasn't until he squatted close to the ground that he finally saw the berries hidden under the leaves.

Seth smiled at the memory. He picked a few and relished their distinctive flavor as he slowly ate them, one tiny berry at a time. He remembered Harold's words and how similar they were to Mark's dad's. At the top of Seth's apartment steps when Harold first moved in, he had said it was amazing what you can see when you slow down and really look. *Hidden treasure.*

The thought felt important. He still believed he was missing something about his dream, or God, or something. He pulled out his pen and tablet from his shirt pocket and jotted a note to look closely for hidden treasure. If nothing else, it was a good reminder for his future job as an investigative reporter.

The sun dipped lower in the sky, and evening shadows crept into the forest. Seth stood, stretched, and headed back to the car. He still wanted to talk to Mark about Jillian, so he pulled out his phone and dialed Mark's number. He answered quickly.

"Hey, Mark. How are you doing?" asked Seth.

"Good, what's up?"

"Are you busy? Can I stop by? Are you at home?" said Seth, rapidly shooting off questions.

"I'm home. Sure. Come around back. I'm in the game room," said Mark, yawning sleepily.

Arriving in no time since the mountain was close to Mark's house, Seth pulled quickly into the driveway, locked the car, and jogged around to the back of the house where the porch light blazed. Since Scooter announced Seth's arrival upon hearing the car in the driveway, Mark was waiting by the door and opened it when he saw Seth approach. The fox terrier yipped incessantly until he walked inside.

"What's up?" Mark asked, shushing the dog and rubbing his eyes as though he'd just woken up. As before, after Seth greeted Scooter, the dog disappeared into another room. The dog seemed to enjoy his role as butler of the house.

Seth watched the dog exit, then said, "I think I messed up."

"Why?" asked Mark, confused.

Seth proceeded to tell him about Jillian, then about the phone call, the letter and the email.

Mark looked slightly amused.

"What possessed you to try to 'fix' their relationship on your own?" asked Mark, trying not to smile because Seth obviously didn't find any of it funny.

"I don't know?" said Seth, in a much-too-loud and whiney voice, thus revealing his frustration and embarrassment.

"Did you pray about talking to Jillian?"

"No. Not specifically about *talking* to her," confessed Seth awkwardly, sounding defeated, "Like I said, I messed up."

Mark sat back on the chair, looking thoughtful and rubbing his chin. "I've definitely, in my zeal to help others, I've gotten ahead of God sometimes…done things without praying about them…tried to take things into my own hands…and usually, it doesn't work out too well for me or the people I'm trying to help, even when my intentions are good."

Seth wasn't sure how to respond, so he didn't.

Scooter walked back into the room and plopped himself at Mark's feet. Mark reached down and ruffled the dog's ears. "I mess up too, but I'm tryin' to learn not to leave God out of the equation and not to run ahead and do things in my own strength. That isn't to say that God wouldn't have led you to do something like this, because He might've. But, well, nothing's too hard for God. We can give this to Him now…and ask for His guidance and forgiveness for not talking with Him about it first. What do you think?"

Seth nodded.

"And, we can get a bunch of people praying for healing in Jillian and Harold's relationship. We don't have to know any details, just that there's something wrong with the relationship— father and daughter. The Holy Spirit will guide the prayer warriors. What do you think? Should I put Jillian and Harold on the prayer list?"

"Yes."

Mark called someone and gave them the prayer request. A simple appeal, he didn't even give last names or details, just a request for healing in a father-daughter relationship—Harold and Jillian.

Then he turned to Seth and asked, "Do you wanna pray about this now?"

Seth nodded in the affirmative, so they did.

A huge burden lifted from Seth's shoulders as he drove home. He appreciated all the supportive and encouraging people in his life. *Hidden treasure.* Seth smiled at the thought. For now, he'd put thoughts about Jillian out of his mind, except for when he prayed for her and Harold.

The next morning during breakfast, Seth casually picked up the newspaper Harold had discarded after reading it. He flipped through the pages, and an advertisement caught his attention. The college announced its sponsorship of a debate on the topic of abortion. Anyone could attend, and it started in about an hour—today. Seth knew immediately that he should go. He never paid attention before, but now abortion seemed like the most important topic on the planet, at least to him.

He showered quickly and once again told Harold that he was going out for a while before work and that he'd see him later at the library.

Seth hurried to the college and arrived in plenty of time. Ample seats remained, so he went right up front because he wanted to hear all of it.

Two long tables lined either side of the stage. At each table sat five people conversing among themselves and studying notes to prepare for the debate.

Soon, it began. Mesmerized, Seth pulled out his pocket notebook and jotted some notes. Though it was hard to say which team held the upper hand, the audience's sympathies clearly lay with the team defending abortion. Shocked at how little he knew, Seth hung on every word. At one point, the pro-lifers vividly described the abortion procedure and marched out large images of aborted babies onto the stage. Nausea consumed Seth. He leaped up from his seat in the front and ran all the way to the exit in the back of the auditorium, not caring who saw him. Worried he might throw up on someone, he ran to the restroom and threw open a stall door just in time. He heaved repeatedly and thoroughly emptied the contents of his stomach. A couple of concerned guys who had seen his fast exit followed him inside. Not having time to lock the stall door, Seth's retching was on display for all the bathroom's patrons.

When the uncontrolled heaving finally subsided, Seth flushed the toilet and sat his quivering body back onto the floor, his face in his hands. The two men sat down beside him and wordlessly handed him some paper towels. After Seth wiped his mouth, they introduced themselves—Steve and Todd—and asked his name. Still shaking, Seth gave his first name. They asked if he was okay. He replied weakly, "I think so."

"Can you stand?" Steve asked and reached out a hand to help. The other guy, Todd, pulled Seth up by his other arm.

"Thanks," offered Seth with a shaky voice. He threw the paper towels away and washed his hands and face with water at the sink. Steve and Todd waited. Seth turned to them. "Hey thanks, I'm fine now. You guys can go."

Todd answered, "Well, we'd like to wait a bit and make sure." He leaned against the wall. "What happened? We saw you run out of the debate."

At that moment, everything came crashing down. The room spun, and Seth wept, his whole body shaking uncontrollably. The men led him quietly out of the bathroom and out a back door into a mostly abandoned courtyard. A couple of college students stood at the other end talking and didn't seem to notice their presence. The three men sat on a bench. Seth once again buried his head in his hands.

After some time went by and Seth continued to keep his face hidden, Steve asked, "Would it be okay if we prayed for you?"

"Yea." Seth croaked.

Steve and Todd prayed for Seth, not having any idea what had upset him so badly.

After the prayer, they explained they were part of a group praying for the pro-life team taking part in today's debate. They asked Seth if he wanted to tell them what was wrong and offered to help if they could.

Eventually, as he had so many times before, he shared his story in its entirety. Neither man seemed surprised. They talked for a long time as Seth sorted through the pain of what he had just witnessed, as well as his own son's abortion. The pictures and vivid descriptions included in the debate brought Seth face to face with the reality of the abortion procedure. Though he thought he had healed, seeing the aborted babies brought everything to the surface again. Widening his eyes in surprise, he put his hand to his forehead and stated flatly, "I'm a murderer." The words shocked Seth even as he spoke them. Sobs wracked his body again. "My son's blood is on my hands. I can't imagine his pain. Abortion is so…brutal…I didn't know." Seth wept. The men left him bare his soul as they realized God was doing a deep work. Healing always comes from an acceptance of truth. But they also reminded him that he was now forgiven by Christ.

"There's no sin too great that the blood of Christ can't cover," explained Steve.

"Oh God! I am so, so sorry. So sorry. My son, I am so sorry." Seth's grief poured out from the depths of his soul. The men stayed with Seth until he quieted. As his senses returned to normal, an embarrassed Seth realized he'd just spilled his guts—literally and fig-uratively—in front of complete strangers. He apologized for all they had just witnessed and heard.

Both men emphatically told him there was nothing to apolo-gize for. "We're brothers in Christ, and that's what we're here for," explained Steve. Todd, a Christian counselor, reached into his pocket and pulled out a business card. He told Seth to call him anytime. Seth thanked him. Steve, an associate pastor at a local church, also told Seth to call or stop in anytime.

Seth thanked them both, and they parted ways. Seth silently offered a short prayer of thanks for these men who had been so help-ful. *Hidden treasure.* He smiled even as his heart grieved about all he had just learned about abortion. His emotions raw, tears streamed down his face again. He wiped them away with his sleeve.

Truth had pierced his heart.

He prayed again for help. And healing.

About a week later, Seth worked the late shift at the library. Harold stayed home. It was too cold outside, and he wanted to do crossword puzzles instead.

A few hours later, a knock sounded at the apartment door, star-tling Harold because in the nearly two months since living here, no one had come to the door when Seth wasn't home. Harold still felt like a guest and, therefore, felt awkward answering the door. But he thought he'd better see who it was, so he slowly pulled himself out of the chair and shuffled to the door. He swung open the door, and there stood his daughter!

"Jillian!" Harold gushed with surprise. "Come in!" He opened the door wider and gestured for her to come inside. "Is everything okay?" he asked with concern.

She ignored the question.

"Where's Seth?" she asked sternly.

"He's working, at the library."

"Good. I need to talk to you anyway. Sit," she commanded.

Harold obediently sat down at the kitchen table, and Jillian sat on the only other available chair at the tiny table.

"I don't know what you two think you're pulling by calling me at work, writing me letters at work, and emailing me at work. Why couldn't you at least contact me at home?" she said crossly.

"What? I don't know what you're talking about?"

"Humph. So you *don't* know. Interesting."

"Know what?" asked Harold, clearly confused.

"Never mind, it's not important. But *this* is. I need to talk to you," she said severely.

"Okay," answered Harold tentatively, not having any idea what was going on.

"I'm going to talk. You're going to listen. Understand?"

"Understood," replied a bewildered Harold.

"You remember your good buddy Dave from the navy? Your drinking buddy Dave? The guy that was always at the house drinking until you both passed out drunk?" Her words dripped with sarcasm.

Harold winced and nodded sadly.

"Your good drinking buddy Dave came to the house *early* one Friday, before you and Mom got home from work, and he raped me. I was only thirteen. I got pregnant to a smelly, fat, gross, disgusting pig Dave whom you loved so much. My friend Lisa's older sister took me for an abortion. The clinic didn't ask any questions. Just took care of it. Before I had the abortion, I told pervert pig Dave that I was pregnant. He said 'So what? Your dad knows we had sex. He said he hoped I enjoyed myself.' Then he laughed. That's why I hate you so much. That's why!" She shrieked uncontrollably as tears ran down her face.

Harold grabbed his heart as a piercing pain and heaviness filled his chest. He tried to catch his breath as the room spun at her words.

"Jilly, Jilly. Oh my god, Jilly. I didn't know this. I didn't know. Why didn't you tell me? I never would have let such a thing happen to you. I love you." And with that, he collapsed onto the floor, just as Seth walked in the door.

Jillian sobbed, glued to the place on the floor where she stood, having risen to her feet by the end of her diatribe.

Seth didn't know why Jillian cried. He didn't hear what she had just told Harold. He only heard Harold's reply and then saw him fall to the floor.

He ran to Harold but realized he was unresponsive. Seth dialed 911, and the ambulance arrived quickly. After carefully carrying him down the outdoor staircase on a stretcher, they whisked him into the vehicle and left, lights and siren blaring.

Seth asked Jillian if she wanted to ride in the car with him to the hospital, but she refused. Seth said, "Well, just stay here then till I get back," and he left for the hospital.

Seth ran into the emergency room when he arrived, asking the receptionist where they'd taken Harold Connar. She told him to have a seat while doctors examined him. After what seemed like an eternity, Seth went back to the receptionist and inquired again. She said she'd check, but when she returned, she indicated Harold was being prepped for surgery, and it would be a while until news of his condition became available.

Seth waited. And prayed. He asked Mark to send another prayer request to the prayer team. Then he waited some more.

Finally after hours of pacing, he asked the receptionist to check again. "He's out of surgery. The doctor will speak with you shortly."

Seth breathed a little easier.

He's out of surgery. That has to be good, right?

Soon, the doctor approached after the receptionist pointed him in Seth's direction. The emergency room technicians had explained to the doctor that after Harold had regained consciousness, he had signed disclosure forms indicating they could talk to Seth about his condition. The doctor introduced himself and asked if Seth was family. Seth explained that Harold's only family was a distraught daughter who didn't want to come along to the hospital and that Harold was his roommate.

The doctor raised an eyebrow at the roommate comment but explained Harold had a heart attack, and they had done a cardiac catheterization and inserted three stents. Harold rested now, and due to his age, he remained in intensive care. Only family could visit while he was there, so his daughter could visit tomorrow.

Seth thanked the doctor for the information and started for home.

When he arrived at his apartment, he heard Jillian crying from the living room. What a sight awaited him there. With swollen red eyes, a flushed, blotchy face, and uncharacteristically messy hair, she sat curled up in the corner of the couch with a blanket and box of tissues. Used tissues lay scattered all over the floor where she had also haphazardly kicked her shoes. Seth didn't know how to react to this strangely distraught Jillian, who was normally meticulously groomed and poised.

"I think your dad's gonna be okay," he said quietly. "He had a heart attack. They did a catheterization and placed three stents in his arteries. He's in intensive care, so only family can see him. They said you can visit tomorrow."

She just cried louder in reply.

Seth didn't know what to say. He didn't know if she cried about Harold's heart attack or something else. Harold seemed really upset, so Seth assumed they'd argued. He remained silent.

Finally, Jillian said between broken sobs, her chest heaving violently. "He didn't know. All these years. He didn't know. I thought he knew." She wailed even louder. She seemed hysterical, and Seth wondered if he needed to call the ambulance again.

"He didn't know what?" Seth wasn't sure what to do or say. He shifted his feet awkwardly.

She just wailed.

Finally, she said, "Nothing. I don't want to talk about it anymore." She seemed to make an effort to calm herself. "Do you have any headache pills?"

"Yea." Seth went to the medicine cabinet in the bathroom to retrieve them. He came back shortly with a small bottle of ibuprofen. "Here," he said, handing it to her.

"Can I have a drink?"

"Oh. Sorry, sure." Seth quickly went to the kitchen and got her a glass of water.

She took some ibuprofen and then said, "Can I sleep on your couch tonight? I'm sorry, but I'm just so tired I don't know if I can get up. Would you mind? I can pay you," she said in a barely audible voice.

"What? Of course, you can sleep here. You don't have to pay me. Don't be ridiculous. The couch folds out into a bed. That's where your dad usually sleeps. Do you want me to fold out the bed?"

"No, too tired, just sleeping right here," she said as she closed her eyes.

Seth turned off the light and went to his own room.

He thought he'd better pray. Things were definitely happening, though he had no idea what. He knew he had to ask God to help both Jillian and Harold tonight.

The next morning, Seth awoke to the sound of clanging coming from his kitchen. Momentarily confused, he crawled out of bed and sleepily made his way there to see what made the ruckus.

Jillian bustled around the kitchen, cooking breakfast.

"Morning!" she said brightly. "I guess you like bacon and eggs with toast and orange juice, since you have all those things in your fridge?"

"Yea," said Seth, stunned.

"Good. It'll be ready soon. Better wash up," she said happily.

Seth walked away but turned to look again at her over his shoulder, not sure if this was the same person or not. *Weird. I hope she's not poisoning my food!* Then he chided himself for that thought, reminding himself this was Harold's daughter, not some serial killer.

Seth wolfed down the enjoyable breakfast. "You're a good cook, just like your dad," said Seth honestly.

"Thanks. Yep, he's a good cook. Mom was too," she answered in a friendly voice. "I called the hospital this morning. They said Dad's doing exceptionally well for his age and that I could come see him this morning, just like you said. Thanks for letting me crash here last night, but I'll get a hotel room for the remainder of my stay."

"Okay, no problem. How long are you staying?"

"Not sure. I guess a lot depends on Dad. We'll see," she said thoughtfully.

"Don't you have to get back to work?"

"I have tons of leave. I never take off, and I'm pretty close to retirement. I'll just have to talk to my supervisor about it," she said vaguely.

"Okay. Well, tell Harold I said hello, and I'll visit him after he's out of intensive care. Would you keep me informed of his progress in the meantime?"

"Sure."

"I have to go to work now." Seth put his dishes in the sink.

"Okay. I'll wash up these dishes then head out. Thanks again for letting me stay last night. I appreciate it. I was pretty upset," she added sheepishly.

"No problem. Just lock the door behind you." Seth waved goodbye.

CHAPTER 22

Healings All Around

…Weeping may last through the night,
but joy comes with the morning.

—Psalm 30:5 (NLT)

Jillian spent every moment she could at Harold's side. When he recovered enough to do so, they spent hours talking about things Jillian had feared talking about before—the pain she had buried deep inside her entire life.

Seth liked what he saw. As though they'd started all over, their relationship blossomed into something fresh and good. He left them to themselves as much as possible so their new bond could flourish.

Upon learning of a hospital release date, Jillian told Seth she didn't want Harold "walking up those rickety apartment stairs anymore." So she found him a temporary residence at a state-of-the-art rehab facility in a nearby city, a little over an hour away. She explained that her dad could continue to recover there with physical therapy. Apparently, Harold also suffered a minor stroke, which resulted in slight loss of motion on the left side. Doctors strongly believed therapy would help him regain full movement.

Harold remained upbeat about the stroke. "I'm just happy it was my left side," he announced while shoveling food into his mouth with the right hand. "Otherwise, how would I eat?" He grinned.

Harold's positive attitude, even in the most difficult circumstances, continually amazed Seth.

In light of Harold's heart attack and stroke, Word of Life Community Church stepped up their efforts to finish Harold's house as soon as possible so he'd have a comfortable place to live after rehab. Since the vandalism incident before Christmas, they put locks on the doors and locked the house when no workers were present. Thankfully, nothing further transpired.

During Harold's recovery, Seth quietly began an earnest job search. He answered a few advertisements for jobs and even had a couple of interviews. He didn't mention it to Harold because Harold had enough on his mind. Seth prayed he would get a good job, the right job. He wanted to surprise Harold with some news that would please him.

Harold and Jillian settled into their new temporary residences, over an hour away (Jillian got a hotel room nearby). Seth marveled at how much he missed his friend even though he had only lived with him for a couple months. The void left by the absence of Harold's towering presence and friendly demeanor loomed large.

The apartment seemed too quiet. And empty.

Seth also realized that, strangely, he missed the dream. For about a year, that dream had haunted him. He had desperately wanted it to stop. And it had. He hadn't had the dream since asking Jesus into his life a couple of months ago. Not once. At first profoundly relieved, he now missed seeing his son. The dream offered an almost tangible connection, and now he longed to see him again.

After church on Sunday, Seth asked Pastor Frank if he could talk with him privately. Pastor Frank agreed and led Seth to his office. Though he hadn't visited the office for months, the welcoming room remained virtually unchanged. Seth sat in the familiar, comfortable, soft burgundy leather chair.

"So, how can I help you?" asked Pastor Frank, smiling and settling himself into the similar chair across from Seth.

"This is going to sound weird. I haven't had that dream since the night I got saved. But now I miss it…I miss seeing my son. It was a connection, I guess. So now I wish I'd have the dream so I can see him. It felt 'otherworldly' somehow. I don't know how to explain it, but I feel drawn to the dream."

"Oh? That's interesting," said Pastor Frank, "and understandable. If I put myself in your shoes, I might feel the same way." Pastor Frank sat back with a thoughtful look on his face, the leather chair creaking as he shifted his weight. "You know, I've always thought you were fortunate to have that dream. Most people don't have such persistent, clear nudging from the Lord like you did with a nearly nightly dream. I'm fascinated by how God used a dream to draw you to Himself."

"Well, people in the Bible had dreams, right?"

"Oh, of course, but not in the same manner or for the same reasons as yours. We need to be careful that we don't attribute a message from God to every dream that comes our way. Certainly, your experience was a bit unusual. But God is amazing in how He works."

"But why do you think God won't let me have the dream again since I miss my son?"

"God does things for reasons we may not understand. He sees a much bigger picture," explained Pastor Frank. "Your yearning for the dream may be more than just a desire to see your son, though I think that is certainly very important to you. I don't want to minimize that feeling in any way."

Trying to understand, Seth shifted in his chair, as though the movement might help with comprehension. He leaned forward, brows furrowed. "What do you mean?"

"Before people know the Lord, they typically spend their lives searching for something, but they don't know what. They look for anything to fill the emptiness or take away the pain in their lives. Relationships, careers, alcohol, drugs, sex, pornography, food, you name it. Something, anything, to make them feel good. But until they find Jesus, none of these things satisfies, at least not for long. When people finally find Jesus, they realize they've found what they were looking for."

Pastor Frank stood and walked to the window. He paused a few moments to gather his thoughts and then continued, "Then what happens next is we start to crave more of Jesus. We long for heaven."

He turned and walked back to his chair and sat down, looking directly at Seth. "So yes, I think it's normal as a Christian to have an 'otherworldly' yearning as you put it. We want to be in His presence."

Seth's thoughts raced as he tried to take it all in.

Pastor Frank interrupted his musings. "So if I were to suggest anything, it would be for you to continue to get to know the Lord more. Spend time in His presence, in praise and worship, in prayer and fasting, in His Word, ask Him to guide you day-to-day. And never be afraid to tell God what's really on your heart. He knows anyway. Tell Him you miss the dream and miss seeing your son. Ask Him to show you why you feel that way and what He desires from you. The dream was no accident. He has your life and future in His hands, and He has great things planned for you. Of this I'm certain."

"Thank you," said Seth sincerely.

Seth pondered the pastor's words on his walk home. Yes, he knew he needed to spend more time in the Lord's presence. He also thought about the need to look closer for hidden treasures. Childhood memories flooded back. On a whim, he stopped at the mini-mart to see if they had teaberry gum. Surprisingly, the store carried the unusual treat. He bought a pack and shoved a piece in his mouth.

Not wanting to miss anything and wanting to be thorough, Seth decided to revisit the last item on his list—look up biblical dreams. After he got home, he read the books of the Bible Harold had suggested, which contained references to dreams. Nothing seemed to apply, but he had not researched biblical dreams beyond Harold's quick suggestions. Seth scoured the Internet for information on biblical dreams, his investigative juices flowing as he munched his teaberry gum.

He found a lot of interesting commentary regarding scriptures and dreams, jotting a few notes to himself:

Dreams are the product of a busy mind when your body rests, but your mind is still active (Ecclesiastes 5:3). Some dreams are meaningless (Ecclesiastes 5:7). What happens in a dream isn't real (Isaiah 29:8). God sometimes used dreams to warn people (Genesis 20:3; Matthew 2:12–13). God sometimes used dreams to foretell the future (Genesis 37:5–10; Daniel). God sometimes used dreams to encourage people (Judges 7:13–15).

Seth yawned and rubbed the back of his neck. He was getting nowhere. None of it seemed to apply. He wrapped his now tasteless gum in a tissue and threw it in the garbage can.

One scripture nagged at Seth. The one in Job 7:13–15: "When I think my bed will comfort me and my couch will ease my complaint, even then you frighten me with dreams and terrify me with visions, so that I prefer strangling and death, rather than this body of mine." Seth remembered how tormented he had felt by his dream, just like Job seemed tormented by his dreams. But it wasn't the same. *My dream had a clear personal message for me.*

Seth prayed about his dream before going to bed, asking God for some kind of closure about it.

Seth slept soundly. When he awoke and realized he'd slept all night and didn't remember having any dreams, he was disappointed.

He stepped into the shower and hummed a praise song he'd learned at Word of Life Community Church. As he rinsed the last of the shampoo from his hair, everything became crystal-clear in his mind. The reason he didn't have the dream anymore is because its purpose had been fulfilled. His dream was not an affliction like Job's but a wooing from a loving God. God allowed Seth to see that his aborted son was with Him in heaven. And God had called Seth to a relationship with Himself. Seth answered the call, and now there was a place reserved for Seth in heaven too.

I'm saved. I'm walking in the light, the same light that's in heaven where my son is, and I'll be there with him too someday.

Seth wondered why it took him so long to see the truth because the evidence suddenly seemed so obvious. The dream wasn't necessary anymore because Seth trusted God now. He knew Jesus was real, and heaven was real. He'd gotten the message. And because he took the time to look deeper, to dig into God's Word, to spend time in prayer, to praise God in song, the presence of the Lord had brought the revelation Seth so desperately sought.

As he stepped out of the shower and grabbed a towel, Seth laughed out loud, whistled, and said a little prayer of thanks.

Harold's house neared completion.

Fortunately, Harold gave Seth full access to his ancient but useful Ford. Now that Harold no longer lived with him, Seth helped the volunteers nearly every day, so the car became invaluable. Continually astonished at how great the house looked and how quickly everything came together, Seth's excitement grew. He couldn't wait for Harold to see his new home. Though work crews called Harold daily about a myriad of details like flooring and paint colors and Harold happily availed himself to their needs, Seth knew Harold couldn't fully appreciate the progress until he saw it for himself.

Seth had just gotten home after painting Harold's new dining room. With paint speckled on his arm and face, he jumped into the shower to scrub off. As he toweled dry, his cell buzzed. Not recognizing the number, he answered tentatively. The editor of the *Upper Forest County Times* greeted him and, wasting no time, offered him a job. Ecstatic, Seth accepted on the spot. Feeling giddy, he whooped and leaped and stomped around the tiny bathroom in celebration.

I have a job! I'm a reporter! Woohoo!

CHAPTER 23

New Beginnings

Forget the former things; do not dwell on the past. See, I am
doing a new thing! Now it springs up; do you not perceive it?
I am making a way in the wilderness and streams in the wasteland.

—Isaiah 43:18–19 (NIV)

Anxious to tell Harold about his new job, Seth made the long
drive to the rehab facility. Even though Harold had progressed
well and was soon being discharged, Seth didn't want to wait to tell
him. He sang loudly to the songs on the radio, tapping the cracked
yellow steering wheel and nodding his head to the beat.

"Hey, Harold," Seth greeted him with a beaming smile, a vigor-
ous handshake and pat on the back.

"My, you're in a good mood today." Harold chuckled.

"I am. Life is good. I hear you're all recovered, and, man, look
at you—better than ever! And your house is all ready for you. I can't
wait for you to see it. Everything's so nice."

"Yes. You're getting me excited. I can't wait to see it. I'm so
thankful for everything and everyone."

"And I have even more good news." Seth could barely contain
himself.

"Oh, what's that?"

"I got a job with *The Upper Forest County Times*!"

"That's great! Doing what?"

"I cover all school board meetings, and there are more schools than I thought in the region. I cover township and borough meetings and also the popular local Historical Society meetings. Those are my routine assignments, but beyond that, they'll assign stories as they come up. They also encourage me to take the lead on finding stories of my own, so I'm real happy about that. Maybe the beginnings of my investigative journalism, eh?"

"Praise God! How I've prayed for you. This makes my day even more than all the other good news, which makes me pretty happy, too." Harold chuckled.

Harold and Seth chatted and enjoyed their visit, and soon, Jillian joined them. She talked about moving Harold into his new home and about how she was working with Word of Life Community Church to plan a big open house. Anyone who helped build Harold's house in any way, or donated time or money or volunteered on a committee, or even anyone who offered prayer cover or moral support was invited to come see the end result of a great community effort.

"Really? That's the first I heard. It's a great idea," said Seth.

Jillian excused herself for a few minutes.

Harold asked, "So when do you start your new job?"

"Not quite two weeks from now."

"I hope you're buying yourself some new clothes," he said in mock grumpiness. He rolled his eyes in an exaggerated manner and pointed at the hole in the knee of Seth's jeans and his shredded cuffs, which dragged on the floor when he walked.

"I am. Don't you worry." Seth laughed. "And not only that, but I have my eye on a new—well, a *used*—car. I'm going to need a car since I have a lot of area to cover. And I'm moving closer to the office that I'm working out of. I just signed a lease on a newer first floor apartment within walking distance to the office. So when you come visit me, you won't have to take those *rickety* steps anymore." Seth grinned.

Jillian had walked in just as he emphasized the rickety steps and said, "Good!"

Harold expressed his gratitude and pleasure about everything Seth shared. Eventually, Seth bid them both goodbye.

* * *

Both Harold and Seth moved into their respective new homes, each helping the other with the process.

A couple days later, Seth drove Harold's car one last time in order to return it to its owner so Harold could be mobile and independent again. When he pulled into the driveway, he noticed a pile of rocks and flowers in the far corner of the backyard that weren't there the last time he'd visited.

Harold stepped out of the house to greet him and noticed Seth's gaze. "I made a grave marker for Rudy. Do you want to see it?"

"Yes, I do." Both men walked slowly to the beautifully decorated corner of the backyard. Flowers, plants and large stones lined the perimeter of the landscaped area with a small plaque showcased in the center. The plaque held the engraved image of a Labrador with an inscription:

RUDY CONNAR
Best Friend and Beloved Yellow Labrador-Retriever
of Harold Connar
See you in heaven, buddy

Seth choked up as he took in the moving sight. Harold put a hand on his shoulder and squeezed. "Jillian and your friend Mark did most of this. I just supervised a little." Harold chuckled a little to try to lighten things up.

"I didn't know Mark helped. He didn't mention it. That's great."

Harold stepped back. "It was kind of a last-minute thing…he was driving by and saw us out here working, so he stopped to help. I sure do miss that dog."

Seth stepped back to join Harold, and they turned and walked toward the house. "Man, I bet you do 'cause I miss him too." They walked in silence for a bit, and when they arrived at the car, Seth said, "Thanks, Harold, so much for letting me use your car. It was a lifesaver."

"Oh, you betcha. Anytime, son. Just bring that new car of yours over sometime so I can see it, and you need to take me for a ride in it too."

"Will do. Sorry I can't stay longer, but I have to get to work to finish up my last shift at the library today. I'll talk to you soon."

"No problem. Good luck with your new job next week." Harold waved goodbye as Seth turned to leave.

"Thanks." Seth waved and walked over the hill toward his new apartment, out of sight.

He and Harold had both moved into new living quarters. Seth had a new used car, and next week he started a new job. Everything felt fresh, new, and exciting.

A couple weeks later, Seth arrived at Harold's packed open house. Having trouble maneuvering around everyone and feeling like a canned sardine, he waved at Harold from across the living room and then escaped to the outdoors. A beautiful spring day, Seth deeply inhaled the crisp, fresh air while relishing the wide-open space.

He found Pastor Frank sitting alone on a swing in the backyard and joined him. "How did you manage to find such a quiet place surrounded by all these people." Seth laughed.

"Oh, this is great, isn't it?" Pastor Frank smiled.

"Yea, definitely. Everyone feels like they're a part of it. We all have a sense of accomplishment, of doing something really good."

"Yes." Pastor Frank smiled. "And I was just thinking about what obedience to God can do."

"You mean all the people with a servant's heart who made this happen?"

"Actually no…er…yes, of course, it's great that all the people involved in this project obeyed the Lord's calling to them. But actually, I'm going back even further," mused Pastor Frank.

"What do you mean?"

"I'm thinking about how Harold obeyed the prompting of the Holy Spirit in the library and approached you about your dream.

Just think how things might've turned out differently if he had not, and the two of you didn't become friends. What if that had never happened? You approached us about rebuilding this house. It may never have been on our radar screen if you had not done so. We have no idea where even the smallest acts of obedience to God might lead. Like I said before, God sees a bigger picture than we do. And I'm so thankful for that."

"That's deep," replied Seth.

"That's our God. Deep but simple too. It's easy to know Him, love Him, and obey Him. He takes care of the depth when all we need to do is follow Him in childlike obedience."

"I never thought of it that way."

"Perhaps I hadn't either." Pastor Frank laughed.

Their reflective time ended as a crowd of people spilled into the backyard, and some of them chatted with the pastor.

Seth decided to try to find Harold, so he made his way back into the living room. Harold stood in the same place he'd left him.

Just then, Seth noticed a familiar face making his way through the crowd toward Harold. Seth's heart raced in fear, and he tried to push himself closer to Harold, wanting to offer protection. As Seth got closer, he saw the man reach out his hand to shake Harold's hand and heard the man say, "I'm sorry." He held onto Harold's hand for a few beats longer than normal.

The man whose angry tirade caused spittle to land in Harold's face at the abortion clinic wore a contrite expression this time. At first, Harold looked surprised, and then he patted the young man on the back and said graciously, "You're forgiven. And you're in my prayers," he added with a smile and a wink.

The young man replied timidly, "Keep praying. I think it's working," and with that, he turned abruptly and left.

Seth stood watching him go with eyes wide and mouth agape.

Harold noticed Seth's shocked expression and said with a chuckle, "The Lord moves in mysterious ways, and for that I'm thankful."

Seth hung around until everyone had gone, and he helped Jillian and Harold clean up. After much urging, Harold finally took a seat in the living room and left Jillian and Seth to the remaining work.

Jillian planned to sleep on Harold's couch for the next couple of nights but then would head back to California. She said she really needed to get back to work now, especially since her dad had safely moved into his new house.

Seth agreed to continue to check on Harold for her.

About a week later, Seth drove his new, used car into Harold's driveway after work. He bounded up to the front door and rang the doorbell.

Harold opened the door before Seth even took his finger off the bell.

"Is that your new car?" asked Harold, happily gesturing toward the Honda. "Did you come to take me for a spin?"

"Yep! Come on!"

"What is it? A Honda? Blue, eh?"

"Yep, it's a Honda Accord. In good shape too. I'm happy with it."

They drove outside of town into the countryside and chatted pleasantly. Harold enjoyed talking about all the gadgetry in Seth's new car, marveling at how modern it seemed compared to his. They arrived back home, and Harold seemed disappointed the ride ended.

"Don't you like your new house?" asked Seth as they walked inside, wondering about Harold's glum expression.

"Oh yes, I do. It's a fantastic house. I couldn't ask for anything more. It's everything I could possibly need or want and even so much more than that. Everyone did such a good job, and I can't believe they did all this for me," he said sincerely.

"You seem kinda down. What's wrong?"

"Oh, I don't know. It's just so quiet here now that Jillian's gone back to California. And I don't have Rudy anymore. The place seems so big. I guess maybe I'm lonely," confessed Harold, "but I'll get used to things."

Seth visited a little while longer but kept thinking about what Harold said. He had an idea, but he'd have to pray about it first.

The next Saturday morning, he pulled into Harold's driveway. This time, Harold opened the door before he even rang the bell. Startled, Seth asked, "How'd you know I was here?"

"Oh, I was sitting in the living room and saw you pull up. That's all."

"Hey, how'd you like to go for a ride?"

"Love to!" said Harold with enthusiasm.

They drove out to the end of town and pulled into the driveway of a small home. Harold turned to Seth with a questioning gaze. Seth chuckled nervously and simply said, "We're here to visit somebody. Come on." He waved in the direction of the house and stepped out of the car. Harold shrugged his shoulders and followed.

Seth waved Harold forward as he walked up the sidewalk to the front door and rang the doorbell. Instantly, a dog barked, and the door was opened by a middle-aged woman. She offered a sad smile to Seth as her face registered recognition. She looked curiously at Harold, studying him in more detail than would be normal under the circumstances. Seth greeted the woman, and Harold shifted awkwardly under the woman's stare but offered up a polite, "Hello, I'm Harold," and extended his hand in greeting. She shook his hand and replied, "I'm Stacy. Please come in." She opened the door wider, and the two men walked inside. A small dog stood by Stacy and barked intermittently at the men until she bent down and said gently, "Shush, Xavier," as she patted his head and hugged his body gently.

The dog quieted and followed her to a chair. She indicated that Seth and Harold should sit on the couch. The dog looked curiously at the two men and walked over to greet them, his tail wagging as he sniffed each of them.

Seth petted the dog and turned to Harold. "I'm sorry I didn't tell you my plans, but I was afraid that if I did, you wouldn't come," he explained sheepishly.

Harold's eyes widened in confusion as he reached out to ruffle the thick blond fur around the dog's neck. The dog licked his hand in response, and Harold chuckled.

"I wanted you to meet Xavier."

Harold's eyes widened further in surprise, and then his brow furrowed as he tried to understand. "Why?"

Seth struggled for words and glanced at Stacy for help.

Stacy explained. "My dad passed away a few weeks ago. Xavier was his. Unfortunately, my husband seems to have developed an allergy to the dog, so I can't keep him. Our son lives in an apartment where he can't have pets. Otherwise, he would love to take him. I've reached out to other families, but so far, no one has shown any interest. A friend of mine made an announcement at her church that we were looking for a home for Xavier." She paused and glanced at Seth.

Seth took over again. "That was my church, and when I heard the announcement, you were the first person I thought of." He paused as he looked intently at Harold. "I know you miss Rudy. And Xavier misses his dad too. I thought you two might be good company for each other?" Seth shifted nervously as he waited for Harold's response.

"Aw, Seth, I don't know. This is so sudden, a lot to take in." He sighed and petted the dog again. Xavier plopped down on his feet. Harold grinned.

Seth chuckled nervously. "A sign?"

Stacy didn't say anything as the men talked, but her expression grew more forlorn.

Harold noticed. "Stacy, I'm sorry about the loss of your father. This must be very hard for you. Can you tell me more about Xavier?"

Stacy's eyes brightened a little. "Dad loved this dog. The two of them were inseparable. He's a Schipperke, and he's so loving and loyal. He misses my dad so much."

"I've never heard of a schipperke before. How long did your dad have him?"

"Oh, a long time, I can't remember. He got him when he was a puppy, and Xavier's getting old now. I have his veterinarian record, and that might tell us how old he is." She started to rise to retrieve the paperwork.

Harold reached his arm out and said, "Oh, Stacy, please sit. You don't have to get the paperwork. That's okay. I don't need to know exactly. He does look old, like me." Harold chuckled with uncertainty.

Xavier licked Harold's hand again as he petted him.

"He likes you," Stacy said sadly as she wiped away a stray tear. "I'm sorry. I'm still grieving."

"No need to apologize," replied Harold. "I completely understand. My wife died a long time ago, and I'm still grieving her death."

Everyone sat quietly looking at the dog who seemed oblivious to the fact that he was the topic of conversation. He stood, stretched, and curled up next to Harold's pant leg for a nap.

After a while, Harold broke the awkward silence. "I honestly don't know what to say. Can you give me a couple of days to think about it?" He leaned back on the couch. "It's just so sudden, and I haven't given any thought to another dog."

"Of course." Stacy smiled gently. "Is there anything else you'd like to know?"

Harold reached down again to pet the sleeping Xavier. The dog peeked at Harold and yawned. "Is there anything I should know? Any problems?"

"No, honestly, he's always been a very good companion for my dad. Other than just being old and moving a bit more slowly, he doesn't have any health problems we're aware of. He can't jump up onto the couch anymore. It's too high for him now, but he likes to sit on the couch with you, so you have to lift him. Of course, he's housebroken. He likes to go for walks, but at his age, he also likes to sleep a lot too." She chuckled. "Do you have any other questions?"

"I can't think of anything right now, but could I have your phone number in case I think of something later?"

"Sure, let me write it down for you." Stacy went to another room for paper and a pen. Harold looked at Seth with mock exasperation. Seth laughed and asked innocently, "What?" Stacy returned with the phone number. They said their goodbyes, and Harold promised to be in touch with an answer in a couple of days.

Xavier had awakened and stood with everyone else. Harold once again ruffled the thick blond fur around Xavier's neck, noticing the color was very similar to Rudy's. He mentioned it to Stacy and Seth.

"My dad always said that blond Schipperkes are rare in the US. Most are black. He got Xavier from a friend who used to live in England where there are a greater number of blond Schipperkes."

"Humph. Interesting," replied Harold as he patted the dog's head goodbye. The dog whined a little as the men walked to the door. Stacy comforted Xavier as the men left themselves out.

They returned to the car in silence. After they were seated and Seth was pulling out of the driveway, he broke the stillness. "I know you miss Rudy. I saw how you look at his pictures and how you look at pictures of dogs on the Internet. Rudy was special to you."

"Yes, he was special. Another dog can't replace Rudy."

"I know, and I don't want to pressure you. I hope I haven't upset you."

"No, you didn't. I just need to think." Harold rubbed his forehead and closed his eyes for a few minutes as though praying. Then he said quietly, "The Lord knows I'm lonely and I miss my Rudy. But a dog is a lot of work. And I don't like the dog's name, Xavier. What kind of name is that for a dog?" he asked grumpily.

Seth was surprised at the annoyance he heard in Harold's voice and wondered if he'd done the right thing. But he had prayed and was sure he sensed this was the right thing to do. Maybe he wasn't too good at hearing from God yet? He sighed.

"Like I said, no pressure. If you don't want him, it's okay. I'm sure they'll find someone."

Harold harrumphed. "Or he'll end up at one of those animal shelters where they'll just put him to sleep."

I hope not.

The next Monday morning, Harold drove himself to the library. He spent a couple of hours looking things up on the Internet. Finally, he stood and looked out the library window. He'd made his decision.

That evening, Seth's cell buzzed. His caller ID showed Harold as the caller.

"Hi, Harold!" said Seth brightly, hoping he was no longer upset.

"Hello, Seth. First, I want to apologize for being a grump. I'm sorry. There was no reason for me to treat you that way."

"No problem."

"I want Xavier," said Harold abruptly, "and I've already called Stacy."

"Oh! That's great! Did you arrange to pick him up?"

"Yes, I'm getting him Saturday. Would you like to come along?" Harold asked.

"Sure, I'd love to. What made you decide to get him after all?"

"Oh, several things, but his name sealed the deal," replied Harold a bit sheepishly.

"I thought you hated that name?"

"I did hate it. But then I looked Xavier up on the Internet to see what it meant. One place said it meant 'new house,' and I thought, well that's appropriate. Another place said it meant 'bright,' and I thought, well, he'd probably brighten my days. And then another place said it meant 'savior.' That one really sold me. I know the dog isn't a savior, but this dog is a gift from my savior…the one who knows me best. So I decided I'd very much like to bring Xavier into my new home to brighten my days and remind me to thank my savior Jesus for all the wonderful gifts he's given me."

"Wow, that's interesting stuff about his name and how it all fit together."

"You taught me good, *Mr. Investigative Reporter.*" Harold chuckled.

On Saturday, Seth pulled into Harold's driveway.

Harold came out the front door and instructed him to pull to the side so he could get his car out. "I want to take my car so Xavier can get used to the smell. Plus, then he won't get dog hair all over yours." Harold's brightly shining eyes, enormous grin, and light and springy gait exuded pure joy in his present activity—bringing Xavier to his new home.

Seth noticed that Harold now had a new fence around his backyard, and he asked Harold about it. Harold grinned. "Remember the guy who wanted his money back when he saw us praying at the abortion clinic?"

Seth nodded. Harold continued, "And he came to my open house, remember?" Again, Seth nodded. "Well, he knocked on my door this week and introduced himself. His grandfather was Xavier's owner! He's the grandson that lives in an apartment that can't have pets. Turns out he loves Xavier, kind of grew up with him, and he was very fond of his grandfather."

Harold's eyes gleamed as he relayed the story. "He asked if I needed help with anything. We hatched this plan for a new fence together. My old fence was damaged by the fire. Now that I'm getting another dog, I want a complete fence again so I can let Xavier outside without worrying about him running off." Harold turned and began walking toward the fence, waving at Seth to follow. "Come on, I'll show you."

Seth and Harold walked around to the back of the house. Harold opened the fence, and they walked inside. "Yep, the young man—Derek is his name—helped me. God brings us opportunities every day to love others. We just need to embrace those opportunities." He winked at Seth. "He's going to come around often to visit Xavier."

Seth laughed. "That's fantastic."

Harold closed the gate, and they walked to Harold's car. "After I met Derek, I knew without a doubt that I was supposed to take this dog. God is good."

Seth agreed as he climbed into Harold's car. *Maybe I did hear from God after all.* He smiled at his thoughts.

Soon, they pulled into the driveway of Stacy's home. Harold jumped out of the car with the speed of a much-younger man.

Anticipating their arrival, Stacy had everything ready. She gave Harold the dog's veterinary record, feeding bowls, food, shampoo, grooming brush, dog bed, toys, and even a small kennel to transport him.

After everything was loaded up, except for the dog and the kennel, Stacy sat down on her living room chair. "Oh, this is so bittersweet. I'll miss him, but I know he'll be well cared for." She covered her face with her hands because she didn't want to say goodbye.

"Remember what I told you, Stacy. You come visit him any time," said Harold sincerely. "Come along with Derek. He says he'll be visiting Xavier regularly."

Stacy uncovered her face and smiled. "I know." She gently picked up Xavier and sat him in her lap. She hugged him and ruffled the fur around his neck. "Good bye, old fella. I'll come see you, I promise." She wiped a tear from her eye, and the dog whimpered, sensing her sadness. You have fun in your new home with Harold. She smiled, and the dog wagged his tail. She carefully put Xavier into the small kennel and carried it out to Harold's car so they could transport him to his new home.

Harold smiled warmly at Stacy. "I promise I will love him with all my heart and take good care of him. And you better visit, a lot."

She smiled in return. "I will." She turned and walked to the house. Harold and Seth got into the car and Harold talked reassuringly to Xavier in his travel crate all the way home.

Seth's heart warmed. *This is good. Really good.*

In no time, they arrived at Harold's house, and Xavier made himself at home. Harold and Xavier were clearly comfortable in one another's presence. Harold had gotten a wide step for Xavier so he could get up onto the couch easily. The dog learned how to use it immediately and curled up on Harold's lap on the couch.

"Well, hey, you two, I'm gonna let you enjoy yourselves," Seth said as he walked to the door.

"Seth."

"Yes?"

"Thank you." Tears welled in Harold's eyes. "And I really mean it."

"You're welcome. And I really mean that too. Call me!" he yelled as he closed the door behind him.

Seth plopped into his blue Honda and whistled to the radio's music all the way home. *Life is good!*

CHAPTER 24

Sorting Things Out

And we know that God causes everything to work
together for the good of those who love God and
are called according to his purpose for them.

—Romans 8:28 (NLT)

One Sunday afternoon, a knock sounded on Seth's new apartment door. He curiously swung the door wide open, and there stood Jillian.

"Hello, Seth," she said with a smile. After a few seconds of Seth's dumbfounded staring, she tentatively asked, "Can I come in?"

"Yes. Yes, come in, come in." He waved her inside. "Sorry. I thought you were in California, that's all," he explained, taken aback.

"I decided to move back east, so I'm moving in with Dad. Then I can look after him. Like you said, he's getting older. He's been through a lot, enough to wear out even the youngest and strongest, let alone someone his age." She sighed sadly.

"What about your job?" asked Seth incredulously, knowing she loved her work.

"I'll be working part-time at the rehab where Dad stayed those couple months. It's an hour away, so it will be a long commute, but I like the schedule. It's three days on, three days off… I'm sharing the job with a woman who just had a baby."

"I'm glad to see things worked out for you two. Your dad's thrilled to have you back in his life."

"I owe a lot of that to you, *Mr. Instigator*." She chuckled.

"Instigator? You're calling me an *instigator* now?" Seth laughed. "I guess that's better than some of the things you called me."

"Sorry about that," responded Jillian sheepishly. "I had a lot of things to work out. I'm glad I did."

"Me too."

"Dad told me about your son," she said quietly.

"Oh, he did?" Seth's cheeks flushed with embarrassment.

"Sorry. I'm being rude. From your expression, I take it Dad hasn't told you about *me* then."

"Uh, no?"

Jillian proceeded to tell Seth about her rape, pregnancy, and abortion. Basically, the same version she told Harold in Seth's apartment, though now a much-calmer rendition.

"Man…I mean…Jillian. Wow, I had no idea. I'm sorry, *really* sorry you had to go through all that." Seth's voice shook slightly. Her confession had rocked him. Goosebumps appeared on his arm. In addition to the shocking nature of Jillian's story—the pain she endured from the rape and then again from the abortion, as well as years of believing a lie about her dad—her story caused an eruption of thoughts in Seth's mind about his own son's abortion.

A crushing ache pressed in on Seth's heart as memories flooded back.

Jillian, unaware of the emotional flood Seth experienced at her words, responded, "For the first time, I can honestly say I'm getting some long overdue and much-needed healing. I attended these weekend retreats for women who had abortions, and they helped. I'm on…on a…truly *remarkable* journey," she said earnestly, searching for words. "I'm feeling whole again. *Better*, I guess you could say. Probably for the first time since I was thirteen. I thought of you with some of the things I learned."

She dug around in her purse and pulled out a brightly colored brochure. "It's recognized in some circles that women may suffer post-traumatic-stress disorder after having abortions. One possible symptom is nightmares, so I thought of your dream. They have retreats for men too, the fathers of aborted babies. I brought you some information." She handed the brochure to Seth.

"Thanks." Seth gave it a cursory, polite look, trying to appear interested while he searched his mind for words. "I don't know if I need something like this. I think I've made my peace," he began tentatively. "The dream stopped after I got saved. I don't think the dream was PTSD, at least not in my opinion. I think God used it to get my attention, about Him and the abortion." Seth put the brochure in his back pocket, crossed his arms, and leaned against the wall. "I know I'm forgiven, but I also know I'd never make the same decision again. And I know I'll see my son someday in heaven." Seth responded with more confidence as his thoughts became clearer. "Hey, have a seat. Would you like something to drink?" He walked into the living room and motioned to a chair.

Jillian followed. "Okay, but I can only stay for a little. I don't need anything to drink, but thanks." She settled into a secondhand but comfortably padded brown armchair that Seth had picked up at the local consignments store. Setting her purse beside her, her gaze returned to Seth as he sat on a small matching sofa. "You're lucky. You know you had a son. I don't know if my child was a boy or girl." She crossed her arms in a protective gesture. "It's good you don't have your dream anymore. I used to have nightmares a lot, but they weren't always the same, and I didn't remember most of them. When I learned about post-traumatic stress, I believed I had some of the symptoms after my rape and abortion. It's still hard for me to talk about." She paused and gazed out the window. "That's why I need these retreats, I guess, but I've come a long way."

"Yes, you're like a completely different person."

Jillian sighed and shook her head in agreement as she pushed her glasses back farther on her nose and turned her attention back to Seth. "Living in California was easier. I pretended I was someone completely different, and that what happened here had never happened." She glanced wistfully out the window again, the sun glinting on her gold frames, then continued. "I made my own new life, or so I thought. But the ache never left." Her eyes clouded at the unpleasant memories.

"I lived in a walled, angry fortress. I hated men and myself. But I loved kids, and I thought maybe God would forgive me if I was just good enough to all those other kids." She smiled with a hint of sadness. "I'm probably the best darn physical therapist for kids you'll ever find. I worked so hard to try to make things right. But now things really are being made right—in my life and with God—but I still have a lot to work through."

"Well, I thank God for all he's done already," replied Seth passionately as he leaned back on the sofa.

"Me too. And heck, look at me." Jillian stood and turned in a circle. "I lost twenty pounds without even trying, and I feel great. I think it's finally getting rid of all that stress, that giant secret, all that guilt."

"You look good. You kinda glow, it's a healthy glow, I mean."

"Aren't you nice?" Jillian laughed appreciatively. "I do feel like I glow nowadays. I'm heading over to Dad's now. I just wanted to stop by, give you the brochure, and say thanks for making me face my demons. You've given me my life back." She turned toward the door.

Seth stood too. She walked toward him and gave him a tentative hug.

Seth awkwardly hugged her back.

She left, not knowing how much she had just rocked Seth's world.

A few days later, Seth visited Harold. Jillian was away grocery shopping. *Perfect*. This gave Seth time to talk with Harold privately. He and Harold sat in their usual places in the living room and exchanged small talk. After happily greeting Seth, Xavier sat contentedly at Harold's feet. Soon, Seth launched into the reason for his visit.

"Jillian stopped in to see me," offered Seth, trying to broach the subject delicately.

"Oh?"

"Yea, she told me what happened when she was thirteen," explained Seth quietly.

"Oh, that's so hard for me to think about. I still can't believe it. But it explains a lot." Harold sighed sadly while rubbing his forehead.

"Yes, it does." Seth cleared his throat and continued. "So…I've thought about a lot of things since her visit. And was wondering… does the fact that your daughter was raped…and got pregnant… and had an abortion…at the age of thirteen…does that change your mind about it? I mean, isn't that one of those 'hard cases' where abortion should be legal? Sorry if the question seems harsh," apologized Seth awkwardly, shifting in his chair. He continued, trying to better explain himself, "Even after seeing the vivid images of dead babies and coming face to face with the horror of what abortion actually is, I don't understand how, but somehow now I'm confused. I'm wrestling with the whole abortion thing for 'hard cases' again since I heard Jillian's story. I wonder what you think, if your views have changed?"

Startled by the abrupt launch into a serious topic after their previous pleasant chatter, Harold paused a moment to gather his thoughts. "I'd be lying if I said my pro-life beliefs didn't waver some when I first found out what happened. It's especially hard when it's your own daughter. Believe it or not, Jillian and I've talked about it. Sometimes it's pretty hard for us both. But you know what? I'm even more pro-life now than before. Mostly because of the pain I've seen my daughter endure, her whole life…how everything she experienced—rape, pregnancy, abortion, lies—shaped her, and not in a good way. I believe if someone goes through such a horrific experience as rape and then discovers she's pregnant…well, I believe giving a baby life would be positive and healing."

"Even if she's only thirteen?"

"Yes," replied Harold without hesitation. "Because I think if someone's biologically mature enough to get pregnant, then she's likely biologically mature enough to give birth. If not naturally, then to have a C-section."

Harold paused and bent over to ruffle Xavier's ears before continuing. "I remember my wife telling me that rape victims recover quicker and better emotionally if they offer their babies for adoption than if they abort their child. And some raise their babies too, quite lovingly and successfully. Abortion is another insult, a tragedy on top of a tragedy, a violation on top of a violation. Two wrongs don't make a right. A baby is an innocent victim, just like my thirteen-year-old daughter was an innocent victim. And you saw those pictures of the dead aborted babies. I've seen pictures too. What could ever possibly justify something like that? To an innocent baby?"

Seth knew he agreed but didn't understand how easily he had gotten confused.

Harold's eyes narrowed and glazed over a bit as though trying to recall something important. He looked out the window and said, "My wife knew a woman who was the product of rape and was adopted. She looked into my wife's eyes one day and said, 'Why shouldn't I have had a chance to be born? What have *I* done wrong?' My wife said that really settled deep in her soul."

Harold turned his attention back to Seth. "And you know what else? The abortion clinic Jilly went to never asked who impregnated her or if she was raped. They didn't care. But if she'd carried her baby to term, the secret would've been out, and I could've dealt with Dave properly. I guess the only saving grace is that monster—Dave—moved away." Harold spat the man's name with contempt. "Before he did, Jilly's friends made sure she was never alone anymore so the abuse couldn't continue. I didn't even have a chance to protect her. She turned to her friends for that," lamented Harold. Tears welled in his eyes, and he grabbed a tissue and blew his nose.

"And he's dead now, so I can't even approach him about it," growled Harold forcefully—his grief turning to anger as he slapped the armrest of the couch. He sighed. "It may be hard for some people to understand, but I'm more pro-life now."

Unbeknownst to Seth and Harold, Jillian had walked in the back door and overheard the end of their conversation.

She interjected, making both of them jump, "I'm really glad to have my dad to talk to, and I'm thankful for his steadfast pro-life views. I've learned that women need love and support after rape, not a quick fix, sweeping everything under the rug. Now that everything's out in the open, Dad's been a loving anchor to me. That's what I'm learning about a lot of pro-lifers. Contrary to the way they're portrayed in the media and academia, they're true lovers of all life, of all people. It's hard to argue with lovers." She smiled wistfully and added softly, "Dad, you would've been a fantastic grandfather."

Silence lingered. Wanting to fill the void, Seth spoke quietly to Jillian, "Well, if it's any consolation, your dad's like a grandfather to me."

"Yes, he is. And yes, it's comforting to know that." Jillian smiled. She cleared her throat and abruptly turned away. "You two keep chatting—I'm going to put these groceries away," she called from the kitchen.

Curious to see if she had brought him any snacks from the store, Xavier joined her in the kitchen. His curiosity was rewarded as they heard rustling, a happy yelp, and the crunching of a biscuit as Xavier chewed loudly. Seth and Harold chuckled.

Harold's demeanor grew serious. "I've been thinking about some things too. How would the world be different if my grandchild had been born? I wish God would give me a dream like he gave you, so I could see this child. No dreams yet," said Harold sadly. "I know I'll meet the little one in heaven, but how I wish the baby would have had a chance to be born. What would've he or she done with his or her life? I'll never know. Such great treasure…lost. No wonder there's a room of tears in your dream."

Once again, unknown to Harold and Seth, Jillian had come back to the doorway and listened, and as she spoke, they both jumped again. "I guess we'll never know those answers until we get to heaven."

The silence stretched, each lost in their thoughts. After a bit, Jillian walked to the window. She turned back to Seth and Harold. "We can't change the past, but I'm so thankful that Jesus is healing me."

"Amen," said Seth, "Me too."

Jillian's gaze returned to the window, and she added wistfully, "I wish it had not been so easy to do. I walked into a clinic at the age of thirteen and got an abortion without my parent's consent. No counseling. No questions asked. I had no idea how dramatically my life would be altered by that decision." Her voice broke.

Harold got up and walked to the window beside his daughter. He pulled her close and gently hugged her. "You were victimized terribly, Jilly. I'm so sorry." His shoulders shook with sobs as Jillian laid her head against his chest, her hands covering her face.

Jillian uncovered her face and lifted her head. "Yes, I was. Twice. I was Dave's victim, but I was also the victim of a society that sells abortion as a solution. I was abused on both fronts. Abortion wasn't the answer. I wish I knew then what I know now."

She stepped away from her dad's embrace. "But my child was a victim too. My baby got a death sentence. Oh, it's so hard to say that and admit it. I know God has forgiven me, but I'm still working on forgiving me." She folded her arms across her chest and added, "I'm getting there."

Harold put his arm across her shoulders, and they both gazed out the window. Seth wondered if he should slip out the back since this seemed to be a private father-daughter moment.

Jillian turned and faced Seth. "And I've forgiven Dave, but it wasn't easy. I'm going to spend the rest of my life doing what I can to bring awareness to sexual abuse and doing what I can to prevent it. I also want to help rape victims heal." She paused, furrowing her brows in thought for a few beats. She sighed deeply and continued, "And I want to keep anyone from experiencing the grief I did. Abortion should not be sold to vulnerable women. It certainly didn't empower me. It nearly broke me. I intend to help women choose life for their babies and do whatever I can to help the world understand that abortion should never be a choice. Not ever," she asserted passionately.

With that, Jillian turned sharply and walked back to the kitchen.

Seth and Harold sat quietly, each lost in his own thoughts. They heard Xavier lapping water from his dish, and he soon rejoined them, lying once again at his master's feet. Harold bent down and petted the dog.

"Before I forget, there's something I want to tell you." Harold sat back and grabbed his Bible from the end table. "A scripture keeps coming to my mind, and I believe God wants me to share it with you. And you already know how I listen to those nudgings," he winked with a gleam in his eye.

Pages rustled as Harold flipped through them, carefully searching. He talked as he looked, "When King David was going to die, he said this to his son, Solomon. Believe me, I'm not in the least, comparing myself to King David. And I'm not trying to say you're

Solomon either." Harold chuckled. "Here it is. 1 Kings 2:2–3: 'I am about to go the way of all the earth…so be strong, act like a man, and observe what the LORD your God requires: Walk in obedience to him, and keep his decrees and commands, his laws and regulations, as written in the Law of Moses. Do this so that you may prosper in all you do and wherever you go…'" read Harold.

Seth's eyes bulged.

"Don't look so scared." Harold laughed. "I'm not dying yet, that I know of. But at my age, you never know. I'm ready when the Lord's ready to take me. I look forward to seeing my wife and Rudy, and now my grandchild too. And I can't wait to meet Jesus face-to-face. But for now, I live day-to-day in obedience to Him." Harold grabbed a tissue and blew his nose again before continuing. "You're like a son…not a grandson, but a son…and I'm thrilled to share my faith with you. It's one of the greatest privileges of my life," explained Harold haltingly as his eyes welled with tears.

Xavier responded to Harold's emotions. He whined, climbed up his doggie stair and onto the couch, and laid his head gently on his lap. Harold absently ruffled the dog's soft ears.

"Thanks." Seth cleared the lump from his throat. "And you're like a dad to me. Truth be told, sometimes I think of you as a brother…and a friend too, of course." He grinned.

"A brother, eh," exclaimed Harold. "I like that." He beamed with joy.

Jillian called from the kitchen to ask Seth if he'd like to stay for supper.

"No, but thanks. I've got writing to do tonight for work," he said, rising.

"Wait a second, Seth, I'm not finished," Harold asserted.

"Oh?" Seth settled back into the chair.

"The part in 1 Kings about walking in obedience to the Lord stood out to me when I read it. I guess I'm worried that we've talked so much about God's goodness and love and forgiveness that I'm worried you might've gotten the impression from me that God's forgiveness gives you permission to sin."

"What? No, I don't think that. Why, do you think I'm sinning somehow? Have I done something wrong?"

"No, I don't think you've done anything wrong, but I just want to be clear. When I wrestled with whether abortion should be allowed for rape victims like my daughter, I began justifying abortion, and the Lord rebuked me. When I heard you ask the same question, I worried you might be going down a path of compromise too. The Holy Spirit convicted me of wrong thinking. Let me explain."

Seth waited patiently while Harold flipped through the Bible again. "Here. Isaiah 5:20 says, 'Woe to those who call evil good and good evil, who put darkness for light and light for darkness, who put bitter for sweet and sweet for bitter.' That's what I did when I briefly thought abortion might be a good choice, under certain circumstances. Murder of the most innocent of human beings—an unborn baby in the womb—is always wrong. It's darkness, and it brought pain and bitterness to Jilly's life."

"Yes, mine too. And I believe it did to Katy's life too, but I'm not sure she sees it yet," acknowledged Seth.

Harold turned back to his Bible, shuffling the pages again. "The Lord led me to Jude. Verse 4 says: 'For certain individuals whose condemnation was written about long ago have secretly slipped in among you. They are ungodly people, who pervert the grace of our God into a license for immorality.' Verses 18 to 19 say, 'In the last times there will be scoffers who will follow their own ungodly desires. These are the people who divide you, who follow mere natural instincts and do not have the Spirit.'"

Jillian listened from the kitchen and came back into the room, again interjecting: "Yea, I went to a pro-choice church in California to make myself feel better, but it didn't work. I only got more confused. But I didn't know the Lord then. I was pretty confused in a lot of ways."

"I don't understand how a church can be pro-abortion," said Harold, shaking his head in confusion. "Some churches are trapped in man's thinking and are leaving God out of the picture."

To Seth, he said, "Please read the book of Jude. It'll make what I'm trying to say clearer. But another point I'm trying to make is that I don't always get things right. If I try to figure things out using my natural, sin-prone mind, I mess up. I need to remember to take everything before God and examine it in the light of His Holy Word."

Xavier yawned and stretched. Harold shifted to accommodate the dog's movement before continuing. "I started to justify Jilly's abortion to make myself feel better and, in my imagination, to make Jilly feel better too. But I'd forgotten that God authors and creates all life. He knits us together in our mother's wombs, and He has a purpose for us before we're even conceived. He doesn't make mistakes. He's God—we aren't. He works all things together for good, and His ways are higher than our ways, even if we can't understand it at the time. All life is valuable and created by God." Harold stood with finality.

Seth rose also, and Harold abruptly stepped forward and hugged him, a big old bear hug, the first time he'd ever done anything like that. Seth choked up as he hugged him back.

"Take care of yourself. Come see me now and then."

"You know I will." Seth swiftly wiped a tear away before it fell.

CHAPTER 25

The Spiritual Battle

"But you belong to God, my dear children. You have already
won a victory over those people, because the Spirit who lives
in you is greater than the spirit who lives in the world."

—1 John 4:4 (NLT)

Now part of his routine on Tuesday nights, Seth looked forward
to working off steam at Word of Life Community Church's
game night. After an intense one-on-one on the basketball court,
he and Mark chatted in the lounge with Pastor Frank as they cooled
down.

Distracted from the conversation by some people in the doorway, Mark turned. He smiled shyly and waved in response to a young
woman his age who had just entered the gym and waved enthusiastically. When she headed in another direction with a friend, Seth
winked and smacked him on the back. "Buddy, you've been holding
out on me. Who's that?" Seth pointed his thumb back in the girl's
direction.

Mark's face turned beet red.

"Ahhhh, spill the beans man." Seth chuckled.

"She's a good friend," replied Mark as his face gradually faded
to pink then flesh toned.

"And?" queried Seth.

"We've gone out a couple of times," admitted Mark reluctantly, his face turning red again.

Seth put his hand over his mouth and tried not to laugh again but ended up snorting in laughter at his friend's embarrassment. Mark's face turned fire-engine red.

"Sorry," muttered Seth as he realized how uncomfortable his behavior was making his friend. "I just didn't know you were dating anyone. It's such a surprise, that's all."

"Yea, it's recent." Mark shrugged.

"She's a lovely young woman," chimed in Pastor Frank calmly. Trying to rescue Mark from his embarrassment, he leaned back in the chair with his fingers entwined behind his head and changed the subject. "You know, Seth, one thing I love about your story is how much people prayed for you. From the moment I met you, I prayed for you, but my prayers only began recently. Mark and his parents prayed for you since you were a child. Harold prayed too, as soon as you started working at the library. At Harold's open house, Marianne Cantor told me a story. Do you know Marianne?"

"No, doesn't ring a bell."

"Her husband's a professor at the college, a math professor, I think?"

"Oh, she's Prof Cantor's wife, that's right. He gave me your name and said his wife attended here."

"Yes, Marianne is on our prayer team. When you talked with him, he told her about your dream. Though he isn't much of a praying man, he knew she'd pray."

"Really?" *I had no idea.*

"Think about all the people who prayed for your salvation: me, Mark and his family, members of the prayer team here at church, Harold, and Marianne Cantor. And these are just the ones we know about. From the beginning, when you shared your story with me, about how you'd been to the psychologist and a psychology professor and a Temple of the Enlightened pastor, I was impressed with your spiritual discernment. You trudged through a lot of confusion. Not many would have made it through unscathed like you did. Others, without as much prayer covering, might have spiraled further into confusion."

A few guys played basketball on the court, and a ball bounced in their direction. Pastor Frank caught it and threw it back to one of the teens who had run to within a few feet of the pastor. "You guys play a mean game. I might join you shortly," he hollered. He turned his attention back to Seth and Mark. "But seriously, Seth, we can go on with the story about how God brought an entire community together to build Harold's house and how He reconciled Harold and Jillian. Not all prayers are answered so dramatically or like we think they should be answered, but God always moves and works every-thing together for good for those who love Him. God's amazing."

"Amen!" exclaimed Seth and Mark in unison.

"On the other hand, I know people who've walked through these doors and shared profound stories of how they came to know the Lord where it seemed as if no one prayed for them. I'm awed at His gentle wooing. And yet, at times, I also wonder how some people miss God or refuse His invitation."

He sighed deeply, then stood and raised his arms over his head, clasped his hands, and leaned to the right in a muscle stretch. "I need to limber up if I'm gonna take on these guys in basketball." He changed the subject as he stretched to the left. "So, Seth, what's the Lord speaking to you lately?"

"Um…well, that His forgiveness isn't permission to sin."

"Good one," agreed Mark.

"And that we need to be careful not to call evil good and good evil like with abortion."

Another good one," interjected Mark again.

"That's Isaiah, I think…Isaiah 5, something." Pastor Frank stopped in the midst of a calf stretch to retrieve a Bible they kept on a nearby shelf in the game room. "Here, Isaiah 5:20."

"And I'm studying the book of Jude."

"How long have you been studying it." Mark laughed. "It's like *one* chapter, I think."

"Hey, no fair," said Seth, "I'm still pretty new to this Bible-studying stuff."

"I know, sorry. Just kidding. I forget what Jude says anyway, so you know more than I do at the moment."

"No problem." Seth smiled.

Pastor Frank opened the Bible to Jude and read the chapter out loud from the New Living Translation.

"I like the way that version reads," said Seth.

"Yep, easy to understand," replied Pastor Frank. "Jude is a somber reminder that, like you mentioned, God's grace, His forgiveness, is not a license to sin or live immorally, and no sin goes unpunished. I think of it this way—I love God so much, and because of my relationship with Him, I want to please Him. I don't want to hurt our relationship by doing something God wouldn't approve of. Everything He asks of me is the very best for me."

"A couple verses jumped out at me, I forget which ones, can I see?" Seth stretched his hand toward the Bible.

Pastor Frank handed it to him.

"Yea, 17 to 19, 'But you, my dear friends, must remember what the apostles of our Lord Jesus Christ predicted. They told you that in the last times, there would be scoffers whose purpose in life is to satisfy their ungodly desires. These people are the ones who are creating divisions among you. They follow their natural instincts because they do not have God's Spirit in them.'"

Seth handed the Bible back to Pastor Frank. "I can't fathom how easily I found abortion acceptable. Partly because I didn't have God's spirit in me, I guess. But I also think about college, how pro-abortion the teachings were and how pro-lifers were mocked. At the time, I didn't care one way or another, but I was still influenced. I also think about my psych professor and how so many of his justifications for abortion would be 'ungodly desires,' like Jude says. This country is divided on abortion and division even exists in churches." Seth furrowed his brows in concern.

Mark joined in, "Yea, this stuff is real heavy. I've always thought abortion was the ultimate form of discrimination—age-based discrimination—against the most innocent, resulting in their death. The unborn have no voice, so they need our voice. The people at the front lines of equality have forgotten about unborn babies. What about forced abortions of female babies in China? What about the disproportionate number of black babies aborted in this country? Did you know the early feminists were against abortion? Susan B. Anthony thought abortion was child murder and that it exploited women and children. Did you know the same arguments used today to support abortion were used to support slavery? About slaves, people said, 'I personally oppose slavery, but I would never tell anyone what to do with their property.' We all agree today that this argument is ridiculous, and we're all relieved we finally got rid of the scourge of slavery, yet pro-abortionists use the same argument. And it's accepted! I don't know how so many people can stick their heads in the sand," ranted Mark.

"Great points, Mark, but it's hard to make them sometimes. When I sit here and listen to us three guys, I think, man I know a lot of pro-choicers who'd say, Will you look at those good ol' boys making decisions for women? Who do they think they are?'" countered Seth.

"True, but funny too," snorted Mark, "Because my mom and sister shaped my views. Pro-life women influence me. It's not some male-chauvinist stance I'm taking. Plus, look at you, Seth. You're a guy, and you're definitely impacted by abortion. Abortion affects everyone, either directly by having experienced it or knowing someone who experienced it, or indirectly by devaluing all life."

Mark sat back in the chair and gazed at the ceiling as he pondered his next words. "As a youth pastor, I have to come at it from a different angle with my teens. I want to help them avoid unwed pregnancy in the first place, so I teach them who they are in Christ...how valuable they are to Him and how He created and purposed them. I help them understand that God created sex for marriage, and we have a lot of discussions about abstinence and the perversion of sex in our society. That's heavy stuff to deal with."

Seth leaned forward suddenly with his elbows on his thighs, hands clasped. "Something's bothering me." His serious and urgent tone grabbed the attention of the two men. They waited expectantly. Pastor Frank sat back down. Seth leaned back and rubbed his face. He continued speaking while animatedly and forcefully flailing his arms to emphasize his words. "After knowing everything I did about abortion, after seeing pictures, I still got confused when faced with a hard case, and I wavered. I'm embarrassed that I did, but I caved to a pro-choice argument, well, almost anyway." He explained what he had learned about Jillian without revealing her identity. "I'm still 100 percent pro-life, but I don't like how easily I almost slipped away."

Pastor Frank looked thoughtfully at Seth for a moment. "Abortion is a spiritual battle. The enemy of God loves abortion because it destroys God's creation, God's beloved. The enemy of our souls will do everything in his power to create confusion and doubt. You learned the truth, and then the enemy came in to confuse you." He opened his Bible but paused. "Many scriptures come to mind. Let me summarize them. In fact, you should write this down. I'll tell you why in a second." He pointed to Seth's pocket notebook.

Seth pulled it out and began writing furiously to keep up as Pastor Frank shared.

He continued slowly. "God is the author of peace, not confusion. The Holy Spirit will help you to remember the truth. Be watchful for your adversary. The devil prowls around like a roaring lion seeking whom he may devour. The enemy comes to steal, kill, and destroy, but Jesus came that you may have abundant life. Do not participate in evil but expose it. Do not be conformed by this world but be transformed by the renewing of your mind. Put on the full armor of God. Those are just a few scriptures, but I want you to research them. Find them. Study them. Spend time in prayer and in the Word because you are in a spiritual battle and need the covering of the Lord. We all do."

Everyone sat in silence for a few minutes until Pastor Frank spoke somberly, "Abortion's a very serious issue facing the church and our country. Perhaps God will use you both in the pro-life movement because you each have so much passion about the issue. For now, let's pray."

EPILOGUE

We can rejoice, too, when we run into problems and
trials, for we know that they help us develop endurance.
And endurance develops strength of character, and
character strengthens our confident hope of salvation.

—Romans 5:3–4 (NLT)

A few years later, Seth walked quickly through the local grocery
store's automatic doors, nearly running into Katy who stood
directly in front of him. Her emerald eyes flickered brilliantly against
the sunlight as they suddenly stared directly into Seth's soul. Startled,
Seth drank in her appearance. She looked gorgeous in a bright-pink
blouse and trendy jeans, and she held a toddler-aged little girl in a
matching pink dress.

"Katy!" exclaimed Seth happily. "How *are* you?"

"Oh my gosh! Seth!" Katy squeezed his shoulder with her free
hand. She turned to a man standing next to her, about her age, who
looked rather curiously at their exchange, and said, "Jeremy, this is
Seth. Oh my gosh!"

She then turned to Seth and said excitedly, "Seth, this is my
husband, Jeremy"—then a pause—"and this is our daughter, Tosha."
Katy smiled brightly.

The room spun. *Husband? Daughter?*

"Your dau...daughter?"

"Yes. Oh gosh. Jeremy, could you take her outside to run
around a bit so I can talk to Seth?" she asked, turning and handing

the grinning little girl with dark curly hair to her daddy, who clearly adored her.

"Nice meeting you," said Jeremy in a friendly voice, as he waved and walked out the door with his daughter.

"How? You? You have a *daughter?*" asked Seth incredulously, his voice quivering.

"She's adopted," said Katy in a serious tone.

"Oh." Seth felt relieved, though he didn't know why. "I didn't know you got married. I didn't know you had a daughter," he said with shock.

"Yea…maybe we could go outside and talk?" she added sheepishly.

"Okay." Seth followed her out the door. *She looks great, and she seems happy, softer somehow, or maybe it's just me, maybe I'm the one who's changed.*

"You seem different," said Seth. "You seem really happy."

"Oh, I am so happy! I'm really, really happy," she gushed. Seth felt a pang of jealousy and a bit wistful about what might've been. "There's so much I should say." Katy tentatively chewed her lower lip as she pondered her words. "Gosh, after we broke up, everything was such a whirlwind for a while. I was in a wheelchair for Merin's wedding. Oh, it's so bittersweet to think about even now, but it seemed too awkward to use crutches while wearing a gown and carrying flowers." She paused and flipped her long, wavy hair over her shoulder in a familiar gesture that flooded Seth with nostalgia. "After a lot of therapy, eventually, I recovered physically from the accident and moved to Oregon. I wanted to make a fresh start."

"Why does everyone move out west?" Seth muttered to himself.

"Huh?"

"Nothing. I'm sorry, go ahead."

"To make a long story short, I struggled with the abortion. I've come to realize that abortion isn't freedom…it's bondage. Abortion is not only a death sentence for a baby, but it's a death sentence for the mother too…something died inside of me. Something good, and I'm not even talking about the baby…I don't even know how to put it in words. It's kind of like an essence, or a light, or a piece of me died."

She paused and gazed into the distance. "I cringe when I think about all the arguments I had in college with pro-lifers. If I could take back those words, I would. Oh my goodness, when I think of all the women I encouraged to have abortions, I am devastated." Katy shook her head.

She sighed deeply and returned her piercing emerald gaze to Seth. "But…eventually, in Oregon, God led me to some meetings for women who needed healing—emotional and spiritual healing from abortion. I started going and eventually started attending a great church. I guess you could say I met the Lord. And I met my wonderful husband. He knows about my past. We married even though he knew I could never give birth to a child."

Her gaze turned to her daughter giggling in a grassy area nearby with her husband. "We decided to adopt, and oh my goodness, our lives are incredibly full and rich since adopting Tosha! We really want to adopt a second child and give Tosha a younger brother or sister."

She looked directly into Seth's eyes and smiled brightly. "Believe it or not, I even volunteer now and minister to women. I've shared my story—*our* story—a few times. I hope you don't mind," she said hesitantly.

"No, I don't mind. I'm glad it—our story—helps others. And I'm happy for you. You have a beautiful family," said Seth earnestly.

"I need to apologize," asserted Katy abruptly. "I was so angry after the abortion. I was mad at myself and *really* mad at you. I blamed you. I know it wasn't fair to blame you, but that's where I was. I kept telling you it didn't bother me, and I was livid that you kept bringing it up. I was eaten alive inside, and now I understand why. I ended a life, a precious life created by God with love and purpose. God never makes mistakes. My child was not a mistake. Deep inside, even though I didn't want to admit it, I knew abortion was wrong. But I believed a lie from our culture that abortion was the best, the *only* right choice. I'm forgiven, I know that now. But I'm so sorry I aborted our baby." She took a deep breath and stared into Seth's eyes. "I'll always remember you. And our son," she added quietly, a slight sob escaping her lips.

Seth stood like a statue, speechless. After a short pause to collect herself, Katy went on, "I've forgiven myself. Jesus's sacrifice was big enough to cover all my sins, even my abortion. I've forgiven you too. I hope you can forgive me?"

"Oh, I do. I have. I forgave you and myself a long time ago." Seth's voice held no trace of anger or accusation. "I'm just glad we'll both get to meet our son in heaven someday." His voice quivered with emotion.

She smiled gently back at Seth and said, "Yes, I'm so thankful for that." Tears welled in her eyes. "God is so good."

"Amen," agreed Seth quietly.

Katy cleared her throat and changed the subject. "So what've you been up to?" she asked with genuine interest. Seth shared enthusiastically about his job as a reporter, volunteer work with Word of Life Community Church, and he briefly explained what happened with Harold's home and with Jillian even though those events happened years ago now. He thought Katy would appreciate them.

"Wow, I'm happy for you, Seth. Have you heard from your dad?"

"No. But he's on my mind a lot," Seth answered longingly.

"I'm going to pray that you and your dad reconcile, just like Harold and Jillian," she said enthusiastically.

"I appreciate that."

"You know, we can pray, but God wants us to take some steps too. You should ask God what He wants you to do about the situation with your dad," she suggested gently.

"I will." Seth nodded.

Katy explained she, Jeremy, and Tosha had come to town for a week to visit family. They chatted a bit more, shared well-wishes, and said bittersweet goodbyes.

After Seth made his purchases, he walked slowly to his car with the groceries, whistling, praying, and thanking God for all He'd done in his life.

A warm dry wind blew. Seth briefly thought of the chinook winds he learned about while reading the placemats at the diner. But then his thoughts turned to the wind of the Holy Spirit. He sensed the presence of the Lord, and he breathed deeply. Peace and joy settled deep in his soul.

He popped the trunk and set the groceries inside. As he slammed the lid, the warm breeze blew again. "Life is good," he said aloud to no one in particular.

Now that I know who holds my future. Seth smiled. *I think I'll call my dad.*

He turned and faced the wind.

Are you facing an unplanned pregnancy?

Reach out to your local pregnancy care center. Services are free and confidential, and they will compassionately assist you in countless ways. These centers go by different names such as crisis pregnancy center or pregnancy resource center. If you aren't familiar with or can't find a local center, these resources can help:

- Care Net: https://www.care-net.org/find-a-pregnancy-center
- Heartbeat International: https://www.heartbeatinternational.org/worldwide-directory
- Option Line (24/7): 1-800-712-HELP or https://optionline.org/ or Text "HELPLINE" to 313131
- Pregnancy Decision Line: https://pregnancydecisiononline.org/ *(Pregnancy Decision Line is the only national hotline offering immediate pregnancy decision coaching to help you through a difficult pregnancy decision. Visit the above website for compassion and confidential support.)*

Have you had an abortion in the past?

There is help to heal your heart. Many pregnancy care centers (above) offer post-abortion healing programs. Below are other organizations offering help:

- Abortion Recovery InterNational, Inc. (ARIN): http://www.abortionrecovery.org/
- Care Net: https://www.care-net.org/i-had-an-abortion
- Rachel's Vineyard: http://www.rachelsvineyard.org/
- Silent No More Awareness Campaign: http://www.silentnomoreawareness.org/search/
- Surrendering the Secret: https://surrenderingthesecret.churchcenter.com/groups/sts-national-leaders

Do you have a personal relationship with Jesus?

Maybe you've attended church your whole life, but still something is missing. You may read your Bible, attend Bible study, or teach Sunday school, but you've never taken personal steps to make your relationship with Jesus real. It's not too late.

Maybe you picked up this novel by chance, or perhaps a friend gave it to you. Possibly, this Jesus stuff is a little foreign. Or maybe you've been hurt by "church folk" or religion in the past. People are imperfect, and Jesus isn't religion. Jesus is the way, the truth and the life, and the only way to heaven.

It's no accident that you're reading this. Today can change your eternity. *But it's up to you.* There's no single, correct "formula" for beginning a relationship with Jesus. But there are some suggestions, such as the "ABC's" of salvation: Admit you've sinned (each one of us has), Believe that Jesus is who He says He is (your Savior who died on the cross for you), Confess that Jesus is Lord of your life (say it, believe it from your heart, and tell others). If that seems like too stringent of a formula, use your own words. Tell Jesus you're sorry, tell Him you know who He is, and ask Him to take charge of your life and begin leading you today. This is the only decision you will ever make that I can guarantee you will never regret. It doesn't mean life won't have difficulties; no one says life is easy, including Jesus. But it does mean your eternity is sealed, and you will have the most powerful, loving source that you can ever imagine guiding you and interceding for you.

The next step: find a Bible-believing church. Ask God to lead you to one...a church that believes the Bible is the inerrant word of God and a church that teaches that salvation is through Jesus Christ alone. Pray from a sincere heart, and you will be led.

ABOUT THE AUTHOR

Deborah Arlene writes about her enduring passion—the beauty and wonder of life. She became pregnant with her son at the age of fourteen. She and her son's father married in 1983, their second child was born in 1988, and they are still happily married today. After high school graduation, Deborah worked for state government for twenty-five years. Her life was forever changed when she met the life-giver, Jesus Christ in 1997, and He began to direct her path. Upon retiring early in her late forties, Deborah attended college for the first time, earning a Gerontology Certificate and an Associate in Arts in Social Science at a community college. She continued her education at Liberty University where she earned a Bachelor of Science in Psychology/Life Coaching with a Minor in Christian Counseling. After graduation, she became the executive director of a pro-life pregnancy care center. She retired again and is currently babysitting her first grandchild. Had she not chosen life for her son in tenth grade, this beloved grandchild would not exist. This is something she is keenly aware of, and Deborah longs for all people to view the life of an unborn child in the womb as irreplaceably precious, just as that child's mother and father are exceedingly precious. Deborah also wants all people to know Jesus, their life-giver, personally. Doing so transforms life into beauty unspeakable, not just for now, but for all of eternity.

If you have had an abortion and want to talk to someone, I'd be honored to be that person.

Rachel Shetterly

rachelshett@gmail.com

CPSIA information can be obtained
at www.ICGtesting.com
Printed in the USA
BVHW071433270519
549345BV00004B/368/P